Christmas in July

Sabine Frisch

Thinking Dog Publishing

Contents

Chapter One   1

Chapter Two   6

Chapter Three   12

Chapter Four   18

Chapter Five   23

Chapter Six   26

Chapter Seven   31

Chapter Eight   35

Chapter Nine   44

Chapter Ten   49

Chapter Eleven   59

Chapter Twelve   64

Chapter Thirteen   71

Chapter Fourteen   76

Chapter Fifteen   82

Chapter Sixteen   92

Chapter Seventeen   98

Chapter Eighteen   115

Chapter Nineteen   125

Chapter Twenty   133

Chapter Twenty-One   141

Chapter Twenty-Two   149

Chapter Twenty-Three   156

Chapter Twenty-Four   161

Chapter Twenty-Five   165

Chapter Twenty-Six   171

Chapter Twenty-Seven   180

Chapter Twenty-Eight   188

Chapter Twenty-Nine   196

Chapter Thirty   201

Chapter Thirty-One   207

Chapter Thirty-two   211

Chapter Thirty-Three   221

Chapter Thirty-Four   226

Chapter Thirty-Five   237

Chapter Thirty-Six   243

Chapter Thirty-Seven   256

Chapter Thirty-Eight   260

Coming Soon   264

Also by Sabine   266

Reviews for Other Books   268

Spotify Playlists   271

Free Bonus Book   272

Chapter One

The warm July breeze carried the faint scent of pine and cinnamon through the streets of Rosewood, putting an unexpected but delightful twist on the usual summer aromas. Sarah Anderson took a deep breath as she stepped out onto the porch of her stately old Victorian home, relishing the festive fragrances. Despite the bright sunshine and humid air of a typical New England summer, there was an unmistakable feeling of Christmas in the air.

Sarah's gaze drifted across her picturesque neighborhood, taking in the twinkling lights and holiday decorations that adorned the well-kept homes. A broad smile stretched across her face as she spotted Emma and Cory, her teenagers, putting the final touches on a life-sized snowman made of cotton batting on their front lawn.

"Don't you two look festive!" Sarah called out with an amused chuckle. Emma rolled her eyes good-naturedly while Cory grinned and struck a silly pose beside their handiwork.

As Sarah headed back inside to grab her Santa hat, the sound of tiny jingling bells made her pause. Pixie, her sassy white and sable Papillon dog, came bounding down the hallway with a red collar covered in tiny bells around her neck.

"Well, hello there, Miss Christmas," Sarah said, scooping Pixie up and nuzzling her velvety red and white fur. Irritated, Pixie plucked at one of the little bells on her collar and shook.

You know I am just doing this for charity.

I do know. And it's very much appreciated.

Discovering her ability to communicate with the little dog had surprised her when she first adopted the papillon, but she now cherished their little mental exchanges."

Everything looks fabulous for Christmas in July.

Cradling Pixie close, Sarah felt an unexpected chill in the air and a tingling spread through her body—the kind of magic that always seemed to accompany her otherworldly friends, Amelia and Simon, whenever they were near. As if on cue, the lights in the entryway began flickering playfully.

"I see you two are getting into the spirit, too," Sarah laughed, looking around for any sign of the mischievous ghosts. They could have crossed over long ago, after Sarah and her kids solved the mystery of Amelia's murder in this very house, but they loved to visit. Besides, Sarah suspected that causing the occasional mischief with electronics and confusing humans appeared to be great fun for the ghosts.

A moment later, the flickering stopped, and the lights remained steady once more. Sarah only shook her head. Having ghostly friends certainly kept life interesting. Amelia and Simon had been an unexpected 'feature' in the home when she'd moved into the old Victorian some three years ago after her twenty-year marriage had fallen apart, but sometimes they felt like family.

Setting Pixie down, Sarah made her way into the living room where Matthew was waiting. Meeting Matthew and her feelings for him had been the other surprise when she moved here, and his warm smile never failed to send pleasant flutters through her chest.

"There's my favorite Santa's helper," he quipped, taking in her festive attire. "I'd say you're more than ready."

Sarah did a playful twirl, letting her red skirt flare out. "I do love Christmas. Even if it is smack dab in the middle of summer."

Matthew chuckled. "Well, with *Creative Charities* donating fifty dollars to the Claremont Children's Hospital for every Santa who shows up, you're doing a wonderful thing. I expect Rosewood will be a sea of red and white today."

He reached out to tuck a stray lock of Sarah's blonde hair behind her ear, caressing her cheek.

"It'll be so much fun," she murmured, rising on her tiptoes to plant a soft kiss on his lips.

She allowed herself to snuggle into Matthew's embrace and momentarily felt his arms around her. When she had arrived in Rosewood Hollow, newly single with two children in tow, she would never have guessed that she would find happiness again. But there he was.

Emma and Cory, now decked out in their holiday best, burst in from outside. Typically cynical, even they couldn't contain their excitement for the unusual July celebration.

"When I called him earlier, Dad said it was nuts that the whole town is dressing up like Santa just to raise money," Emma laughed, adjusting the fuzzy white trim on her hat.

"The neighborhood kids are going to lose their minds seeing a whole herd of Santas roaming around," Cory added with a grin. "I can't wait!"

Sarah's face lit up as she watched her typically cool teenagers join in the fun. With a wink at Pixie, she dangled the festive red and white walking harness in front of her and headed towards the door.

"Who's ready to spread some early Christmas cheer?" she called over her shoulder.

Sarah felt a surge of pure joy as their festive little troupe began the short walk toward the town square. Rosewood was certainly in for a merry surprise!

The pleasant stroll down tree-lined streets soon led to a lively scene in Rosewood's bustling square. Sarah grinned as they turned the corner, a seasonal wonderland unfolding before them.

Crimson-clad Santas with cottony beards mingled among twinkling lights that cast a warm glow on the glossy leaves of flowering vines. Plastic reindeer, their antlers gleaming in the late afternoon sun, shared lawn space with moss-covered garden gnomes and candy-striped umbrellas. The air buzzed with joyful laughter and holiday cheer, tinged with the fragrant blend of warm cider and the sweet perfume of blooming roses.

Sarah and Matthew, their fingers intertwined and palms slightly sweaty in the summer heat, joined the festive throng. They marveled at the delightfully bizarre yet perfectly fitting juxtaposition of yuletide spirit and midsummer charm that only their beloved town could conjure.

"Sarah! Matthew! Over here!"

The familiar voice of Lily, Sarah's dearest friend, rose above the jovial cacophony. Sarah turned to see her beaming and waving energetically from beside an elaborately decorated snack table overlooking the square's central fountain.

Weaving through the crowd of revelers, Sarah drank in all the sights and sounds around her. The pure, childlike joy in the faces around her was contagious.

Pixie wagged with delight and jumped at Lily, the little bells on her collar jingling merrily.

"Is your store closed today?" Sarah asked her friend. "I would have thought with the town square full to bursting..."

"Nah..." Lily shook her head and offered them a few festive cookies on a paper plate. "They're all here to be part of the spectacle, not to buy books. Tomorrow will be a different story."

Behind Lily, her Rosewood Hollow Bookstore was draped in garland and featured a sign reading, "Christmas in July—Commemorative Posters Available. "I might need Emma to help at the store."

"You got it," Emma beamed before Sarah could even open her mouth.

Helping out at the bookstore just might be one of her teen's favorite activity, right after reading itself.

The cheerful hubbub in the town square gradually died down as Mayor Tom Aldridge took the stage. His bright red suit and fluffy white beard made him look every bit the part of a real-life Kris Kringle.

Chapter Two

Mayor Aldridge tapped the microphone a few times with his finger, creating a horrible feedback screech, and spread his arms.

"Ho, ho, ho! Merry Christmas in July, Rosewood!" the mayor's jovial voice boomed over the loudspeakers. "What a splendid sight to see so many rosy-cheeked Santas gathered here today."

He paused, opening his arms wide with a broad smile as he surveyed the crowd. "Christmas in July – what a crazy idea! But you've all outdone yourselves."

Scattered cheers and applause rippled through the gathered Santas in appreciation. Sarah pulled Pixie a little closer, the dog's tongue lolling happily as she looked up at the mayor.

"Thank you," Mayor Aldridge continued. The good folks at Creative Charities and Innovatech will be making a sizable donation to Cedar Ridge Children's Hospital for every Santa who is here today, so let's hear it!"

The crowd erupted in cheers and whistles, dozens of burgundy-sleeved arms shooting skyward to ring the dangling bells on their hats and belts hard. Sarah felt her chest swell with hometown pride, exchanging a warm look with Matthew, who had taken off his own hat and swung the little bell as hard as he could.

As the mayor launched into the activities and photo opportunities schedule, Sarah felt a gentle tug on her sleeve. She glanced down to see Emma leaning in close.

"Hey, Mom?" The teen's voice was low, barely audible over the crowd's noise. "I know Jen said she wasn't going to make it, but do you think it'd be okay if I slipped away for a bit to see if she's at her place? She's been really down lately."

Sarah's brows knit together slightly at the mention of Emma's conspicuously absent best friend. Jennifer came from a rough home situation, which had Sarah worried for the girl's well-being when she missed events like this.

"Of course, sweetheart," Sarah murmured, reassuringly touching her daughter's arm. "Just let me know if you need anything, okay? And be careful on those side streets."

Emma nodded gratefully, giving her mom's arm an affectionate squeeze before melting back into the crowd of revelers. As Mayor Aldridge's voice faded into the background, Sarah felt an odd shiver creep down her back. Nothing good ever happened when she had these premonitions, and she quickly glanced around for Matthew, Cory, and Lily.

A moment later, Matthew handed her a cup of iced hot chocolate and toasted her with his own. Sarah sipped her decadent drink and idly scanned the busy scene around the Rosewood Common.

Her eyes briefly landed on a pair of skinny Santas in identical costumes making their way toward the far end of the square, checking back over their shoulders now and then.

There was something...off about their purposeful strides and furtive glances. It didn't quite mesh with the carefree, jovial atmosphere surrounding them. Again, that indefinable prickle of unease crept up Sarah's spine.

"Matthew?" She touched his arm lightly, nodding toward the two departing figures. "Did you see where those Santas were headed in such a hurry?"

Matthew followed her line of sight, squinting slightly against the bright sunlight ricocheting off the tinsel-draped lampposts. "Nothing back there but the Junction side street. Weird that they would head that way. Maybe they're just looking for a convenient place to take a leak."

"That's gross."

Sarah elbowed her partner in the side and made a face, trying to find the two again. There was a perfectly good lineup of bright blue porta-potties on the other side of the square. Gross.

Before she had a chance to say just what she thought of that idea, on such a joyous, festive summer day, the two Santas slipped around the corner and out of sight.

"Better hope they get back for the final 'hat tally'," Matthew grumbled and sipped his chocolate. "I can see it in your eyes; you want to give them a piece of your mind."

"I still think it's gross. How would you feel if Cory..."

"Let it go..." Matthew pulled her close and put his arm around her waist. "Put the mom hat away for an afternoon and have fun."

At the same time, he pulled his Santa hat to sit a little askew over one eye, and Sarah had to laugh. How well he knew her. Solving their first mystery together just over two years ago, when Sarah discovered she had access to powers others did not have, bonded them in a way nothing else could. Or, as Matthew would put it, a single left shoe and a single right shoe suddenly found one another in the middle.

How very true.

A hush fell over the throng of Santas in Rosewood Hollow's town square. Hundreds of red-suited figures, a sea of beards and belly pads, shifted their weight in anticipation. Sarah pulled a bit on her red felt dress, letting the air cool her sweaty skin. The smell of popcorn and roasted chestnuts mingled with the cloying sweetness of cotton candy, a peculiar perfume for a summer Christmas.

Mayor Tom Aldridge, a portly man with a perpetually jolly twinkle in his eye, tapped the microphone on stage once again. As it crackled to life, his booming voice filled the square.

"Alright, folks! Time to judge the best Santa costume of our very special Christmas in July! Remember, folks, the jollier the better, so please come up and vote, and the winner takes home a nice little gift certificate from Jepson's Country Store!"

A smattering of applause and good-natured ho-ho-hos rippled through the crowd.

Sarah squeezed Matthew's hand. She glanced around, searching for Cory, who'd split off with a friend to talk basketball just moments ago. Emma must have connected with her friend; she was nowhere to be seen.

Just then, the air split with a scream. A high-pitched, panicked cry that clawed its way through the festive cheer. Sarah's smile vanished, replaced by a mask of terror. The scream—it was Emma's, unmistakably. The world seemed to tilt on its axis. The jolly Santas, the twinkling lights strung across the square, the scent of summer treats—all of it dissolved into a mad background blur. All Sarah could focus on was the raw fear in her daughter's voice and the primal urge to get to her.

Ignoring the bewildered stares of the people around her, Sarah shoved through the crowd, her heart a frantic drum solo against her ribs.

"Emma!" she screamed, her voice hoarse with a terror she couldn't contain. The garish red and white costumes blurred into a sea as she fought her way deeper, the echo of the scream a beacon guiding her through the panicked throng.

Sarah shoved her way through the startled crowd, not caring who she jostled in her frantic attempts to get to her daughter. Matthew and Lily rushed to keep pace, their own faces etched with fear.

"Sarah, over here!" Matthew called, grabbing her arm and pulling her toward a side street just off the square's perimeter.

The narrow alleyway seemed to echo with an eerie silence in the wake of Emma's scream. Sarah felt her heart hammering against her ribcage as they raced forward, the sound of their steps echoing off the high walls.

And then they saw her. Emma, clutching the front of her Santa dress with trembling hands, her eyes wide with terror. She stood unmoving, fixated on something just ahead that Sarah couldn't see yet.

"Emma, sweetheart!" Sarah rushed to her daughter's side, framing the girl's pale face in her hands. "What happened? Are you hurt?"

But Emma seemed too shocked to speak, merely shaking her head mutely as tears streaked down her cheeks. Exchanging a worried glance with Matthew, Sarah turned to follow her daughter's haunted gaze.

That's when she saw it—or rather, him. A crumpled, lifeless form in a Santa suit lying face down on the grimy pavement in a slowly spreading pool of red. Sarah's hands flew to her mouth to stifle the scream bubbling up in her throat.

"Dear lord..." she breathed, her whole body numb with disbelieving horror. The man could not be alive, not like this.

Panic erupted all around them as others caught sight of the disturbing scene. Some brave souls inched closer to get a better look, while others turned away. Shrill cries and hysterical sobs pierced the air as the reality set in.

One of the Santas was dead.

Chapter Three

In the chaos, Sarah distantly registered the authoritative voice of Officer Penny Harding cutting through the bedlam. Just ten minutes earlier, the seasoned policewoman had been sitting in a camp chair outside the police station, waving to the townspeople and making sure no one overdid it on spiced cider.

Now she leaped into action, her hair whipping wildly as she rushed toward them with her radio clutched to her lips.

"This is Officer Harding; I need all available units at the northwest corner of the town square immediately! We have a 10-54, possible 10-57; I repeat, we have a body!"

Penny's gaze landed squarely on Sarah's stunned face, a million unspoken questions passing between them. In that moment, Sarah knew their charming town's joyful Christmas in July had taken a dark, sinister turn.

The next several minutes were a blur of flashing lights and barked orders as Rosewood's tiny police force swarmed the alleyway. Sarah felt numb, her senses overwhelmed by the cacophony of chaos that had erupted.

She clutched Emma protectively to her side, her daughter's slight frame trembling violently against her own. Matthew hovered close behind, his jaw set in a hard line as he surveyed the grisly scene with a mixture of disbelief and simmering anger.

Officer Harding rapidly took charge, ushering the growing throngs of gawkers away from the area and barking instructions into her radio. Two more uniformed officers hurried over, urgency etched into their weathered faces.

"Gavin, Marcus... secure the perimeter and start clearing these by-standers out!" Penny ordered in a tone that left no room for argument. "And somebody get the EMTs over here ASAP!"

The two men jumped into action, pushing their way through the stunned crowd with firm but gentle insistence. Sarah could only look on numbly, her mind still struggling to process this turn of events.

Only moments ago, they had been basking in the joy and cama-raderie of their town's whimsical Christmas in July celebration. Now, a gurney was being wheeled to the edge of the alley, its harsh metal clanking sending a chill down Sarah's spine.

Just at the edge of her awareness, she could sense Amelia and Simon, their presence crackling with intensity. The ghostly duo sensed the roiling waves of unease and despair washing over Sarah, but she barely registered their attempts to soothe her rattled nerves.

Her eyes were inexplicably drawn to the crumpled Santa suit lying so sickeningly still on the pavement. Whoever that poor soul was, their holiday cheer was cut brutally short. They did not deserve to end like this, and at that moment, Sarah burned with the need to find out who had done this.

A firm hand on her shoulder made Sarah start. She turned to find Officer Harding's gaze boring into her own, a silent understanding passing between the two women. The policewoman's expression was grim but determined.

"We're going to need to ask you and your family some questions," Penny said in a low, measured tone. "Anything you might have seen or heard, no matter how insignificant it seems."

Sarah opened her mouth to respond, but the words seemed to catch in her suddenly parched throat. She could only manage the smallest of nods.

As the gurney bearing the shrouded form disappeared around the corner, a pall of silence settled over the alleyway like a heavy fog. Sarah drew Emma closer, her embrace a shield against the encroaching darkness.

What should have been a day of twinkling lights and warm laughter had twisted into something far more sinister. As Sarah gazed at the crime scene tape fluttering in the breeze, a sickening premonition crept over her. This wasn't an event any of them would forget soon.

Just as Matthew placed a gentle hand on the small of her back to guide her and Emma away from the traumatic scene, Officer Harding's radio crackled to life again.

"Unit 321, this is dispatch," the tinny voice rang out, cutting through the heavy pall lingering in the alleyway. "We've got a 10-90 in progress, repeat, bank robbery alarm at Rosewood Bank and Trust on Chestnut Boulevard."

A tense silence hung in the air for a beat before Penny cursed under her breath, her shoulders slumping ever so slightly. Lifting the radio to her lips, she spoke in clipped, authoritative tones. "10-4 dispatch, I'm splitting my unit to handle both situations. Roll additional units for backup."

She turned to the two patrolmen still on the scene. "Gavin, you're with me. Marcus, stay here and coordinate with the EMTs when they arrive. Full lockdown until we get forensics in."

With a curt nod to Sarah and Matthew, a silent apology in her eyes, Penny spun on her heel and rushed back toward the square with Gavin in tow. Her urgent footfalls soon faded into the distance, leaving an uneasy hush in their wake.

Sarah felt her stomach twist into fresh knots of dread. A body showing up at their community's proudest event was harrowing enough. But a bank robbery on top of it all?

She exchanged a loaded look with Matthew, his expression mirroring the disbelief and trepidation roiling inside her own mind. What was happening to their peaceful little town?

A heart-wrenching sob erupted from Emma's chest, shattering the stillness. Sarah pulled her daughter close, cradling her as she wept, her slender body trembling with grief.

"Shhh, it's okay, baby...I'm here," Sarah murmured, running a soothing hand over Emma's silky hair. But her own voice sounded unconvincing to her ears, laced with the same horror they were all grappling with.

Over Emma's shoulder, Sarah locked eyes with Lily, and they took Emma between them, slowly walking out of the alley.

Just as they entered the now-empty village square again, Sarah felt an icy chill around their little group. Amelia and Simon. The two ghostly presences radiated waves of protective energy, clearly sensing the danger in the once-festive atmosphere.

The town square now starkly contrasted to the festive scene from earlier. An eerie, unsettled silence had descended, wrapping the empty space in a heavy shroud of disquiet.

Discarded novelty hats and tinsel garlands littered the brick pavers, trampled underfoot in the crowd's exodus. Wisps of red and green crepe paper streamers danced mournfully in the warm breeze, drifting across the now-abandoned snack tables like ghostly apparitions. Crumbs and sticky spills were the only evidence left of the holiday treats that had been hastily abandoned.

The merry tunes of carol singers had given way to an ominous quiet, punctuated only by the occasional metallic rattle of loose aluminum chairs rocking back and forth. A few scattered jingle bells lay forlornly on the cracked asphalt, their cheerful, tinkling laughter now muted.

Crime scene tape erected around the mouth of the alleyway danced in the breeze like a menacing streamer, a garish reminder of the horrors unfolding just out of sight.

From out of nowhere, Pixie materialized by her side, and Sarah bent down to pick up the little papillon.

There you are. I was worried about you. I am sorry for...

Don't you worry about me, Pixie answered gently and placed a little kiss on Sarah's cheek. *Emma is the one who needs you right now.*

As if she had heard, Emma stopped and reached out. Sarah held out her arms to allow Pixie to transfer into Emma's, and the little dog snuggled tightly against the girl, sharing comfort and warmth in that way only dogs can.

More police vehicles arrived on the scene in a shriek of sirens, their piercing wails cutting through the unnatural hush. Reinforcements from Claremont PD by the looks of it. The flashing lights strobed in frantic patterns, casting the entire area in an otherworldly crimson glow one moment, only to leave it cloaked in deep indigo shadow the next.

As the black-and-whites screeched to a halt across the square, doors flew open, and uniformed officers spilled out in a flurry of shouted orders and radio chatter. Their hurried footsteps crunched across the scattered remnants of holiday decor, the otherwise undisturbed silence only compounding the bizarre dichotomy.

Drawing a deep, steadying breath, Sarah straightened her spine and lifted her chin. She was no stranger to mysteries and the darker elements that sometimes shadowed their tight-knit community. But this...this took things to a whole new level of darkness. One she wasn't at all prepared for.

Chapter Four

Officer Harding approached the distraught little group with a solemn expression, her eyes reflecting a mixture of professionalism and empathy. She crouched down to Emma's eye level, placing a gentle hand on the trembling girl's shoulder.

"Emma?" she spoke in a low, soothing tone. "I know this has been incredibly traumatic for you. But I need to ask if you're feeling up to answering just a few questions about what happened."

Emma's lower lip quivered as she lifted her gaze to meet the officer's. Sarah could see the storm of emotions swirling in her daughter's eyes—fear, confusion, and the struggle to comprehend her morbid discovery. Instinctively, she pulled Emma a little closer, offering what little comfort and protection she could.

Penny's knowing gaze flickered up to meet Sarah's. "Of course, only if you're okay with it, Sarah. I want you to be part of this interview all the way. We can wait until she's had more time if needed."

Sarah's chest constricted painfully at the thought of subjecting her baby girl to any further trauma, but she also knew the sooner they could get answers, the sooner this nightmare could be over.

Squaring her shoulders, Sarah gave a tight nod of affirmation. "It's alright, Penny. Let's just...get this over with."

With a grateful dip of her chin, Penny rose to her feet and motioned for them to follow. The small group made their way across the eerily vacant square, Matthew keeping a supportive hand anchored at the small of Sarah's back.

Within moments, they were ensconced in the cramped confines of the Rosewood Police Station's tiny entryway. The harsh fluorescent lighting cast an unflattering pall over the drab space, adding to the already oppressive atmosphere.

"Can you hang on for just a sec?" a kindly older deputy with a grizzled beard asked. "I'm sorry, but I have someone waiting in the interview room for Officer Harding."

Penny Harding glared daggers at him and squeezed Emma's shoulder. "Why was I not told?" she snapped and turned back to Emma.

"I'll be right back," she said under her breath, disappearing into a room just off the hall. Emma barely nodded. The door swung shut behind Officer Harding, but it didn't latch all the way. Sarah, seated closest to the door, heard every word spoken inside.

"Chloe," she heard Penny say quite kindly. "I didn't realize my officers would bring you right over and leave you waiting."

"Your deputy..." The woman's voice trembled, and a sob escaped her. "He said you'd want to know what happened inside the bank right away. Before I forgot. I just... it was..." A strangled sob escaped the woman.

Chloe, probably the bank teller at Rosewood Savings, Sarah thought.

"Take your time," Penny said gently. "Just tell me everything you remember."

Chloe cleared her throat and began. "It was so unreal. Two Santas came in—identical red suits, white beards, the works. I even laughed at them. I assumed they were headed for the Christmas in July event. But then I wondered why stop at the bank first—is that weird?" She paused, blowing her nose.

"Anyway, before I could ask what they needed, one of them pulled out a gun. He was so calm, almost cheerful, making a joke of it. The other robber, though... that one seemed really anxious."

Penny's pen scratched quickly across the paper. "What happened next?"

"The one with the gun, he kept saying, 'Relax, you know nothing's gonna happen.' But he was pointing the gun right at us, so how could we relax?" Chloe's voice quavered. "Then he winked at Deanna, she's another teller. She's real pretty, I guess, and he liked her. But still, it was... odd. Like maybe he knew her from somewhere?"

"Interesting," Penny murmured. "Go on."

"Nothing. They took the money and ran. Deanna started fussing and making a huge scene. I think she was in shock. Because of that, I was... I was late hitting the alarm." Chloe sobbed again and blew her nose. "I'm so sorry."

Penny placed a reassuring hand on Chloe's arm. "It's okay. You did your best in a scary situation. Was there anything else?"

Chloe nodded. "Just as I finally hit the alarm, I heard what sounded like a pop from outside. It was faint, and I didn't know if it was a shot, or maybe fireworks from the event, but..." She trailed off and blew her nose again.

Out in the entry, Sarah's mind raced. A dead Santa in an alley, two Santas robbing a bank, and a gunshot. Obviously related, but how?

"Thank you, Chloe," Penny said, closing her notebook. "You've been very helpful. We'll get to the bottom of this."

Moments later, Emma huddled into herself on the vinyl sofa in Penny's office, knees tucked up under her chin. Sarah slid in beside her, wrapping a protective arm around her shoulders as Penny settled into the chair opposite them.

"Whenever you're ready, Emma," the officer prompted gently. She flipped open her small notebook again, pen poised to jot down the details.

Emma worried her lower lip, her eyes welling with fresh tears, her arms holding Pixie in a tight stranglehold as she began.

"I-I'd gone to Jen's house, looking for her..." Her voice trembled as she paused to collect herself. "When she didn't answer, I decided to cut through that alley on my way back to the square. It's faster, and... I didn't want to miss the event."

Sarah rubbed soothing circles across her daughter's back, her own gut twisted in protest at having to make Emma relive those horrible moments. But she remained silent, allowing Emma to unveil the truth at her own pace.

"I could hear the mayor starting his speech, thought I'd see the voting after all, and then... That's when I... I literally stumbled over..." Emma's words caught in her throat as a strangled sob escaped. Swiping furiously at the tears streaking down her flushed cheeks, she soldiered on. "Over his body. Just lying there, face down on the ground. I thought I should... All that stuff you learn in first aid, you just don't remember it when you... You know?"

A heavy silence fell over the room, punctuated only by Emma's ragged breathing as she struggled to regain her composure. Officer Harding remained a stoic, impassive presence, her dark eyes registering every detail while betraying no emotion. The harsh crackle of the police radio suddenly sliced through the tension, causing them all to start. Penny's hand flew to it to turn it off, but not in time.

"Unit 321, this is dispatch. We've got an ID on that 10-54 from the square. Victim's name is Tyler Robinson, a twenty-two-year-old male. You know him?"

Sarah felt the blood drain from her face as the name struck her like a physical blow: Tyler. A local delivery driver who worked part-time at the museum for Matthew. He'd done small favors for them now and then, even returned to her house when she'd missed a delivery. He always carried treats for Pixie, and the little dog had always greeted him eagerly.

Sarah was only vaguely aware of Penny's muffled response to the radio.

Tyler was just a few years older than Cory, with everything ahead of him. Who and why? Emma started trembling again, and she gave her shoulder a comforting little squeeze.

Out of the corner of her eye, she saw a wispy, translucent little cloud forming, glowing and glittering for a moment and disappearing again.

Amelia and Simon, she could feel their presence thrumming with outrage around them. Amelia specifically had a deep connection with Emma that Sarah did not understand entirely, and she was certain just then that Amelia could move mountains with her outrage. Carefully, Sarah let out a harsh breath. *We'll find who did this*, she thought, and felt the electric connection with Amelia and Simon, causing her to shiver and raising the hair on her arms. *We'll find the identity of Tyler's killer and what's behind all this.*

The wave of energy ebbed again, and Sarah had to pull herself back to the conversation. Officer Harding only had a few more questions, and then she released them back into the hot July afternoon.

Chapter Five

As they stepped out of the police station, the weight of the day's events pressed down on both Sarah and Emma like a physical burden. The sun was setting, casting long shadows across the parking lot and painting the sky in glorious orange and pink hues that felt at odds with the somber mood.

Emma suddenly stopped, her hand tightening around Sarah's. "Mom," she said, her voice so small and vulnerable that something inside Sarah clenched hard.

"I didn't want to tell Officer Harding, but when I got to the alley... I heard something."

Sarah knelt down to eye level with her daughter, her heart aching at the fear she saw in Emma's eyes.

"You mean like a shot or the shooter running? Why wouldn't you ...?"

Emma shook her head, her eyes welling with tears. "No. Mom. I think I heard Tyler, though I didn't know it was him then. And I didn't really hear him. It was... more the way you hear Pixie." Emma put an impossibly small and fragile hand over her heart, and Sarah shivered. The cold, hard fist that gripped her heart when she couldn't sleep at night was back.

Knowing that she herself had abilities beyond what science and biology could explain was one thing, and frequently she struggled to deal with it, but Emma had been displaying similar talents for the last year or so. Tyler's spirit? Could she have felt it? Sarah fought a shiver.

"What...what did he say?" she asked tonelessly, and Emma shook her head.

"It didn't make a lot of sense." She closed her eyes, took her mother's hand, and took a few deep, steadying breaths.

"It sounded sort of like, 'I thought it was supposed to be fun, just a joke. You said it was just a publicity stunt.'"

Sarah hesitated, torn between her instinct to protect her daughter and her desire to get the information to Penny Harding. She had promised herself she wouldn't get involved in any more dangerous investigations, not with the kids to think about.

"Emma, honey, maybe he was just referring to the Santa event, you know?"

Nobody in their right mind would really see this as just a publicity stunt, would they?

"Don't just dismiss it," Emma interrupted her musings, her voice barely above a whisper. "I don't believe he was talking about the actual event. You have... powers. You can figure out what it means. If I tell Officer Harding, well, she will just..."

Sarah squeezed Emma's hand hard. Penny Harding had both feet planted firmly in the here and now. Talking about 'powers' and 'messages from beyond' would not sit well with her.

Sarah felt a lump form in her throat. The innocence of Emma's sweet face, juxtaposed with the very real horror she had witnessed, nearly broke her heart. She pulled her daughter into a tight hug, feeling Emma's silent tears dampen her shoulder.

After a long moment, Sarah pulled back, looking into Emma's eyes with determination.

"Please, Mom."

"All right, sweetheart. I'll do what I can to help figure this out, all right?"

I don't know myself where these powers came from or why I have them, she thought. But if there's ever any danger to my children... Her fist automatically clenched.

Emma nodded vigorously, a glimmer of relief shining through her tears. "Thank you. If anybody can figure this out, it's you."

As they walked to the car, Sarah felt a mixture of apprehension and resolve settle over her. She had really had her fill of mysteries, unsolved crimes, and strange happenings in the past few years, but for Emma's peace of mind, she could take up the mantle once more. Whatever darkness had descended upon their town, Sarah was determined to bring it to light, no matter the cost.

Chapter Six

The heavy silence between them on the short walk home was nearly suffocating. Sarah kept stealing glances at her daughter, her heart clenching at the hollow, haunted look in Emma's eyes.

Her sweet daughter had witnessed the kind of trauma no child should ever have to endure and, at the same time, connected to powers she didn't understand. Sarah ached to pull her into a fierce embrace, to shield her from the harsh realities that had come crashing into their world.

But she knew there would be time for that soon enough. Once Matthew and Cory joined up with them, Emma seemed to take some small comfort in her brother's sturdy presence beside her.

Sarah's gentle son had been uncharacteristically quiet since rejoining them at the police station. No doubt he, too, was processing the gut punch of learning their friendly young delivery driver, Tyler, was the one lying lifeless in that grungy alleyway.

Didn't Tyler play hockey and basketball at the community center as well? Sarah felt her heart lurch again, thinking that he and Cory might have played on the same team, maybe assisted each other's plays, celebrated wins, and bemoaned losses together.

As they walked up the driveway, Cory put his arm around Emma's shoulder and walked as close as he could. Sarah felt her eyes prick with tears at the tender gesture.

Matthew fell into step beside her as they followed the kids up the front walk. His jaw was set hard, eyes narrowed in that intense way that meant his mind was racing with unanswered questions.

In the games room, Pixie immediately hopped up beside Emma, cuddling in close and offering what doggy comfort she could. It was Matthew who finally broke the silence.

"I just...I can't wrap my head around it," he murmured, his brow furrowed deeply. "Tyler was a good kid. Why would anyone want to hurt him?"

Sarah knew how much Matt had come to care for the sandy-haired boy who'd worked part-time in night security at the museum.

Clearing his throat, Matthew continued. "He told me he just needed a little extra cash, working shifts at night to help make ends meet. Talked about wanting to see the world once he had got out of this tight spot he was in..."

His words trailed off, leaving them all to envision the bright future that had been so brutally snuffed out. Sarah swallowed hard against the lump in her throat.

Cory idly played with one of his game controllers without turning it on. "You don't think...you don't think he got mixed up in anything bad, do you? With that bank robbery and all?"

Sarah felt her stomach twist at the implication, at the very idea that Tyler could have been embroiled in something so nefarious. But before she could respond, Matthew nodded slowly, pushing his glasses up on his nose.

"It's a possibility we might have to consider, Cory. The timing seems too coincidental not to be connected, doesn't it?"

Just then, Sarah felt the hairs on the back of her neck prickling. She was acutely aware of the ethereal presence of Amelia and Simon hovering nearby, no doubt having absorbed every disturbing detail.

The notion that Tyler Robinson—seemingly a gentle, kindhearted soul—could be entangled with Rosewood's shadowy underbelly seemed a little far-fetched. Yet, as Sarah stared at her little family in the cozy games room, an eerie chill crawled up her spine. Had desperation driven Tyler to such extremes? And if so, had that fateful choice sealed his doom?

Sarah shuddered, feeling as if icy fingers were tracing patterns on her skin. Logic told her not to leap to conclusions, but intuition—that same sixth sense that had guided her through countless mysteries—screamed that something was terribly amiss. The facts were as clear as they were chilling: a young man lay dead in the heart of their quaint town, his life snuffed out mere moments after the bank's alarm had pierced the sleepy afternoon air.

Finally, Cory retreated to his room with a late-night snack, and Sarah and Matthew exchanged a long look. Sarah wanted to say something, spin a theory that had been nagging at her, but Cory reappeared in the doorway, his expression uncharacteristically serious.

"Mom, Matthew," he began, his voice low and intense, "Emma told me what she heard, and that just makes no sense. We need to find out who really did this. Who killed Tyler and robbed the bank? Because it was not him."

Sarah felt a pang of concern at the determination in her son's eyes, and she tried to tell him the same thing she had told Emma.

"Honey, the police are handling the investigation. It's not our place to—"

"Right, the police," Cory interrupted, his voice rising slightly. "Like they got it wrong when they accused Katelyn, and then again with Lily. Super. They'd never listen if Emma told them what she heard. You know what they'll do, they'll just say, oh, Tyler needed money, so he went and robbed a bank, all done. We're not buddies or anything, but I really don't think he would do this."

Matthew placed a gentle hand on Cory's shoulder. "We understand you want to protect your friend's memory. But poking around in these situations..."

Cory shook his head vehemently. "No, you don't understand, Matt. I played hockey with Tyler. He wasn't the kind of guy to take the easy way out. Someone else did this, and they're out there getting away with it."

Sarah felt her heart twist at the frustration in her son's voice. She glanced at Matthew, who gave her a slight nod of understanding.

"Look," Cory continued, his voice softening, "I know you guys think I'm still just a kid, but I want to help. You and Emma... you do things with your mind, don't you? To figure out what really happened? And I want to know that. What really happened? For him... and for me."

A moment of silence spread as Sarah and Matthew absorbed Cory's words. Finally, Matthew spoke, a hint of amusement in his voice despite the serious situation.

"Well, Sarah," he said, turning to her with a raised eyebrow, "it looks like both your kids want you to get to the bottom of this mess."

"I don't do things with my mind," Sarah muttered. "I just... And Emma... she's only beginning to figure it all out. I can't..."

Pixie picked that moment to hop up on her lap and paw her forearm.

Yes, you can. And then there's me, and Amelia and Lily. We made an awesome team before.

Sarah couldn't help but smile slightly at that, even as she felt the weight of responsibility settling on her shoulders. She looked from Matthew to Cory, seeing the expectation and hope in their eyes.

With a deep breath, she closed her eyes and spread her hands. "Alright," she said softly. "We'll look into it. But," she added, fixing Cory with a stern look, "you have to promise me the same thing as Emma did... no foolish risks—ever. This isn't a game, understood?"

Cory nodded eagerly. "I promise. Thanks, Mom."

As Cory headed back to his room, visibly relieved, Sarah turned to Matthew.

"I guess I don't have a choice, huh? Another mystery we're going to have to figure out, whether we want to or not."

Matthew wrapped an arm around her shoulders. "You've done it before. For your kids... and for Rosewood.".

Sarah leaned into his embrace and closed her eyes for a moment. Figuring out a mystery was one thing; she just hoped she could guide Emma as she discovered more of her own abilities. The blind leading the blind, she thought, closing her eyes for a moment. I don't even know myself why I can do what I do.

Chapter Seven

B ack on the couch, she pulled her knees up under her chin and wrapped her arms around her legs, letting her gaze drift sightlessly across the room. The jovial, happy mood from this morning had disappeared completely, replaced by a somber heaviness that hung in the house that night. Even Cory had lost his teenage sarcasm and gone to bed early. Sarah did not think he'd appreciate her checking on him.

His voice was changing; he'd asked Matthew to teach him how to drive—her little boy was ready and eager to be a man. But what would happen if the answer to this mystery wasn't what he thought?

Beside her, Matthew sat staring blankly, a half-empty glass of merlot in his hand.

"I just can't wrap my head around why someone would want to hurt him," Matthew said, his voice thick with emotion.

"I saw Tyler as a good kid just trying to make ends meet with those jobs after he'd lost some money in a scam of sorts."

Sarah nodded, handing him a fresh glass of wine before settling beside him on the couch.

"You don't think his money troubles had anything to do with it, do you?" she asked carefully. "If that failed investment scam lost him a lot... well, maybe..."

Matthew shook his head firmly. "I don't think so. He was a hard worker. Determined to pay it all back. His background check came back totally clean, and he swore to me this was just a tight spot because of one dumb decision. Somebody talked him into it."

Draining her own glass, Sarah felt a wave of distress from Emma upstairs in her room. Finding a body, hearing the deceased's final words, that would be tough on anyone. She put a hand on Matthew's shoulder, excused herself, and headed upstairs to check on her girl one last time.

∞

Emma didn't like closed doors; they made her feel shut in and cut off from everyone else. Her bedroom door was slightly ajar, with a beam of light creeping out through the gap. Sarah pushed it open gently and stopped in her tracks, feeling her eyes well with tears at the sight before her.

There, sitting cross-legged at the foot of Emma's bed, was the ghostly form of Amelia. The playful spirit had one transparent hand gently stroking Emma's leg in a soothing gesture as the girl slept fitfully.

Amelia looked up with an uncharacteristically soft expression. Her usual calm, composed expression was replaced by a tender smile. She turned her head, and Sarah found the spectral form of Simon standing at the foot of the bed, his hands by his side, watching over the two ladies he felt were his to protect.

"The poor dear," Amelia whispered. "The young man from the alley keeps visiting her dreams. I couldn't bear the thought of her suffering through any more nightmares tonight."

Sarah mouthed a silent "thank you" as Amelia gave Emma's leg one last comforting pat before rising up.

"She's very special," Amelia said softly. "Remember that you have the power to ease her pain."

With that, she joined Simon, and they drifted ethereally away and through the wall.

You have the power.

Sarah sat on the edge of the bed, just as Emma moaned in her sleep and tossed restlessly. She reached out and gently stroked the messy blonde curls. Emma felt sweaty and pained.

Sarah drew back her hand and stared. Just normal, everyday fingers. In times of great need or emergencies, however, what they could do frightened her.

You do know that Amelia's right. You have the power.

Pixie strolled into the room and smoothly hopped onto Emma's bed to curl against the girl's back.

To help her? Sarah asked.

To help anybody. If you would stop doubting yourself and just trust it.

Just then, Emma turned again, and Sarah put her hand just above the girl's heart.

When she had moved to Rosewood Hollow after her divorce and into this house, she'd discovered... abilities she'd never known she had. If someone threatened her family, she seemed to release something she herself feared.

But in her hands, she'd also discovered a power to heal. Instinctively, she drew back from those powers and tried every day to figure out where they came from.

Just then, Emma moaned in her sleep again, and Sarah splayed her fingers.

"Peace," she said softly and saw Pixie crowding in even closer, touching her entire body to Emma's.

"Peace."

Emma sighed, and she sank deeper into her bedding softly, as if a pressure had been released.

That's it, Pixie said softly.

Sarah withdrew her hand, resisting the urge to look at her fingers again. "Stay with her," she said softly, but she need not have. Pixie had cuddled up so tightly to Emma that a force of nature couldn't pry her away.

Her heart was heavy but reassured; Sarah rose, pulled the door almost closed again, and returned downstairs to Matthew's comforting embrace.

∞

The big grandfather clock in the entry chimed softly, announcing the end to a day she'd rather not remember.

"How is she doing?" Matthew asked, and Sarah only shrugged.

"She has a tough road ahead. But there are a lot of...individuals rooting for her."

Matthew only stared into the dancing flames of the fireplace. He knew enough not to question that sentence, and Sarah squeezed his hand hard.

Chapter Eight

T he next morning broke dark and gray, as if reflecting the previous day's events. Sarah had made breakfast, but neither Cory nor Emma did more than move food around on their plates in silence.

Matthew decided to work from home so he could be there for them just in case they needed him.

Sarah cleaned the dishes and tidied her kitchen, feeling footloose. Much as she wanted to stay at home for her kids, she knew what they really wanted was a solution to the mystery surrounding Tyler's death. And that required her.

She stood at her kitchen window, staring into the yard until she felt the gentle tap of a paw on her leg.

Looking down, she met Pixie's inquisitive dark eyes.

So... are we going to take a walk into town, or what?

You think?

Pixie spun around in a dizzy circle and sat again, looking up at Sarah from dark, glittering eyes. And the tip of her fluffy white tail began to glow ever so gently. Her sign of magic.

"All right," Sarah said, winked, and reached for the leash. "You and me, girl."

The town square, which had been a festive scene of joy and holiday cheer only a day earlier, now stood eerily devoid of all traces of the much-hyped Christmas in July event. Not a stray decoration or abandoned lawn chair remained. The space had been meticulously cleared overnight as if to erase any hint of the previous day's chaos.

Sarah shuddered involuntarily as she passed the entrance of the alleyway where Tyler's body had been discovered. Yellow police tape still cordoned off the area, serving as the only visible reminder of the grisly crime. The dank, narrow passage seemed to pull her in with a sense of dread and foreboding.

"Well, Pixie," she said out loud, stooping to scoop up the small dog into her arms, "I was kind of hoping they'd leave the crime scene untouched, and we could look around a bit."

Pixie responded with a serious side eye and a lick on Sarah's cheek, as if offering reassurance.

Since when have you needed human crime scene clues?

Right.

Stroking the dog's silky fur, Sarah's gaze drifted three blocks over to the unmistakable facade of Rosewood Savings & Trust. The impressive stone edifice practically loomed over the surrounding buildings, its stately columns and carved gargoyles casting long shadows in the morning light. The hairs on her arms stood on end as she remembered the terse alert from the police about the daring bank robbery taking place around the same time as Tyler's murder.

"Too many coincidences for my liking," she muttered under her breath, taking a few steps away. A million thoughts careened through her mind at breakneck speed. Could Tyler have been involved in the heist, acting out of desperation? His financial troubles could support that theory. However, he might also be an unlucky bystander in the wrong place at the wrong time. Her heart—and indeed, her kids—wanted to believe that second option so badly.

With a determined nod, Sarah tightened her grip on Pixie and set off toward the bank, her sensible flats clicking rhythmically against the sidewalk as she scanned the scene from left to right. If there were answers to be found regarding these bizarre crimes, the bank seemed as good a place as any to begin her search.

As she drew closer, Sarah had to avert her gaze. She always felt that eerie sensation that the ornately carved stone figures adorning the roof seemed to watch her every move, their snarling faces menacing against the bright summer sky. She quickened her pace, Pixie tucked securely in the crook of her arm.

Matthew had explained the history of carved stone gargoyles to her at least a dozen times, yet she still found them to be a little ominous.

They had only traveled a couple of blocks from the town square when a familiar voice called out her name.

"Sarah! Sarah Anderson, wait up, would you!"

Lily. Sarah turned and waited as Lily hurried up the sidewalk, clutching a zippered bank bag to her chest. Lily's curly red hair bounced with each step, and her cheeks flushed from the exertion.

"Well, if it isn't the owner of Rosewood's best little bookshop," Sarah said as Lily pulled up beside her. "How are you? You already opened the store again after... You know."

Lily rolled her eyes good-naturedly. "What good would closing the shop do anyway, other than hurt the business? People who come in to gossip might buy something. I was just headed over to make my daily bank deposit. Missed it yesterday." She gave the bulging bag a little shake, the contents clinking faintly.

At the mention of the bank, Sarah felt her pulse quicken a bit. She regarded Lily with lowered eyelashes.

"Does it not worry you? I mean... to go into the very bank that was robbed yesterday."

To Sarah's surprise, Lily seemed unbothered and simply shrugged her slender shoulders.

"A bit, I suppose. But you can't let that stop you from doing what you need to do. Did you know that bank robberies are, in fact, on the decline? A rarity, almost. Cashless society and all that." Her gaze sharpened as she eyed Sarah and Pixie carefully. "But your interest seems... keener than expected, somehow."

Sarah felt a blush creep into her cheeks as Lily's astute perception hit a little too close to the truth. Her best friend didn't miss much, especially if it concerned Sarah on the trail of the latest mystery.

"I wasn't going to get involved, I swear to you," Sarah said with a rueful chuckle. "But then both Emma and Cory wanted me to check it out, and I can't help but wonder about the connection between the murder and the robbery, given the timing. There... I said it."

Lily's eyes widened in surprise. Then, a slow smile curved her lips as she gave an approving nod.

"Emma and Cory, uh-huh. I didn't think you could resist the sheer temptation to see if there's anything the police might have missed. Although after what happened last time, with Vincent..."

"Not doing anything like that," Sarah said and winked. "I was just going to drop in, have a little look-see."

"I still have my deposit to make, so what are we waiting for?" Lily looped her free arm through Sarah's as they continued on their way, Pixie keeping a relaxed trot beside them.

"I actually have a lot of fun every time I get to be the backseat driver on one of your investigations."

Sarah laughed and elbowed Lily in the side, equal parts exasperated and deeply grateful for her friend's unwavering support.

Lily and Pixie, she corrected in her mind, when the little papillon jumped against her knee and winked at her. Best sidekicks a girl could have.

❧

The stately Rosewood Savings & Trust building dominated the square, striking a balance between old-world charm and modern amenities. Constructed in the late 19th century from sturdy gray stone quarried locally, the three-story edifice stood as a testament to the town's historic roots, as a plaque out front proudly proclaimed.

Tasteful renovations and modern touches ensured the venerable institution could provide updated services and security worthy of the present day.

Despite the dramatic heist that had occurred just 24 hours earlier, there was no sign of disruption or disarray inside the lobby of Rosewood Bank & Trust.

If Sarah didn't know better, she'd never guess that this was the very site where armed robbers had stormed in and allegedly made off with thousands in cash and valuables from the vault.

"Did you hear that the security tapes in the lobby were not working yesterday?" Lily whispered while they waited for their turn. "Bit odd in a modern bank, don't you think?"

"I hadn't," Sarah said softly. "Where did you get that?"

Lily simply shrugged. Having lived here all her life, she had her sources. The security cameras weren't working, which was definitely odd. That screamed inside job, didn't it?

Sarah looked up at the cameras covering the customer service area, their little red eyes blinking rhythmically. Creepy that, she thought, when a door at the far end of the lobby opened.

Time seemed to slow as Sarah watched the lone teller's coworker, Deanna Barnes, emerge from a staff door and start tidying her workstation for the day.

'Deanna started fussing and making a big scene. I think she was in shock. Because of that, I was late hitting the alarm.' Wasn't that what Chloe, the bank teller, had said? And how come Deanna was already at work again today, one day after the robbery? Sarah cocked her head and she watched the other woman's precise little movements. Her breath caught in her throat when Deanna's gaze flicked up and met hers across the empty lobby.

Suddenly, Sarah found herself locked in the woman's piercing stare. Deanna's eyes, a striking shade of pale green, bore into her with unsettling intensity. A tremor of unease rippled through Sarah as a strange sensation washed over her—a jarring flicker of familiarity, as if she innately recognized this stranger on a deeper, almost primordial level.

The moment stretched on infinitely until Pixie gave a short little whine, jolting Sarah back to the present. She blinked rapidly, the eerie spell broken, as Deanna abruptly turned and disappeared through the staff door once more.

Sarah's mouth went dry as she unconsciously gripped Lily's arm, her knuckles whitening. What had just happened? What was that feeling of unexplained recognition? And why did the sight of Deanna Barnes unravel a tangled thread of unease deep in her gut?

Lily, still waiting her turn, leaned in close, lowering her voice urgently.

"What was that all about? That staring contest that just went down between you and that other teller?"

Sarah could only shake her head slowly, her pulse thrumming in her ears as she struggled to find the words to describe the peculiar, somewhat unnerving transcendent moment she had just experienced.

"I know Deanna from when she volunteered at the museum's fundraising gala last year," Sarah explained in a hushed tone. "I'm pretty sure she's married to a civil engineer by the name of Tom. I think he's quite a bit older than her."

Lily arched an eyebrow. "What was that strange look she gave you just now? It seemed like she was challenging you or something. So odd."

Sarah shrugged, still feeling unsettled. "I don't know, honestly. Maybe she recognized me from the gala, too? Though I can't imagine why she'd react that way."

"I think she was on duty yesterday when the robbery went down," Lily reasoned. "Might be a normal reaction to feel a bit jumpy and suspicious of everyone right now, especially with someone in the bank who doesn't have an account here... like you, for example."

Lily's eyes darted to her hairline.

"Don't know why she's already back," Sarah said tonelessly.

Worrying her lower lip, she looked back and wasn't quite convinced. There had been something more, an uncanny sense of knowing behind

Deanna's penetrating gaze. She couldn't put a finger on it, so she nodded slowly.

"Yeah... maybe that's it."

Through the glass wall, she saw Deanna walking down the hall toward what she believed was the staff room.

Deanna Barnes cut a striking figure, even in her neat black pantsuit and crisp white blouse. In her early 30s, she possessed the kind of cool, polished beauty that turned heads, from her sleek blonde bob to her impeccably applied makeup.

Her fashion sense was decidedly trendy yet professional. She wore designer accessories like the buttery-soft leather tote slung over one arm and the chunky gold watch peeking from beneath her cuffed sleeve. Even her black kitten heels looked like they cost more than Sarah's monthly grocery budget.

But it was Deanna's eyes that were genuinely arresting—a pale, sparkling shade of green that seemed to miss nothing as she surveyed her surroundings with a somewhat haughty, watchful gaze. There was an intensity, an almost predatory quality about how her stare could pin someone in place.

Though she appeared young enough to still be starting her career, the substantial diamond solitaire on her left ring finger suggested her marriage to an evidently wealthy older man. Sarah struggled to remember Deanna's husband and could recall little more than his name, Tom, and that he worked as a civil engineer.

While working at the fundraising gala, she had picked up bits and pieces of town gossip, like the rumor that Deanna had only married Tom for his money and would certainly leave him the moment a younger, good-looking fellow caught her eye. At the time, she had dismissed it as envy; the Barnes family certainly had money, didn't they?

The ice queen, Sarah had dubbed her then.

It was hard to imagine this elegant, affluent woman involved in something as tawdry as a bank. And yet, Sarah couldn't quite shake her nagging suspicion that Deanna knew more about the previous day's events than she let on.

Chapter Nine

The lone teller on duty, a friendly-faced woman in her fifties named Cassie, welcomed them with a warm smile as they approached the counter.

"Come right up, Lily! Here for your deposit?" Cassie asked, her tone bright and familiar as she accepted Lily's zippered bank bag.

"Always glad to do it," Lily replied with an easy grin. "My little bookstore has been keeping you all plenty busy lately."

Cassie gave an impressed whistle as she began counting out the cash. "I'll say! I'm glad you're doing so well!"

Her gaze then shifted curiously to Sarah and Pixie, cradled comfortably in her arms. "Are you looking to open a new account with us today?"

Sarah shook her head and chuckled. "Oh no, I was just out with Lily, that's all. Enjoying the summer sunshine with Pixie here."

As if on cue, Pixie let out a cheerful yap and wagged her feathery tail excitedly. Cassie melted instantly, emitting an admiring coo as she leaned over the counter for a better view.

"Well, hi there, beautiful! Aren't you just the most precious little thing?" She straightened up, giving Sarah an inviting smile. "Please feel free to stop in anytime. We love having furry friends visit the bank... and their owners, too, of course."

She gave Pixie one last admiring look. "In fact, with that cute little pup sniffing around, I'll bet you customers would line up to say hi to her!"

Cassie's eyes sparkled with amusement as she pushed Lily's deposit paperwork across the counter. "You know, after yesterday's wild events, I'm glad you came in today to bring some normalcy! I think some of our senior customers are a bit worried."

She leaned over the counter again and gave Pixie another gentle tap on the nose with her manicured red nail. "I hope this gets resolved soon, so we can return to normal, don't you, little pup?"

As Lily thanked the teller and gathered her things, Sarah's gaze was once again drawn to the staff door from which Deanna had emerged earlier. She couldn't shake the peculiar sense that Mrs. Barnes would not return to the bank lobby until she and Lily had left.

⁂

Later that evening, Sarah and Matthew relaxed together on the porch swing, enjoying a glass of wine as the fireflies began blinking their magical lights in the dusky yard.

"Matthew, do you remember Deanna Barnes from when she volunteered at the museum's gala last year?" Sarah asked, breaking the comfortable silence between them.

Matthew frowned in thought for a moment before nodding. "Yeah, of course. Tall, blonde, dressed to the nines as always. Why do you ask?"

Recounting her unusual encounter with the bank teller earlier that day, Sarah described the unsettling vibe she had received from Deanna's intense, scrutinizing gaze.

"It felt as if she recognized me, yet there was something more present, too. An undercurrent of...I don't know, perhaps tension?"

To her surprise, Matthew let out a bark of laughter, shaking his head adamantly. "Oh, I seriously doubt Deanna Barnes would ever be mixed up in anything as pedestrian as a bank robbery," he chuckled. "That woman is too busy maintaining her perfectly highlighted hair and manicured nails to get her hands dirty with anything illegal."

Sarah arched one sculpted eyebrow curiously. "You seem awfully certain about her."

"Please," Matthew affirmed with a nod. "Deanna and her husband are the kind of people who have serious money. Money with a capital M, if you will. Barnes inherited a fortune from his parents. They're members at the historical society and never let me forget their donor status."

He took a sip of his cabernet, considering his words carefully. "No. If I had to guess, whatever you sensed from her was probably just her usual attitude of superiority. She can be a bit...aloof at times. Snooty Cory would say. And you did have a dog in your arms." Matthew rolled his eyes and winked. "Hard as it may be to believe, some people do not take to Pixie."

Sarah scoffed, yet she couldn't dispute that assessment based on her brief encounter with the stylish Mrs. Barnes. Being a snob didn't automatically imply guilt. Unfortunately.

With a slight shake of her head, she let the topic go for now. Matthew's expression had turned slightly wistful as he gazed up at the darkening sky.

"I do wish Cory wasn't taking Tyler's death so hard," he murmured after a moment. "I didn't realize they were friends over and above playing on the same rec hockey team despite the age difference."

Sarah ached for her teenage son. At seventeen, losses like this could be particularly hard to process. He would tell her it wasn't necessary, but she wanted to check in with Cory again before bed.

Resting her head on Matthew's shoulder, Sarah watched the fireflies winking in and out of existence like tiny harbingers dancing among the shadows. The world could be so peaceful and beautiful out here on her porch; if one didn't think of the mysteries lurking in those very same shadows, just waiting to be unraveled.

Matthew chuckled softly as he swirled the rich cabernet in his glass.

"Any news about that bank robbery being tied to Tyler's murder?"

Sarah frowned slightly and shook her head again.

"I honestly don't know...There's no clear connection, and it feels like a stretch to relate the two. However, it's a strange coincidence if they are not." She paused, reflecting on her unusual encounter with Deanna at the bank earlier that day. "Deanna Barnes and Tyler Robinson are as different as two people could possibly be."

"No, not exactly the likeliest pair of criminal conspirators." He gave Sarah a sidelong glance, one eyebrow raised knowingly. "But then again, perhaps stranger things have happened?"

"Or neither one of them has anything to do with the other," Sarah countered, looking down at her hands. "Just a coincidence. Wrong place, wrong time."

"I used to think there was no such thing as coincidence," Matthew said. "But in a small town like Rosewood Hollow, sometimes the odds of crossed paths are higher than you'd expect."

Matthew smiled fondly and wrapped an arm around Sarah's shoulders. Resting her head on his shoulder, Sarah's gaze drifted over the darkened treeline, where the fireflies continued their mesmerizing dance.

Chapter Ten

The next morning, sunrise found Sarah and Lily lacing up their runners for their customary morning walk through the flower-lined streets of downtown Rosewood. The two friends strolled leisurely along the sidewalks, with Pixie trotting happily beside them, taking in the picturesque New England scenery.

Towering maple and elm trees arched overhead in sprawling canopies of green, dappling the antique brick walkways with lacy patterns of shifting sunlight. Hanging baskets overflowed with vibrant petunias and geraniums, perfuming the air with their sweet fragrances. Quaint shops and boutiques housed in beautifully preserved 19th-century buildings lent a timeless, almost storybook charm to the downtown thoroughfare.

As they passed by the white-steepled town hall and neatly manicured public green, Sarah glanced sidelong at her best friend.

"Help me understand this, a robbery and a murder on the same day. Are they connected or not? I'm driving myself crazy."

Lily arched one perfectly groomed eyebrow quizzically.

"And they both happened at the Christmas in July event. Maybe that's the key to it, before everything... went sideways."

"Sideways, good word."

Sarah nodded, worrying her lower lip between her teeth.

"It seems so improbable that these two crimes occurred almost simultaneously. Then there's Matthew and Cory, insisting that Tyler was merely an innocent bystander. Help me make sense of this!"

"Sorry, I'm stumped," Lily shook her head. "But everything happened at the event. Why don't we visit the folks who organized all the craziness?" Lily suggested slowly. "Creative Charities, right? That PR agency that has taken over a number of local events and fundraisers lately?"

"Right..." Sarah quickened her pace slightly. "Is there any chance you could help us arrange a meeting with them? I recall you mentioning that you had worked with Creative Charities before for something at your store."

Lily waved one hand and grimaced.

"Only in that they drastically overcharged me for designing a single promotional flyer many years ago. But I'm still friendly with the owner, Gina Eastbrook. She comes in to shop now and then. Want me to finagle us an appointment there?"

A smile curved Sarah's lips as she watched Pixie pause to sniff inquisitively at a vibrant flower basket. Whoever had committed these crimes had used the event as a cover. That was as good a place to start as any.

"If you wouldn't mind. Maybe something will shake loose."

With Lily already pulling out her phone to tap out a text, Sarah gave the quaint downtown street one last appreciative glance. Finally, Lily peeled off to open her bookstore.

"I'll let you know when Gina from the agency gets back to me," she called over her shoulder with a cheerful wave. "Meantime, try not to magically solve the entire case without me."

"As if!"

Pixie gave a spirited little yip, and she and Sarah turned and headed back home.

∽

Sarah approached her cheerful blue house with its tidy lawn and flower boxes overflowing with petunias.

She called out upon entering the cool entry hall, with its black and white mosaic tiles and massive double staircase, but received only silence in return. In the kitchen, she discovered a page torn from one of Matthew's yellow legal pads, pinned to the table with a metal tin of tea.

"Gone to the lake with Emma and Cory for some entertainment. See you later," she read aloud.

Matthew. He knew the kids were troubled by Tyler's death and tried to distract them.

"Now I feel guilty," she said to Pixie. "I should have thought of that myself."

Matthew thought of it, Pixie answered. *And your kids admire it when you get to the truth.*

Still.

Sarah tapped the note against her finger.

The rush of affection for Matthew warmed her from the inside out. After the turmoil of her marriage to Michael, the divorce, and moving, finally finding a caring, supportive partner felt like the greatest of second chances. She smiled wistfully, looking forward to hearing all about their lake outing when they returned home later.

Sarah was just pulling out her phone to text Matthew when an icy vise gripped her heart with a hard squeeze. The air around her suddenly grew still and inexplicably chilled, and the fine hairs on her arms prickled with apprehension.

Sarah knew that visceral feeling all too well, the telltale sign Amelia was about to manifest in the here and now.

Sure enough, as Sarah pivoted slowly on her heel, a faint mist began to coalesce in the corner of the dimly lit kitchen. The vapor swirled and thickened, gaining a more opaque form. Slowly, the hazy white cloud started to take on a human shape - that of a woman in an elegant floor-length dress from the early 1900s.

Her gown was an ethereal white, and the fabric shimmered and flowed like actual smoke. The high collar accentuated her long, graceful neck. Lace accented the sleeves and bodice in delicate floral patterns. As the misty form solidified, Sarah could make out her refined facial features: high cheekbones, pale skin, ruby-red lips, and eyes that seemed to contain infinite sadness behind their beauty.

Her hair was pinned up in an elaborate style, and a few strands had begun to loosen, and wisps danced around her face as if in a slight breeze.

A wry smile played across Amelia's cherubic features as she swept into the kitchen.

"Why, my dear Sarah, all alone at home on this fine summer morning?" The spirit's face sparkled with mischief. "Did everybody depart in the hopes you would solve this dreadful mystery by the time they returned?"

Sarah rolled her eyes good-naturedly, long ago becoming accustomed to Amelia's flair for the dramatic.

"And hello to you too, Amelia," she replied, shoving her phone back into her pocket and gazing at a point just behind Amelia.

"Where is Simon today? Did you leave him... home?"

She barely bit off the phrase, Is he unwell. Was there such a thing, Sarah wondered. Could ghosts be unwell?

Amelia's ruby lips curved into a melancholy smile.

"Ah, Simon. He tries now and then to convince me to say farewell to this earthly plane and to you—forever—now that we can." Her voice carried a melodic, otherworldly lilt. "To answer your question, he is otherwise occupied today. He has also developed quite a fondness for engaging with the things you call…electronics. They can be quite entertaining."

"Don't remind me," Sarah said, gripping the phone in her pocket a little tighter, feeling instant empathy for the poor soul whose computer or phone Simon was 'playing with' today. The memory of how Amelia and Simon had basically disabled the entire police station last winter to buy some time for her friend Lily still sent shivers down her back. If Detective Penny Harding ever found out…

"She won't," Amelia said simply. "And even if she did, nobody would believe her and send her off to be treated for – what do you call it again – stress-related issues."

I know the feeling, Sarah thought, and rubbed the spot between her eyebrows.

"I keep forgetting you can sense my thoughts," she said instead.

"You could shield them, you know."

Another thing that was supposed to be within her abilities. Sarah smiled and tried to hide the fact that she had never heard of the practice before.

"As for your other question, yes, sometimes even we Spectrals prefer to remain undisturbed, though it is more an ailment of the mind…"

Made sense.

"Not that I'm not delighted to see your mischievous face, Amelia," Sarah said, arching one eyebrow curiously, "but what brings you flitting about my kitchen today? Surely you're not just here to tease me mercilessly."

Amelia's expression turned momentarily somber as she clasped her translucent hands together.

"Actually, I had hoped to check on young Emma's well-being after that dreadful trauma she experienced. The poor dear looked so distraught when I paid her a visit last night to gently watch over her dreams."

A lump formed in Sarah's throat at the tender gesture from her impish friend. For all Amelia's puckish antics, she harbored a well of empathy, particularly when it came to protecting the innocence of children.

"That's very kind of you," Sarah replied, her voice catching slightly with emotion. "Emma was certainly shaken, but I think having you there to ward off any nightmares helped tremendously. Thank you."

Regaining her customary buoyant air, Amelia gave her wrist a dismissive flick.

"Oh, think nothing of it! Emma is a... very special, gifted young lady, and I try to look after her whenever I can."

Her expression turned sly as her luminous eyes danced with mirth. "Speaking of looking after matters...I may have also done a bit of spying about town regarding that dreadful business at your Christmas in July festival. Such a shame to have it ruined."

Sarah felt her pulse quicken at the prospect of a lead from her otherworldly ally.

"Did you find anything interesting? Anything important?"

Amelia sparkled in a particular shade of lavender and silver, which could mean she was either amused or angry; Sarah could never really tell.

"I happened to pay a little visit to that charming institution you humans are so obsessed with, the bank," Amelia replied airily. Her pearly features crinkled into an impish grin. "And I may have caught wind of a most intriguing conversation between two of the employees there."

Pixie barked emphatically, her fluffy tail swishing to emphasize the ghost's tantalizing implication. Sarah poured a glass of water to hide her impatience. Had Amelia been there at the same time she and Lily had, she wondered, but didn't ask.

"So," she said instead, taking a sip of her water. "Don't leave me hanging, then. What did you find? A banker with his hand in the till? What?"

With an impish giggle, Amelia drifted closer until her wispy form hovered mere inches away.

"Well, for starters, my dear, I know that you and Lily visited there just yesterday." She paused deliciously before whispering, "It would seem not all is as it appears with that frosty teller who gave you the cold shoulder."

Sarah's breath hitched in her throat, and an icy tingle danced along her spine. Her unsettling interaction with Deanna Barnes had sparked an instinctive prickling of suspicion. Amelia drew back a little, as if the entire thing had suddenly bored her. She just loved to tease Sarah, especially if she knew she had information Sarah wanted.

"Tell me everything you heard, Amelia, please," Sarah said now. "And spare no details, even if they seem strange – especially if they are strange."

Amelia's sculpted features twisted into an expression of exaggerated contemplation as she recalled the overheard conversation.

"Well, it seems your frosty Miss Deanna is quite the topic of speculation amongst her coworkers," the ghost began, a hint of relish in her tone. "I materialized in that horribly drab little staff room the tellers use and overheard two of the younger women gossiping away like squawking hens!"

Sarah tried not to appear too eager as she waited for Amelia to continue. The spirit paused for dramatic effect before obliging.

"The first girl-a petite little thing, I can't recall her name—was saying how Deanna always acts as if her designer shoes and bags elevate her above the rest of them." Amelia rolled her eyes emphatically. "Putting on airs as if she's the queen of the bank and they're mere paupers, presumably."

"And the other gossipy teller?" Sarah prompted, unable to repress her investigative zeal. "What did she have to say about Deanna's supposed haughtiness?"

"Ah, yes!" Amelia's eyes glittered with mischief. "Well, this second young lady, a bubbly redhead with a smattering of freckles, if I recall correctly, seemed to agree that Deanna could be maddeningly superior at times. But she also mentioned having noticed Deanna acting rather... strangely, I believe her word was. Secretive. They speculated that perhaps there was a new man in her life."

Sarah felt her heartbeat quicken as the pieces began falling into place. "Acting strangely, how exactly? Any details? And who would that new man have been? Does he have a name? Don't make me pull this out of you one word at a time."

Amelia gave an airy shrug of her slender shoulders. "That's just the rub of it, my dear, I couldn't quite make out any more details before those chatty tellers dispersed again. But it does seem our prim and proper Mrs. Barnes may have been behaving rather uncharacteristically as of late."

"You know, complaining about a coworker is kind of normal on this plane. I've been there."

It certainly was not a lot that Amelia had brought her: envy and gossip amongst coworkers.

Amelia's spectral form shimmered and glittered for a moment, and she rose a few feet to stare down at Sarah, a sure sign she disagreed with something Sarah had just said.

"Perhaps that is so in your world, but I do not generally miss it when someone says, acting funny, and actually means it."

The glitter died down again, and Sarah raised her hands a bit.

"Sorry. Do you think you might be able to visit the bank again and keep an ethereal ear to the ground?" she asked, trying to process what little she had just found out. "Any other gossipy tidbits about Deanna could potentially lead us to an answer. Both Emma and Cory are quite adamant that Tyler is innocent—and that I should prove it."

The mischievous spirit's face broke into a devilish grin. "Why, Sarah, I thought you'd never ask! Creating some harmless chaos and adding delicious intrigue to your mundane lives is one of my greatest pleasures."

Sarah closed her eyes and tried not to think about what she had just unleashed. A ghost with a mischievous streak, inside a bank. Still, Amelia was an invaluable ally when it came to these mysteries, even if her methods were rather... unconventional.

"Wonderful. Thank you!" Sarah bent to scoop up Pixie, cradling the tiny pup against her chest. "And while you check around, Pixie and

I will see if her exceptional sniffer can help find the solution to the mystery."

Pixie yipped in seeming agreement, somehow always privy to the secrets Sarah was trying to unravel.

With a wink and a swirl of incorporeal mist, Amelia vanished from sight, off to stir whatever spectral chaos she deemed necessary. She relished creating disorder. Her antics could be silly and annoying, yet Sarah understood the ghost adhered to strict principles regarding injustice and outright deception.

Sarah stroked Pixie's soft fur, her mind already filled with questions about the elusive and enigmatic Deanna Barnes.

Was it mere dislike, or did that elegant, aloof teller really have a few things to hide behind that frosty veneer? Was it gossip, or could the ice queen truly be involved in a tawdry affair? And was said affair possibly tied to the chaos of the bank heist and Tyler's murder?

Chapter Eleven

A s Sarah pondered the implications of Amelia's gossip while doing mindless busywork in the kitchen, she heard the sound of tires crunching on gravel. Accompanying it was the cheerful cacophony of Matthew and the kids returning from their lake outing. The front door burst open, bringing in a wave of laughter and excited chatter.

"Mom! Mom! You should've seen the fish I caught!" Cory's voice rang out, filled with teenage enthusiasm.

"He nearly fell in," Emma said, sounding almost like herself again. "And I found the prettiest shells on the beach!"

In her hand, she held a fistful of brightly colored shells, and her eyes lit up with plain joy once again. Sarah couldn't help but smile at their exuberance.

"That's wonderful, you two! Why don't you go upstairs and get cleaned up? I'll be up in a bit to hear all about your adventures."

As the kids thundered up the stairs, Matthew approached Sarah, his hair still damp from swimming. He planted a quick kiss on her cheek.

"Hey, babe. How was your morning?"

Sarah's expression turned serious as she led Matthew to the kitchen for some privacy. "Well, it was certainly... informative," she began, leaning against the counter. "Amelia decided to come and visit."

Matthew's eyebrows shot up. "Really? What did our resident ghostly troublemaker have to say?"

Sarah recounted Amelia's eavesdropping at the bank, particularly the gossip about Deanna Barnes and a potential lover. As she spoke, Matthew's brow furrowed in concentration.

"Usually when somebody says a person is acting strange, there's something to it," he mused. "And it does seem to line up with the odd vibe you got from her yesterday."

Sarah nodded. "Exactly. You think she could be behind the whole thing? And then, given the timing of the bank robbery and Tyler's murder..."

Matthew held up a finger to stop her.

"Now, let's not jump to conclusions. A little strange behavior doesn't automatically equate to criminal activity. While having an affair is certainly not nice, it is not, in fact, criminal."

"Well, it should be," Sarah snapped, remembering her ex-husband. "But you have to admit, it's a lead worth pursuing. We don't have much else to go on right now."

Matthew wrapped an arm around her shoulders, giving her a gentle squeeze. "I just want you to slow down and be careful, okay? I know how you get when you're on the trail of a mystery."

Sarah leaned into his embrace and took a deep, slow breath.

"I will, I will. I'm just frustrated."

As they stood there in the kitchen, the sounds of the kids' laughter drifting down from upstairs, and Matthew running his hands through his damp hair, Sarah felt a rush of gratitude for them.

"You know," Matthew interrupted her thought, "in all my years of studying local history and observing human nature, I've found that murders usually boil down to a handful of main motives: jealousy, envy, hatred, or revenge."

Sarah secretly grinned at his analytical approach. "Is that so? And what about the motives in robberies?"

"Robberies are a bit simpler," Matthew replied with a wry smile. "They almost always come down to the obvious thing: money."

Sarah's eyes lit up for a moment, and she nodded.

"Meaning, if Deanna's involved in either the murder or the robbery—or both—we need to have a serious look at her financial situation and her personal life."

"If you can," Matthew agreed cautiously. "If she's been acting strangely, that could point to money troubles or problems at home. Either of those could potentially drive someone to desperate measures."

Sarah began to pace the kitchen, chewing on her lower lip. "That wouldn't explain why Tyler was shot, though. I need to find out if Deanna's having any financial difficulties. Maybe unexpected debts, gambling problems, or expensive habits she can't afford?"

"And her home life," Matthew added. "She's married to an older man—that engineer, Tom. There's some gossip she had an affair. Trouble in paradise?"

Sarah drummed her fingertips together with impatience. "Good point. Maybe Lily can help. She seems to know everyone's business in this town."

Matthew chuckled. "Just be careful, Sarah. Digging into people's personal lives can be dangerous, especially if they really do have something to hide."

"I know," Sarah assured him, reaching out to squeeze his hand. "But if Deanna is involved in Tyler's death or the robbery, I want to find out. Christmas in July was supposed to be a happy, fun event. Instead, it turned my kids' lives upside down and gave them nightmares. I want to know."

Matthew gave her a quick kiss on the cheek.

"Sometimes, I think there's an FBI undercover agent lost in you and your canine sidekick. You two are ruthless."

Sarah smiled up at him, feeling a surge of affection for this man who supported her even in her most unconventional pursuits. "Aw, thanks for the compliment."

She could still hear Cory and Emma's laughter drifting down from upstairs, and a bit of her earlier guilt went away. She now had a plan: investigate Deanna Barnes's financial situation and home life. Deanna could be the key to this thing—or an entirely uninvolved third party who was going through a rough patch. Either way, she'd find out.

Sarah's phone buzzed, shattering the peaceful evening. "Michael," she mouthed, closed her eyes briefly, and stepped onto the porch.

"Hello, Michael," she answered, her voice as cool as the night air.

Matthew watched from the doorway, worry deepening the line between his eyes. Even from a distance, he could almost hear Michael's booming voice through the phone.

When Sarah finally hung up, she turned to Matthew with a weary sigh. She pressed her fingers against a spot on her temple and muttered a few unkind words under her breath.

"Typical Michael," she said, shaking her head. "He's up to his old tricks, using the awful events of the last few days as an excuse to meddle. Says he wants the kids in Florida until it's all sorted out."

Matthew's face darkened. "He can't do that, Sarah. No."

"He'll certainly try," Sarah replied, her voice gaining strength. "Which means we've got our work cut out for us. We need to solve

this mystery fast. It's the only way to keep Rosewood—and our family—safe and sound."

Chapter Twelve

After dinner, Sarah and Matthew sat quietly on the front porch. The summer evening was pleasantly warm, with a gentle breeze carrying the scent of blooming jasmine from the garden.

They could hear the muffled sounds of Cory and Emma's familiar bickering from upstairs.

Sarah chuckled softly.

"As much as their squabbling can drive me crazy sometimes, it's oddly comforting to hear them at it right now. It's… normal."

Matthew nodded, understanding in his eyes.

"It means life goes on, even in the face of unsettling events. Kids have a way of grounding us in the everyday, don't they?"

"They certainly do," Sarah agreed, leaning her head on Matthew's shoulder.

After a few moments of comfortable silence, Matthew stirred. "Since it's such a beautiful evening. Why don't we take Pixie for a walk?"

Sarah looked up curiously, then caught the glint in Matthew's eyes and grinned broadly.

"Yes. That sounds perfect right now. I could use a walk, and so could Pixie, I'm sure. And also," she grinned at Matthew and rubbed her hands. "Wouldn't you know it, the Barnes' house isn't too far from here, is it?"

Matthew raised an eyebrow, a knowing smile playing at his lips. "Sarah Anderson, are you suggesting we just happen to stroll by her place?"

"Well," Sarah said, feigning innocence, "it would be purely coincidental if our evening constitutional took us in that direction, wouldn't it?"

Matthew laughed, shaking his head. "You're incorrigible, you know that? But I can't say I'm not curious myself."

Sarah grinned, already standing up to fetch Pixie's leash. "Great minds think alike, Dr. Matthew Turner."

∞

After letting the kids know they were heading out for a short walk, Sarah and Matthew set off down the tree-lined street, Pixie trotting happily ahead of them. They chatted casually as they walked, but Sarah could feel the anticipation building as they approached Deanna's neighborhood.

As they turned onto Elm Street, Sarah's keen eyes scanned the houses. "There," she whispered, her eyes widening as she tilted her head towards a stately two-story colonial. The house gleamed with a coat of fresh paint; its expansive lawn bordered by perfectly manicured hedges. Precise geometric flower beds, bursting with color, added a touch of perfection to the scene. In the drive, two gleaming vehicles demanded attention. A sleek Porsche SUV sat beside a bright yellow sports car that looked impossibly low to the ground, its aerodynamic curves hinting at raw power and speed.

"That's the Barnes' place," Sarah whispered, her voice tinged with a hint of awe.

Matthew let out a low whistle. He couldn't tear his gaze from the cars. A wry smile played on his lips for a brief moment before his expression turned serious.

"My entire salary as a history professor wouldn't even cover the maintenance for those two," he muttered, shaking his head slightly.

They slowed their pace, trying to appear nonchalant as they passed by. The house was mostly dark, except for a soft glow from an upstairs window.

Suddenly, Pixie's ears perked up, and she let out a low growl. Sarah and Matthew exchanged a look of surprise.

"What is it, girl?" Sarah murmured, bending down to soothe the agitated dog.

As if in answer, the sound of raised voices drifted from an open window. Though they couldn't make out the words, the tone was unmistakably angry and confrontational.

Sarah's heart raced as she strained to hear more. Was this the first piece of evidence suggesting trouble in Deanna's personal life?

As they lingered for a moment in front of the Barnes' house, the rhythmic snip of hedge clippers caught their attention. An older gentleman with salt-and-pepper hair was meticulously trimming his boxwoods a few houses down.

Noticing Sarah and Matthew, he paused his work and offered a friendly wave. "Evening, folks! Are you looking for someone?"

Matthew's face flushed with embarrassment at being caught seemingly snooping, but Sarah smoothly stepped in.

"Good evening! We're just out for a walk with our little dog. Thought to turn down this street. It's such a lovely neighborhood."

The man nodded approvingly. "That it is. Name's Frank, by the way. Frank Henderson."

"Nice to meet you, Frank," Sarah replied warmly. "I'm Sarah, and this is Matthew."

Frank's eyes darted briefly to the Barnes' house, then back to Sarah and Matthew. His voice lowered to a stage whisper. "Couldn't help but notice you folks slowing down there. Heard the commotion, did you?"

"I was actually admiring the cars," Matthew said a little uncomfortably, but Sarah saw an opportunity.

"Sounds like somebody is having a bit of a row now, doesn't it? Is everything alright over there?"

Frank shrugged, leaning on his hedge clippers. "Oh, it's not uncommon 'round here. Tom Barnes, he travels a lot for work. Engineering consultant or some such. Gone for weeks at a time sometimes. Puts a strain on things, I imagine."

"That must be difficult for Mrs. Barnes," Sarah said.

"I'd say so. Young woman like that, left alone so often. Can't be easy." Frank shook his head slowly. "Shame, really. They seemed like such a nice couple when they first moved in."

Matthew finally recovered from his initial discomfort. "How long have they lived here?"

"Oh, going on five years now, I'd reckon," Frank replied. "But in the last year or so, well..." He trailed off, glancing again at the Barnes' house. "Let's just say the arguments have become more frequent. They're not from around here, the Barnes', though, Tom's parents were. Wealthy people, I tell you. He inherited quite a bit, though his father... he was a hard head." Frank shook his head and stared down at his hedge clippers. "All about family and traditions, he was."

Something shattered over in the Barnes' house, and Frank winced a little. Sarah took Matthew's hand, filing away this valuable information.

"We should probably be on our way. It was lovely meeting you, Frank."

"Lovely couple," she whispered as they continued their walk. "He's away a lot, and their relationship seems to be just a tad strained."

Once they were out of earshot, Matthew finally slowed down.

"Neighbors," he whispered. "Aren't they always a regular goldmine of information?"

Sarah grinned, still rolling what she had just heard around her mind.

"Frank more than some," she mused. "But this opens up a whole new avenue of possibilities."

She stopped and looked back down Elm Street, worrying her lower lip until Matthew gently tugged on her arm. "Come on," he said softly.

"We shouldn't linger. People might get suspicious."

Reluctantly, Sarah nodded, and they continued their walk, Pixie still on high alert. Matthew only relaxed when they were back on the porch.

They were arguing about a man, Pixie said, twisting her large ears this way and that. *I don't miss much with these, but they didn't mention a name. Unless stud has become popular recently.*

I don't think so, Sarah answered and grinned. *Safe to say Deanna might be having an affair.*

Safe to say. Pixie shook and yipped at Matthew a few times. Her way of apologizing for leaving him out of the conversation.

∞

Sarah was sitting in the games room, her feet tucked under her, when a wild thought struck her. Could Tyler have been involved with Deanna somehow? It was far-fetched given their age difference and disparate social circles, but nowadays...

Lost in thought, Sarah barely noticed when Cory wandered into the living room, headphones dangling around his neck.

"Hey, Mom," he said, heading for the kitchen. "Any leftover pizza?"

The bottomless pit of a seventeen-year-old. Sarah saw an opportunity and tried to keep her tone casual.

"In the fridge. Hey, Cory? Do you know... did Tyler ever mention if he was seeing anyone?"

Cory paused, his hand on the refrigerator door, and gave his mother a quizzical look.

"Tyler? Dating?" He snorted. "Mom, Tyler was way too busy and too broke for that. Between his two jobs and helping coach the junior league, when would he have time?"

"But surely he must have had some interest in girls... or guys," Sarah pressed gently. "You two were friends, right?"

Cory rolled his eyes in classic teenage fashion and turned away. "Mom, gross. We didn't talk about that kind of thing. Tyler was cool, but he wasn't like spilling his love life to me or anything."

Realizing she might be pushing too hard, Sarah backpedaled. "Of course. I was just curious."

Cory shrugged, pulling out the pizza box. "I mean, I guess there were some girls at hockey who thought he was cute or whatever. But Tyler was all about work and saving up to pay off that debt. He wasn't into the whole dating scene."

As Cory retreated to his room with his late-night snack, Sarah exchanged a look with Matthew.

"Mom, gross," Matthew mouthed and tried to hide his grin.

"I thought he might know." Sarah sighed. "It was worth a try. But it does seem to rule out any obvious romantic entanglements for Tyler."

Matthew nodded thoughtfully. "Which brings us back to Deanna. If there's a connection there, it's not an obvious one."

"No," Sarah agreed, her brow furrowed in concentration. "But there's definitely something going on with Deanna Barnes. And I intend to find out what it is."

Chapter Thirteen

T he next morning, Sarah bustled about the kitchen, the aroma of freshly brewed coffee and sizzling bacon filling the air. She had planned to do something good for the children. Instead, she was surprised to see Cory already up and hunched over his laptop at the kitchen table, his brow furrowed in concentration.

"You're up early," Sarah said, sliding a plate of eggs and toast in front of him. "What's got you so focused?"

Cory barely looked up, his fingers flying across the keyboard. "Just doing some research."

Curiosity piqued, Sarah peered over his shoulder. Her eyes widened as she saw the name, Deanna Barnes, in the search bar. "Deanna Barnes? Why are you looking her up?"

Cory finally tore his gaze away from the screen, looking slightly sheepish.

"I, uh... I kind of overheard you and Matthew talking last night. About Mrs. Barnes maybe being connected to what happened to Tyler. And then you thought..."

Sarah felt a mix of concern and admiration for her son's initiative.

"Cory, we will have a talk about eavesdropping."

"I know," Cory interrupted, his expression earnest. "It's not cool at all. But Tyler was a friend. If there's something going on, I want to help figure it out."

Sarah sighed, recognizing the determined look in her son's eyes—a trait he'd clearly inherited from her. "So, what have you found out?"

Cory turned back to his laptop, eager to share. "Did you know Mrs. Barnes used to live in Boston? And she worked for this big investment firm there before moving to Rosewood."

Sarah's eyebrows shot up. This was new information. "Really? That's... interesting. Anything else?"

"Not much," Cory admitted. "She doesn't have much of an online presence. There's some gossip on her friends' social media that she was pretty ambitious there. But Mr. Barnes... It seems he hit the jackpot right around then. Inherited a boatload of dough from his parents. And that seems to be about when the two of them hooked up."

Sarah placed a hand on Cory's shoulder, equally proud of him and concerned about his involvement.

"Cory, I appreciate your help, but I don't want you getting too wrapped up in this. This is not your problem."

Cory looked up at her, his eyes shining with determination. "I am seventeen, remember? Besides, I want to help. For Tyler."

Sarah took a step back. She couldn't entirely stop her son from looking this up. Not when he was so invested in the outcome.

"I do understand. Just... don't do anything outright illegal, please."

Cory grinned a little and looked back down at his tablet. "As if. But honestly... there's not much here, unless you count your Mrs. Barnes being after a rich husband."

As Sarah moved back to the stove, her mind was racing. Deanna Barnes, formerly of Boston... working for a big investment firm, trying to land a wealthy husband. Like everything else about that woman, it could mean everything or nothing. Barnes had money—lots of it, from the sounds of it and from what Frank had told her. Why would she feel the need to rob a bank, then?

Quite suddenly, she felt a familiar chill run down her spine. The temperature in the kitchen seemed to drop several degrees in an instant, and the fine hairs on her arms stood on end.

Amelia was making herself known again. But unlike her usual dramatic appearances, the mischievous ghost didn't materialize this time.

Sarah glanced around the kitchen, half-expecting to see Amelia's impish grin in the dramatic gathering of a mist cloud. But there was nothing. Just the lingering cold and an inexplicable feeling of unease.

"Amelia?" Sarah whispered, careful not to draw Cory's attention. "Are you there?"

The chill intensified for a moment, as if in response, before gradually fading away. Sarah couldn't shake the feeling that Amelia was trying to communicate something, but for some reason couldn't—or wouldn't—fully manifest.

This was unusual behavior for the typically gregarious spirit. It would bring her the greatest joy if she managed to startle Sarah. Something was up, and the creepy feeling in her gut wouldn't let go. She would have to try to contact Amelia later when she was alone.

"Anything else interesting over there?" she asked Cory, trying to keep her voice steady despite the unsettling encounter. "I really don't see Deanna Barnes as the social media type."

Cory had only a few more details he had found in an online article, and Sarah's mind raced with possibilities.

Upstairs, the sound of slamming doors echoed through the house. Sarah startled, but the thundering of feet down the double staircase told her it was only Matthew and Emma racing into the kitchen.

"Beat you," Emma declared triumphantly, slapping her hand onto the big, scarred harvest table they used for everything in this house. Matthew threw up his hands and grinned. Pixie darted in behind them and came to a screeching halt by her bowl, looking at Sarah with her tail wagging furiously.

"I concede," Matthew said with a laugh. Sarah's heart warmed as she watched the lanky historian with her children. He brought out the best in them.

"Racing before breakfast?" she asked, holding up a teapot.

"Yup," Matthew nodded and took one of his favorite mugs off the shelf. "Emma is showing me up, though. Must be age."

Sarah chuckled as Emma speared a blueberry with her fork and held it out towards Matthew, pretending it was a microphone. "So, Matthew," she said in a mock-serious tone, "how does it feel to be beaten in a footrace by a little girl?"

Matthew, ever the good sport, feigned offense. "Little girl? Young lady, you run faster than anyone else I know." He winked at Sarah, who couldn't help but smile.

"Alright," Emma conceded, giggling. "Thanks for the race." The lighthearted moment didn't last, though; almost immediately, a shadow fell over her features.

"This whole thing is still crazy. Sometimes I think it was all a nightmare and Tyler isn't really..." Her voice trailed off, sadness flickering across her face.

"It's a lot to take in," Matthew agreed gently. "But you know what helps? A good distraction. So, what's on the agenda for today, everyone?"

Emma's eyes lit up. "Can I hang out at the bookstore? Maybe help Lily shelve some new releases?"

Sarah raised an eyebrow playfully. "Always looking for an excuse to sneak a peek at the latest YA novels, are we?"

Emma grinned. "Matthew said a distraction would help! Besides, you know I love helping out."

Cory, who had been digging into a stack of pancakes, looked up. "I've got basketball practice this afternoon," he announced around a mouthful of food. "But I can help out around the house this morning if you need anything."

Sarah felt a surge of warmth. Thankfully, a sense of normalcy was slowly returning. "Thanks, honey," she said, reaching across the table to ruffle his hair. "But I think I will meet Lily. Go ahead and do something fun."

A message arrived on his phone, and Cory merely gave her a thumbs up, already answering with the staccato thumb typing Sarah knew she'd never master.

Chapter Fourteen

When the last of the dishes had been cleared a little while later, silence settled over the house, broken only by the rhythmic tick-tock of the grandfather clock and Pixie's contented snores as she curled up at Sarah's feet. Cory had left for the community center for a pickup game with friends, Emma had taken her e-scooter into town to hang out at the bookstore, and Matthew was working upstairs in his home office.

Sipping the last of her lukewarm coffee, Sarah contemplated the day ahead. So many loose ends of this mystery still needed to be tied up, and she didn't know where to start. Perhaps a walk in the park would clear her head. The fresh air and sunshine might be just what she needed, and Pixie would certainly appreciate it.

As she reached for her Jacket hanging by the door, a sudden gust of wind slammed the kitchen window shut. Pixie yelped, startled awake, and scrambled to her feet. Sarah whirled around, heart pounding. Had she not just locked the back door? The kitchen remained empty. Then, a voice, ethereal and laced with amusement, echoed from the corner.

"Lovely weather for a walk, wouldn't you say, Sarah?"

Amelia materialized by the window, a translucent figure framed by a swirling vortex of icy air. Pixie, fur bristling, let out a couple of low barks that sounded like a reprimand of the mischievous ghost.

Sarah sighed, a mixture of exasperation and amusement bubbling up inside her. "Amelia, you scared the living daylights out of me!"

"Oh, come now, Sarah," Amelia teased, her voice tinkling like wind chimes. "Don't tell me you haven't gotten used to our little theatrics by now."

Sarah couldn't help but crack a smile. "I should have by now," she conceded. "But next time, maybe try a less dramatic entrance?"

Amelia chuckled, the sound like rustling leaves. "Where's the fun in that, dear?" she quipped.

Sarah shook her head. "Was that what your appearance this morning was all about, startling the bejesus out of me?"

Amelia tilted her head, a grin spreading across her translucent features. "Not at all. Something just came up right at that moment. But I've come to tell you something of great importance. Something regarding our little mystery."

Sarah dropped back into her chair. "Alright... shoot." She raised her hands to her head. "No—don't shoot. Do not shoot—tell me what you found."

The ghostly woman's face was a mix of excitement and urgency. "I do indeed have some news," she announced, her voice echoing slightly. "Remember yesterday you asked me to do some... ethereal eavesdropping?"

Sarah raised an eyebrow, both curious and wary. Now alert, Pixie positioned herself protectively in front of Sarah, eyeing the spectral visitor with a mix of familiarity and caution.

"Go on," Sarah prompted, knowing that once Amelia had gossip to share, there was no stopping her. She just hoped whatever the ghost had to say was worth postponing her peaceful morning walk with Pixie.

Amelia's ghostly form shimmered, her Victorian-era dress rustling despite the absence of wind. She leaned in, a mischievous glint in her otherworldly eyes. "My dear Sarah, I've made a most interesting discovery about our suspect, Deanna Barnes, and her husband, and it would tend to confirm what their neighbor told you. Their coffers are far from empty, I assure you. In fact, their bank balance would make even the most prosperous merchant in my day green with envy. I saw more than fifteen million dollars."

Sarah's brow furrowed, her coffee mug frozen halfway to her lips.

"Amelia," she began, her voice low and cautious, "You know their exact bank balance?"

The ghost waved a translucent hand dismissively, causing a nearby dish towel to flutter.

"Oh, you know, a little peek here, a little glance there. These modern computing machines are quite fascinating. All those numbers and figures, just floating about in the ether."

Sarah's eyes widened, her mug clattering against the countertop.

"You didn't! Amelia, tell me you didn't hack into the bank's computer system!"

Oh, she most assuredly did, Pixie said, crowding closer to Sarah's leg, and shook dramatically. *You know that woman and her newfound joy with computers.*

"Lord love us," Sarah palmed her face.

Amelia's form wavered slightly, her expression a mixture of confusion and amusement.

"Hack? My dear, I simply... observed. These mortal concerns about privacy are so quaint."

Sarah ran a hand through her hair, exasperation etched on her face. "I'm not supposed to be privy to that information. Amelia, please tell me you didn't change anything or move any money? Do you have any idea what kind of trouble this could cause? Not just for me, but for the bank, for Deanna and her husband. For everyone involved!"

The ghost's laughter tinkled like icy wind chimes. "Trouble? Oh, Sarah, you worry too much. I'm incorporeal, remember? What are they going to do, arrest a spirit? Besides, I just looked. I didn't change a thing."

Sarah's frustration mounted as she watched Amelia's nonchalant attitude. Amelia wouldn't, she thought. She wouldn't move money around... just for fun. Maybe give it to someone deserving, would she?

Sarah paced the kitchen, up and down, while Pixie trailed after her, sensing her owner's agitation.

"Amelia," Sarah began again, struggling to keep her voice level, "I understand you're trying to help, but this isn't like peeking through windows or eavesdropping on gossip. We're talking about highly sensitive, encrypted information. If anyone finds out—"

The ghost interrupted with a tinkling laugh that sent a shiver down Sarah's spine. "Oh, pish posh! You mortals and your rules. In my day, a lady's personal correspondence was sacred, yet here you are, broadcasting your every thought on that thing you call social media. Besides..." Amelia paused with a toss of her hand and looked away. "You read my diary."

Sarah pinched the bridge of her nose, feeling a headache forming.

"That's not the same thing at all, and you know it. Look, I appreciate your initiative, but we need to solve this case legally. If you did any funny business in there, if anybody finds out the banking records were compromised, any evidence we gather will be inadmissible."

Amelia's form flickered, her expression shifting from amusement to a hint of contrition.

"I did not change a thing. Although surely the end might justify the means? We now know the Barneses aren't in financial straits. Doesn't that rule out monetary gain as a motive?"

Sarah sighed, leaning against the counter. The cool surface grounded her, helping to organize her thoughts. "It's a piece of the puzzle, yes, but we can't use it without revealing that I have... access to the Barnes' bank balance."

As if sensing an opportunity, Pixie trotted to the back door, looking expectantly at Sarah. The morning walk they'd planned suddenly seemed like a perfect escape from this latest quandary.

Amelia noticed the dog's movement and huffed, a gust of cold air ruffling the curtains. "Fine, fine. Go on your walk. But don't come floating through my walls when you need more information!" With that, she began to fade, her form dissolving like mist in sunlight.

Sarah reached for Pixie's leash, her mind whirling. As she clipped it to the dog's collar, she muttered, "What I wouldn't give for a nice, beautiful house that wasn't haunted."

No, you wouldn't. You won't admit it, but secretly, you love that ghost.

Well... She is entertaining.

And she helped us get the sapphire and return it, and Mort Jenkins...

Pixie looked up at her, brown eyes wise and knowing. Sarah could almost swear the dog was smirking.

As they stepped out into the warm July morning, Sarah took a deep breath of fresh air. The walk would do her good, clear her head. Maybe by the time they returned, she'd have figured out how to proceed with her investigation without getting herself or any of her family in trouble, and preferably without any more ghostly intrusions. However, Pixie was not half wrong.

"Deanna did not have any apparent financial issues. And from what I see, she didn't even know Tyler or associate with him in any way. So how does this all hang together, Pixie?"

Chapter Fifteen

Sarah and Pixie ambled down Rosewood's main street, the beautiful sights passing unseen. The morning sun cast long shadows across the sidewalk, and a gentle breeze carried the scent of freshly baked bread from the corner bakery. Pixie trotted along, her nose twitching at every new smell, while Sarah's mind whirled with the complexities of her investigation.

Question is, she said to Pixie in her mind. *Are the two crimes related or not?*

It would be an awful coincidence if they were not, don't you think?

But where is the common thread, Pixie? The thing that connects a middle-aged bank teller with more than enough money and a young, broke delivery driver slash security guard. I just can't find it.

Maybe it's not the people who are connected.

Sarah stopped and stared down at Pixie for a moment.

Mmmm, she thought and kept walking.

They approached Rosewood Books, its quaint storefront adorned with colorful displays of new releases and local author spotlights, when the door chimed. Sarah looked up, momentarily startled out of her reverie.

Emma emerged from the bookstore, a paper bag clutched in one hand and a bright smile on her face. Her hair, usually pulled back in a neat ponytail, fell in loose waves around her shoulders, giving her a more grown-up look that caught Sarah by surprise. When had her little girl started looking so mature?

"Mom! Pixie!" Emma called out, her voice clear and strong—a far cry from the croaky whisper of breakfast. She bounded down the steps, narrowly avoiding a collision with Mrs. Fitzgerald, who was attempting to enter the store.

Sarah's eyebrows rose as Emma approached.

"Well, look at you! Feeling better, I take it?"

Emma nodded enthusiastically; her cheeks flushed with excitement rather than fever.

"A morning in the bookstore was exactly what I needed!"

"And you found a few new treasures," Sarah said and pointedly looked at the bag in Emma's hand.

"Um..."

"No worries, you've earned it."

Pixie, who had been patiently sitting at Sarah's feet, now stood and gave a soft woof of greeting to Emma. The girl bent down to scratch behind the dog's ears, cooing softly.

As Sarah watched her daughter's enthusiasm, a warm feeling spread through her chest, momentarily pushing aside her worries about ghostly interference and bank records. Here was a reminder of why she did what she did—to make Rosewood safer for Emma, Cory, and all the other residents who called this quirky town home.

"Well," Sarah said, reaching out to tuck a strand of hair behind Emma's ear. "Are you headed home already? We can all walk together, unless you're meeting some friends?

"Actually," Emma said slowly, looking left and right as if to make sure no one was listening in on their conversation. "I thought we could stop by Rosewood Bank, get some financial advice, maybe look around a bit?"

Sarah's eyebrows shot up, a mix of surprise and concern crossing her face. Now it was her turn to look around quickly, left and right. The bustling street continued its morning routine, oblivious to the scheming taking place on the sidewalk.

"Emma," Sarah began, her voice low and measured, "I appreciate your enthusiasm, but we can't just waltz into the bank under false pretenses. Besides, Lily and I were there... and we didn't find anything.

Emma's face fell slightly, but the determined glint in her eye remained. "Who's talking about false pretenses? I do need financial advice, remember? For my college fund?"

Sarah bit her lip, considering. It was true that they had been meaning to start planning for Emma's future education. The responsible parent in her warred with the curious investigator. Then it dawned on her.

"Amelia, right? It was Amelia who told you what she'd been doing at the bank. She just showed up at the house, filling me in."

"I told her you wouldn't like it," Emma said, looking down at her shoes. "But... she was excited and happy to contribute and—"

Sarah drew her daughter into a quick hug and held her hard. Don't grow up, please don't grow up, her mom instinct screamed. Then, she let go of Emma and looked at her long and hard.

Coming to terms with her own powers could be hard enough at times, but finding out that Emma shared some of the same talents frightened the living daylights out of her.

"She didn't mean anything by it," Emma now said and took her mother's hand. "And she swore to me she hadn't manipulated anything."

Pixie, sensing the tension, let out a small whine and looked up at them both, her tail swishing back and forth uncertainly.

"Besides," Emma continued, warming to her idea, "you're always saying how important it is to be proactive about financial planning. This way, we're killing two birds with one stone."

Sarah couldn't help but smile at her daughter's logic. The more Emma discovered her connection to the spirit world, the less she'd be able to hide from her.

"Well then... you've clearly been paying attention to my lectures," she said, a note of pride creeping into her voice.

They paused at a crosswalk, waiting for the light to change. The bank's imposing facade loomed across the street, its large windows reflecting the afternoon sunlight.

Sarah sighed, her resolve weakening.

"Alright, let's say we do this. We'd need to be very careful. No obvious snooping, no pointed questions about Deanna. We're there for financial advice, nothing more. Understood? If something falls into our laps, so be it."

Emma nodded eagerly, barely containing her excitement. "Absolutely, Mom. I'll be the picture of innocence."

As if to prove that she could pull it off, she smiled up at Sarah in the most serene way, her blue eyes soft and gentle, and blonde hair curling down her back.

Pixie trotted alongside them, her leash jingling softly. Sarah took a deep breath as they approached the bank's heavy doors. "Okay, here's the plan. We go in, ask about setting up a college fund consultation, and keep our eyes and ears open. But if I say we leave, we leave. No questions asked. Deal?"

Emma nodded solemnly, though her eyes sparkled with excitement. "Deal."

Sarah pushed open the door, the cool air-conditioned interior a stark contrast to the warm July morning outside. As they stepped into the bank's polished lobby, Sarah couldn't help but feel a mix of trepidation and exhilaration. Whether this impromptu visit would yield valuable information or complications, only time would tell.

She glanced down at Pixie, who looked back at her with what Sarah could have sworn was a knowing expression. Sometimes, she mused, the most unexpected partners in crime were the ones right under your nose—or, in this case, at the end of a leash.

∞

The interior of the bank was awash in muted beiges and soft blues, clearly designed to project an aura of calm professionalism.

To their right, a long marble-topped counter stretched the length of the room, punctuated by four teller stations. The gentle clinking of coins and the rustle of papers created a soothing white noise. Overhead, recessed lighting cast a warm glow, softening the edges of the modern decor.

A young woman with a polished smile approached them. Her navy blazer bore a shiny name tag that read, "Jessica." Fortunately, she was not the same teller who had greeted her and Lily just the day before.

"Good morning," she greeted them warmly. "How can I assist you today?"

Sarah cleared her throat. "We'd like to discuss setting up a college fund for my daughter."

Jessica nodded. "Certainly. Our financial advisor is with another client at the moment. Would you mind waiting for a few minutes?"

Sarah agreed, and Jessica directed them to a seating area tucked away in the far corner of the lobby. The chairs were sleek and modern, upholstered in a soft, cream-colored leather that creaked slightly as Sarah sat down. A glass coffee table in front of her held neatly fanned magazines, their glossy covers reflecting the overhead lights.

Emma, restless with anticipation, stood up almost immediately. "I'm going to look at those brochures, okay?" She pointed to a display near the entrance, a rotating stand filled with colorful pamphlets.

Sarah nodded, her eyes scanning the room as Emma walked away. The bank was relatively quiet for a weekday afternoon. An elderly couple huddled with a loan officer at a desk near the center of the room, their whispered conversation occasionally punctuated by the shuffle of papers.

Near the teller counter, a man in a crisp business suit checked his watch impatiently, his polished shoe tapping a staccato rhythm on the marble floor. Behind the counter, Sarah could see Deanna Barnes, her head bent over a computer screen, fingers flying across the keyboard.

The air was thick with the scent of paper, ink, and the faint traces of lemon-scented cleaner. Every few moments, the soft ding of a computer or the whir of a printer would break the hushed atmosphere.

Sarah leaned back in her chair, affecting a casual pose while her mind raced. She watched Emma out of the corner of her eye, noting how her daughter was doing an admirable job of appearing absorbed in a brochure about retirement planning while sneaking glances around the room.

Two female employees stood only a few feet from Emma, separated from her by a few potted palms, chatting beside a coffee maker. Was that why Emma had moved over there?

She takes after you, Pixie said, and Sarah detected a trace of amusement in her voice.

Is she snooping?

Pixie only shook and gracefully hopped into Sarah's lap, giving her a quick kiss on the cheek.

So smart. Nobody is going to look at a fifteen-year-old girl.

Pixie, I really wanted to—

Sarah barely had time to register Emma's sudden reappearance before her daughter was at her side, clutching a handful of glossy brochures to her chest. Emma's eyes were wide, a mix of urgency and something else—was it excitement? —flickering across her face.

"Mom," Emma said, her voice pitched slightly higher than normal. I completely forgot about sports practice. We need to go—now!"

Before Sarah could respond, Emma had already turned towards the teller counter. "I'm so sorry," she called out, her voice carrying across the quiet lobby. "We have to reschedule. Thank you for your time!"

Sarah found herself being tugged to her feet, Emma's hand gripping her arm with surprising strength. Pixie had to scramble in a hurry down to the ground, looking as confused as Sarah felt.

"Emma, what—" Sarah began, but her daughter was already steering her towards the exit, moving at a pace that was just shy of running.

The cool air of the bank gave way to the humid July heat as they burst through the doors. Emma didn't slow down, practically dragging Sarah and Pixie down the sidewalk. Pixie almost had to run to keep up, her leash tangling around Sarah's legs.

It wasn't until they had turned the corner, the bank no longer in sight, that Emma finally slowed to a stop. She was slightly out of breath, a sheen of sweat on her forehead that Sarah suspected wasn't entirely due to the summer heat.

"Emma Jean Anderson", Sarah said, her voice stern but tinged with concern. "What on earth was that about? You don't have sports practice today."

Emma glanced around, checking to see if anyone was within earshot. The street was relatively empty, with just a few cars passing by and an older man walking his dog on the opposite sidewalk.

"Mom," Emma said, her voice low and urgent. "I heard something. In the bank. And I don't think it was meant for my ears."

Sarah's eyebrows shot up. She crouched down slightly, bringing herself to eye level with her daughter. Sensing the tension, Pixie pressed against Sarah's leg, her ears perked forward attentively.

"What did you hear?" Sarah asked, her heart beginning to race. Had Emma stumbled upon a crucial piece of evidence? Or had her amateur sleuthing gotten them into trouble?

Emma took a deep breath, her eyes darting around once more before meeting her mother's gaze. "It's about Deanna," she said. "And I think... I think it might explain a lot."

Sarah looked at her daughter expectantly, noting the mix of excitement and nervousness in Emma's eyes. They had moved a safe distance from the bank, standing in the shade of a large oak tree on the quieter side street.

"Alright, Emma," Sarah said, keeping her voice low. "What did you hear? Take a deep breath and tell me."

Emma inhaled deeply, then exhaled slowly. Pixie sat at their feet, her tail swishing back and forth on the sidewalk as she looked up at them attentively.

"Okay, so," Emma began, her words tumbling out in a rush, "I was pretending to look at those brochures, right? But then I overheard these two tellers who were on their break. They were gossiping in the corner, just past those plants, thinking no one could hear them."

Sarah nodded, her curiosity piqued.

"I saw that. Good thinking. What happened?"

Emma leaned in closer, her voice dropping to a whisper. "They were talking about Deanna. They really don't like her. But that's not the weird part. They were saying how they thought during the bank robbery, Deanna wasn't scared like all of the other tellers were!"

Sarah's eyebrows shot up. "What do you mean, not scared?"

"That's just it," Emma continued, her eyes wide with excitement. "One of the tellers said she heard that, unlike everyone else, Deanna didn't have to lie down on the ground. Can you believe that? Everyone else was terrified, but Deanna... it was like she wasn't afraid of the robbers at all!"

Sarah's mind raced with this new information. It was odd, certainly, but what did it mean? "Did they say anything else about it?" she asked.

Emma shook her head. "Not that I heard. They just seemed really suspicious about it. Like, why would the robbers treat Deanna differently from the others?"

Sarah placed a hand on Emma's shoulder, both proud of her daughter's observational skills and concerned about the implications of what she'd overheard. "That's a good point. But remember, this is just gossip.

For now. Much as we want to help Tyler's family, we have no idea if any of this is actually true or if they just dislike Deanna Barnes."

Emma nodded, but Sarah could see the wheels turning in her daughter's mind.

"What do we do now?" she asked, her eyes bright and her voice eager.

Sarah straightened up, her investigator's instincts kicking into high gear. "Now," she said, "we figure out what this could mean."

Sarah bought them ice cream cones from a local vendor, and they sat on a bench, watching the coming and going across the Rosewood Hollow common. Even Pixie was allowed a lick or two of ice cream. To a casual observer, it all looked so peaceful and wholesome. But inside, Sarah's mind clicked through all of the possibilities.

Deanna Barnes might have issues with her husband, but they appeared financially set. Why then would she take a risk like that of a robbery? And Tyler and Deanna? No... she dismissed that possibility as soon as she'd thought of it. Even as a theory, that one didn't make any sense.

Sarah wadded up their napkins and tossed them into the nearby bin. This was getting stranger by the minute.

Chapter Sixteen

As they approached the intersection where they would normally turn towards home, Sarah felt a knot form in her stomach. Just ahead lay the alley, where Emma had made that grim discovery not so long ago. The memory of her daughter's scream and her pale, shocked face that day was still fresh in Sarah's mind.

Sarah slowed her pace, gently tugging on Pixie's leash. "Hey, Em," she said, trying to keep her voice casual, "why don't we take the long way around today? It's such a nice day for a walk."

It's not surprising that Emma saw right through her mother's ruse. She squared her shoulders and set her jaw, shoved her hands into her pockets, and walked away.

"It's all right. We can go this way. I'm fine and can't take the long way around for the rest of my life."

Sarah studied her daughter's face, searching for any signs of distress. "Are you sure?"

"I'm sure," Emma interrupted, her voice steady. "It happened, and avoiding an alley won't change that. Besides," she added with a small smile, "We're helping Tyler and his family find the truth, remember?"

Pride swelled in Sarah's chest, mingling with a touch of concern. When had her little girl grown up and matured? She reached out and squeezed Emma's hand. "Alright, if you're sure. But you tell me if you want to turn back, okay?"

Emma nodded, and they continued forward, Pixie padding along between them. As they neared the alley, Sarah felt Emma's hand reaching for hers. The entrance loomed ahead, a narrow gap between two brick buildings, dark and shadowy, foreboding somehow. Yellow police tape still fluttered from one wall, a stark reminder of the tragedy that had occurred there.

Sarah held her breath as they passed, her eyes still scanning Emma's determined face. But Emma kept her gaze forward, her steps never faltering. It wasn't until they had walked past completely that Sarah felt her daughter let out a long, slow breath.

"You okay?" Sarah asked softly.

Emma nodded, a small, triumphant smile playing at the corners of her mouth. "Yeah, I'm okay. It's just an alley now."

Sarah smiled and took her daughter's hand, swinging it gently. The alley might be 'just an alley' to Emma, but to Sarah, it represented something more, a reminder of how quickly life could change, and how strong her children could be in the face of adversity.

Sarah wanted to say something to that effect, when Pixie suddenly barked up a storm that shattered the quiet morning air. Before either of them could react, the little dog lunged and gave a powerful tug, and the leash slipped from Sarah's grasp.

"Pixie!" she called out, but the tiny Papillon was already darting into the alley, her white and sable fur a blur of motion, her leash flapping wildly behind her.

Emma drew back a bit. "Mom, what's she doing?"

Without thinking, Sarah ran after her dog, Emma close on her heels. The alley's shadows enveloped them immediately, and the air was noticeably cooler between the tall brick walls. The sound of Pixie's excited barks up ahead echoed off the buildings.

They rounded a corner to find Pixie circling a large, dented trash bin, her tail wagging furiously. The dog's paws scrabbled against the metal as she attempted to jump up.

"Pixie, down!" Sarah commanded, reaching for the leash that trailed through a puddle, slick with something greasy and disgusting.

Pixie only shook and kept going. With a surprisingly graceful leap, she managed to hook her front paws over the bin's edge. Her head disappeared inside for a moment, and when she emerged, she was clutching something red and white in her mouth. Sarah froze.

"Is that... a Santa hat?" Emma asked incredulously as Pixie pranced back to them, clearly proud of her find. Her little white face had a smear of grime across it, but her eyes sparkled with triumph.

Sarah crouched down, gently prying the hat from Pixie's mouth. It was indeed a Santa hat, slightly dirty and torn but unmistakable, with its white fur trim and bright red fabric. She turned it over in her hands, her mind instantly sorting through a dozen possibilities.

"A Santa hat? Here?" she asked, a deep line forming between her brows.

Emma clapped a hand to her mouth. "This is where I found Tyler. Do you think there's a connection?"

Sarah dipped her head slowly, her gaze shifting between the hat and the spot where Tyler's body had been found, remembering the scene she had found that day. "But Tyler's hat was beside him on the ground... Why would this be here? And why now?"

Pixie sat at their feet, looking up at them expectantly, as if she knew she'd uncovered something significant.

"Somebody just tossed it. It's actually a miracle it's still here, the garbage service must have missed this bin." Emma said her voice hushed with excitement and a touch of apprehension. "Hardly surprising...." Her nose wrinkled a little at the general filth of the alley.

"Or they were told to leave this alley alone for a bit – either way..." Sarah carefully placed the hat into a plastic bag from her purse. "I'm not sure yet what it means. But Pixie might have just given us another piece of the puzzle. We need to give this to Detective Harding right now."

Sarah and Emma walked into the Rosewood Police Station, the old wooden doors closing behind them with a soft creak. The familiar scent of coffee and paper filled the air as they approached the front desk.

Officer Thompson looked up from his computer and smiled as he recognized Sarah and Emma.

"Mrs. Anderson, what brings you here again today? Have you not had enough of us yet?"

Sarah cleared her throat. "We need to speak with Detective Harding, please. It's about the Robinson case."

A few minutes later, they were ushered into Detective Harding's office. The detective's salt-and-pepper hair was slightly disheveled, and dark circles under her eyes suggested she'd been working long hours.

"Sarah," she greeted, her voice a mix of exhaustion and wariness. "And Emma. I hope you are feeling better after everything that's happened. What's this about?"

Sarah carefully pulled the Santa hat from her purse and held it out. "We found this in the alley where Tyler's body was discovered."

Harding's eyebrows shot up. She quickly donned a pair of latex gloves before taking the hat.

"What in the world? Where and how? Why were you even in there?"

"Actually, Pixie found it," Emma piped up. "In a trash bin in the very alley where... You know."

Harding's frown deepened as she examined the hat. "And you handled this without gloves, Sarah? You should have known better. Anyone who watched half an episode of Law and Order would have."

Sarah winced slightly. "I know, I should have been more careful. But I thought it was important to bring it straight here. In case something else happened."

The detective sighed, carefully placing the hat in an evidence bag. "This is potential evidence. I wish you had called me the moment you saw it. This could compromise any forensic value it might have had."

"I'm sorry," Sarah said, her voice only a little contrite. "But isn't it odd that it wasn't found during the initial search? Careless, even?"

Harding nodded only grudgingly.

"It is. And I suppose we should be grateful you brought it in before the trash service took everything away." She paused, fixing Sarah with a stern look. "But I need not remind you, this is an active investigation. You can't just go poking around crime scenes. You're making a habit out of this."

Sarah nodded, but her right hand made a loose fist in her pocket. Loose enough to cross her middle and forefinger.

❧

A few pleasantries later, they left the station. Emma took her mother's hand and gave her a long, curious look.

"That was weird. What's the deal with that hat, do you think?"

"Some random festival goer could have just... tossed it, I suppose."

"But you don't think so?"

Sarah glanced down at her daughter, a small smile playing at the corners of her mouth.

"You got that right. You see, most of the hats we were all wearing for the charity event were provided by Creative Charities, and their logo was pinned on them just to give an idea of the number of people attending and to maximize advertising for the agency."

"But this one didn't..." Emma said and grinned. "Good eye, Mom."

"Not that it was mandatory to use their hats..."

"I had my own costume... and hat."

"And..." Sarah prodded. "You took it back home, didn't you? Because it goes with the rest of your costume."

They walked home in thoughtful silence, both mulling over the potential significance of their discovery. It was still a little thin. Indeed, somebody could have just tossed their Santa hat on the way home or found it lying there on the ground and disposed of it. It was possible—but in a dirty, dark alley, it didn't seem quite likely.

The summer sun beat down on the sidewalk, but Sarah shivered suddenly. Much as this entire case was still a puzzle of too few pieces, they had just found another one thanks to Pixie's curious nose.

Chapter Seventeen

Sarah's phone buzzed on the kitchen counter as she was preparing dinner that night. She wiped her hands on a dish towel and answered.

"Sarah, it's Detective Penny Harding," came the familiar voice on the other end.

Sarah's eyebrows rose in surprise. "Detective Harding, what can I do for you?"

"I wanted to thank you again for bringing in that Santa hat earlier," Penny said, her tone professional but with a hint of warmth. "It was... unexpected, and still not properly handled... but potentially useful."

Sarah leaned against the counter and let the silence drag on for a moment.

"Have you found anything new, then?"

There was a pause on the other end of the line.

"You know I can't really discuss details of an ongoing investigation," Penny replied, a note of caution in her voice. "I know you are curious, and I know your children were involved."

"More than that," Sarah said.

"But I want to emphasize how important it is that you stay away from this case."

Sarah bit her lip, resisting the urge to protest.

"I understand, Detective. But surely you can see why I'm concerned. This happened right in our town, and-"

"Understood," Penny interrupted gently. "But we're handling it. Our primary theory is that Tyler and one of his friends were motivated by money and chose the event to maximize on chaos and confusion. His accomplice possibly became greedy and shot Tyler for his share. I know this is not the popular opinion, but this fits the evidence we have."

Sarah's mind raced, thinking of the gossip Emma had overheard at the bank. She opened her mouth to share it, but stopped herself. She could almost hear Penny reprimanding her for sharing idle gossip.

"I know you're concerned, that's why I'm sharing this with you. That said," Penny continued, "We still need to apprehend Tyler's accomplice. We're being thorough. We're not ruling anything out at this stage."

As you shouldn't, Sarah thought. It had only been a few months ago that Detective Harding had suspected her friend Lily of another serious crime, and between the Christmas Holidays and her stubborn insistence it couldn't be anyone but Lily, it had taken two ghosts and a small miracle to convince her otherwise.

Finally, Sarah nodded, even though Penny couldn't see her. "I appreciate you keeping me in the loop, Detective."

"Just... promise me you will leave this be," Penny said, her voice softening slightly. "I know you have a knack for this sort of thing, but it's dangerous. Leave the investigating to us, okay?"

"Of course," Sarah replied, her fingers crossed again behind her back. "Thanks for calling, Detective Harding."

As she hung up, Sarah stared at the phone for a moment, lost in thought. The official theory didn't sit right with her. There were too many loose ends, too many strange coincidences.

"Mom?" Emma's voice called from the living room. "Who was that on the phone?"

Sarah took a deep breath, composing herself before answering. "Just Detective Harding, honey. Thanking us for the hat."

"Did she find anything?"

"Not yet, Em. Hopefully soon."

Pixie sat up straighter, draping her fluffy white tail around her back paws just so.

A little too obvious, and a little too easy, don't you think? she asked, with a mix of excitement and sass. *And what's up with that 'official warning' to stop us? Stay out of it... Please!*

Sarah tossed Pixie a piece of carrot she had been chopping and winked at her.

Of course, I'd like to find out who actually killed Tyler. I don't for a minute believe that story. But we can't go charging in like a bull in a China shop.

Please, Pixie scoffed, pawing at the piece of carrot in front of her as if to decide whether to eat it or not. *I'm a Papillon, not a bulldog. Subtlety is my middle name.*

No, I think your middle name is Trouble, Sarah teased, and tossed another carrot piece, even though Pixie was eyeing the plate of cookies on the counter.

The point is, we've got a mystery to solve, and a nose that knows. She raised her head as if testing the air.

So?

So, I know it wasn't Tyler's hat, and not that woman from the bank. Her perfume would have given me a sneezing fit.

But you remember the scent?

Did you really just ask that?

Pixie finally took the pieces of carrot, knowing there was no cookie in her near future, although she chewed with much more effort than strictly necessary.

"Am I interrupting anything?" Matthew strolled into the kitchen and gave her a quick kiss on the cheek. "It looked like you and Pixie..."

"No worries," Sarah chuckled. "Wait until you hear what our little canine detective here found today."

Quickly, she caught Matthew up on what they had heard in the bank, and Pixie finding the discarded Santa hat in the very alley where Tyler's body had been discovered.

Matthew's eyes widened, his jaw slackening as he leaned forward.

"And the police never spotted this?" His voice cracked slightly, disbelief etched across his features.

A sly grin crept over Sarah's face. They locked eyes for a moment before she simply shook her head and murmured,

"Nope."

"Well, I hope Detective Harding was suitably embarrassed about it."

"Somewhat," Sarah quickly recounted her conversation with Penny Harding, keeping her voice low. "She thinks Tyler and some friend did this for the money, but to my mind it just doesn't add up."

Matthew's frown deepened, and he blew out a big breath.

"You do have a point there. I interviewed Tyler for the job. He wasn't perfect, but he sure didn't seem the type to rob a bank or... well, you know." He trailed off, unable to voice the thought of murder.

"Exactly," Sarah nodded emphatically. "And here's the kicker, Pixie says the scent on the hat isn't Tyler's."

Matthew raised an eyebrow, a small smile playing at the corners of his mouth. Sometimes he still found it surreal that Sarah could talk to her dog, but he'd long since learned to trust Pixie's insights.

"That is indeed curious," he mused, stroking his chin thoughtfully. "A Santa hat in July, found in the alley where... where it happened. And it's not Tyler's?"

Nope, Sarah heard in her mind. *Definitely not Tyler's scent. And before you ask, it's not just because the hat was in the trash. I know my scents, thank you very much.*

Wouldn't dream of doubting you.

Sarah leaned back, her mind whirling with possibilities. "So, we have a mysterious Santa hat, a bank robbery, and a..." she glanced towards the living room, where Emma was still watching a nature program, "a murder. And they are probably connected... but not necessarily."

Sarah sank deeper into her chair, absently toying with a discarded spoon on the kitchen table. "It makes sense if you assume Tyler and a friend robbed the bank for money..."

"Which we don't," Matthew interjected.

"Right, which we don't," Sarah agreed. "But follow that logic, the friend then shot Tyler to keep all the loot. Bingo bango. I can see why Penny Harding thinks that's the case."

Matthew sighed and forked his fingers through his hair.

"Tyler made a split-second dumb decision? And got shot for it?"

Sarah fell silent, her fingers still fidgeting with the spoon. After a moment, she looked up, her eyes sharp.

"But why would Deanna Barnes be oddly familiar with one of the robbers?"

"Is that a confirmed fact?" Matthew asked, leaning forward.

"No," Sarah admitted, her shoulders slumping slightly. "But I intend to find out."

Matthew's face tightened, and he looked at her for a long moment over the rim of his reading glasses.

"And I'm sure Detective Harding wants you to stay as far away from her investigation as humanly possible."

As if on cue, Pixie shook, a faint shimmer of gold glitter appearing at the tip of her tail—her magic at work. Sarah recalled Pixie's earlier sassy thought, *As if a little thing like 'official warnings' has ever stopped us before.*

She couldn't help but grin at Pixie's attitude, but Matthew's worried expression didn't change, and he didn't appreciate her grin.

"Sarah, I know it sounds like fun, but please don't take it lightly," he urged. "This isn't just about solving a puzzle. It could be dangerous, especially after what happened last time with Vincent Carlisle catching you snooping around his past."

The memory of that showdown at the police station still made him pale, even though he hadn't witnessed the full extent of what had transpired between Sarah, Pixie, and Amelia.

"I'm not taking things lightly," Sarah sighed, reaching out to squeeze his hand. "But I don't want to just let it go. Something's not right here, and if we don't figure it out, who will?"

Matthew nodded slowly, his expression softening.

"I figured you'd say that. Just... promise me you'll be careful?"

Sarah had just finished her morning coffee the next day when her phone buzzed with an incoming call. She smiled when she saw Lily's name on the screen.

"Morning, Lily! I didn't miss a walking date, did I?"

Lily's voice crackled with excitement over the line.

"Not at all! I've got fantastic news!"

Sarah leaned against the kitchen counter and grinned at her friend's enthusiasm.

"Oh? Hit me!"

"Well," Lily began, barely containing her glee. "You know how I've been volunteering at the animal shelter, right?"

"I remember," Sarah said and automatically reached down to caress Pixie's velvety head, as always close to the kitchen counter, hoping that something would fall.

Lily's best friend, Pixie's former owner, had passed away in an accident, leaving Pixie stranded at the shelter until Sarah adopted her. The animal shelter had been Lily's heart project ever since.

"So," she continued now, "Yesterday, I was chatting with one of the other volunteers, and it turns out her sister works at Creative Charities!"

"The ad agency that put on the Christmas in July event?" Sarah asked, her pulse quickening.

"Exactly!" Lily confirmed. "I knew you wanted to look around there, and I didn't get an answer from Gina, sooo, I may have... embellished a little. I told her that you and I were considering starting our own small charity event and looking for professional advice."

Sarah raised an eyebrow, impressed by her friend's quick thinking. "Lily, you didn't!"

"Oh, but I did," Lily chuckled. "And it worked like a charm! We're invited to visit their office this afternoon for a tour and a chat about event planning. So, tell me, are you up for it, or are you up for it?"

Pixie perked up her ears at Sarah's excited tone and put her paws on her knee.

What's the scoop? she asked, sliding down in a long stretch. *Good news?*

Sarah covered the mouthpiece of her phone for a moment. "We might have a way into Creative Charities," she whispered to Pixie before returning to her call.

"Lily, that's brilliant! What time should we be there?"

As Lily rattled off the details, Sarah's mind clicked through the potential outcomes. This could be their chance to gather more information about the day of the robbery and Tyler's death. She just hoped they could pull off the ruse without arousing suspicion.

"You are a genius, my friend," Sarah said as she ended the call. She looked down at Pixie, who was wagging her tail expectantly.

"Girl, looks like we've got an appointment this afternoon."

Pixie's eyes sparkled with mischief.

Sneaking into the lion's den under false pretenses? One of my better-developed abilities!

Sarah tapped Pixie's little nose gently and winked.

"Just remember, we need to play it cool. We're there to learn about event planning, nothing more."

Right, right, Pixie nodded sagely. *Just two totally normal humans and their incredibly charming and good-looking dog, definitely not investigating anything suspicious at all.*

∞

Their appointment had been set for early afternoon. Since Matthew was working at the museum, and Cory and Emma were having fun at a local pool with their friends, Sarah and Lily decided to drive to Claremont and Creative Charities together.

Pixie, in a new stylish pink purse carrier, rode on Sarah's lap, taking in her surroundings like a queen being chauffeured.

About half an hour later, as they approached the modern building, the sleek glass doors of Creative Charities Agency loomed before them.

Sarah smoothed down her sensible blouse and skirt, feeling a touch self-conscious next to Lily, who was decked out in a vibrant floral dress that seemed to embody the essence of summer.

"Ready for this?" Lily whispered, her eyes sparkling with excitement.

Sarah nodded, trying to project more confidence than she felt.

"Ready as I'll ever be. Though I wish someone had told me this was dress up," she said with a sideways look at her friend.

"Come now. I'm the one who's usually told she dresses like a bird of paradise..."

Pixie shook and trotted between them, her white and red fur gleaming in the afternoon sun. The little Papillon held her head high, tail swishing regally as if she owned the place.

The cool air-conditioned breeze ruffled Sarah's hair as they entered the lobby. The interior was a showcase of modern design—all clean lines, abstract art, and sleek furniture. A receptionist looked up from behind a curved desk.

Sarah was about to make a comment to Lily about the woman's business suit being worth more than her car when her professional smile suddenly widened as she caught sight of Pixie.

"Oh, my goodness, what an adorable dog!" she exclaimed, her composure momentarily slipping.

Pixie, ever the diva, gave a delicate woof and pranced in place, basking in the attention.

"This is Pixie," Sarah introduced, trying not to roll her eyes at her dog's antics. "I hope it's all right that we brought her?"

"Goodness, of course!" the receptionist assured them, already reaching for a treat from a drawer. "We're very pet-friendly here. Welcome to Creative Charities. You must be Sarah and Lily?"

As the receptionist called their contact, more employees drifted over, drawn by Pixie's charm. The little dog was in her element, accepting pats and coos with gracious nods, as if she were royalty granting audiences to her adoring subjects.

"Please do leave your contact info when you leave," a young woman in her twenties said to Sarah, just as Pixie climbed onto her arm and turned, as if asking for a close-up. "Our photographer would just jump if she got her for a model."

"Would you look at that," Lily murmured, amused. "Pixie's stealing the show already."

Sarah nodded, grateful for the distraction. It gave her a chance to scan the lobby, noting the "Christmas in July" posters still adorning one wall. Her eyes lingered on a group photo, wondering if any of those smiling faces held the secrets they were seeking.

"Sarah Anderson?" A voice called out, breaking into her thoughts. A tall woman with a sleek bob and a tablet in hand approached them. "I'm Vanessa, Event Coordinator. Welcome to Creative Charities!"

As they shook hands, Sarah took a deep breath, still trying to figure out the best way to get the information she needed.

"Thank you for having us," Sarah replied with a smile. "We're excited to learn more about your work."

Pixie gave another regal woof of agreement, earning more chuckles from everyone around. As they followed Vanessa deeper into the office, Sarah kept looking left and right, as if she were hoping to uncover something big. In the spectacular boardroom of glass and chrome, Vanessa showed them a video presentation of some of the more successful events the agency had put together, and quite suddenly, the conversation began to lag noticeably.

"So why don't you tell me exactly what you had in mind?" Vanessa said, tapping the button to let the presentation screen disappear into a clever little cabinet of lacquered black wood again.

"What is your event all about, your target audience, your budget, that kind of thing? I can tell you if we can help you at all."

"Well, actually...." Sarah said, and Lily grabbed her hand under the table.

"I own the bookstore in Rosewood Hollow," she said smoothly. "And I was thinking of a literacy program for teens, you know. Something to get them interested in reading again. Any ideas in that direction?"

"I see." Vanessa folded her hands, and Sarah couldn't take her eyes off the massive diamond on one finger. "It looks like you are still in the idea-finding phase. There's no shame in that, but perhaps what you want to do first is take some of our brochures, read through events we have put on before, and see if anything there inspires you."

"Didn't you just put together the Christmas in July event in Rosewood?" Lily asked, and Vanessa's face visibly darkened.

"Yes, such a wonderful project. I personally worked on the execution. Too bad it was... marred in such a dreadful way. Shame..." Her beringed fingers waved away the memory of the event, and the smile returned. "It's still hard to speak about it. You have to understand that Christmas in July was sponsored by some very large corporations. Perhaps start with something smaller".

"Perhaps."

She really thinks you two are a couple of bored housewives from the sticks, Sarah suddenly heard and bit her lip to keep from laughing.

Pixie, of course.

She has no idea who she is dealing with.

"Every bit of information we can gather will be of value," Sarah said out loud and rose. "Why don't you show us some of your brochures, and we will get some inspiration. Perhaps it will be just what we need."

Lily stared daggers at her. She had no intentions of leaving yet.

Nothing. They had discovered absolutely nothing, Sarah thought, frustration gnawing at her. Lily's ruse, the cover story, the entire trip to Claremont... apparently all for nothing.

When Vanessa rose and turned toward the door, Lily gestured wildly with both hands.

"What the heck?" she whispered into Sarah's ear. "You want to leave already? Now?"

Sarah only shrugged. They followed Vanessa out of the conference room, their spirits about as low as they could get.

If they ever did decide to run an event, they now had a massive amount of knowledge to do so, but not a single clue about the Christmas in July event or Tyler's death. Sarah tried to hide her disappointment, forcing a polite smile as Vanessa chatted animatedly about fundraising strategies.

"Oh, before you go," Vanessa said, pausing by a door marked Private. "Let me grab some of those event brochures for you. They might help with your planning." She disappeared into the office, leaving Sarah and Lily alone in the hallway.

Lily leaned in close to Sarah, whispering, "Thanks, that was a bust. I really hoped we'd find something."

Sarah nodded, her shoulders sagging slightly. "So did I, but there's nothing to find. Maybe we're barking up the wrong tree entirely."

Pixie, who had been trotting alongside them, looked up indignantly. *Hey, watch the canine jokes, will you?*

As they continued down the hallway, waiting for Vanessa to return, a strong aroma suddenly filled the air. The rich, inviting smell of freshly brewed coffee wafted towards them, growing stronger with each step.

Sarah's nose twitched, and she saw Lily inhale deeply, a small smile crossing her friend's face despite their disappointment. The scent was so potent, so alluring, it seemed to push away their frustration for a moment.

Just as Sarah was about to comment on the heavenly smell, she noticed Pixie's behavior change. The little dog's ears perked up, her nose working overtime as she sniffed the air intently.

"Pixie?"

Sarah stumbled forward as Pixie suddenly lurched ahead, the leash nearly slipping from her grasp again.

"Pixie! Darn it. What on earth?" she began, but her words were cut short as the little dog all but dragged her down the hallway.

Lily hurried after them, her colorful dress swishing as she tried to keep up. "Sarah, what's gotten into her?"

They rounded a corner, the scent of coffee growing even stronger. Pixie made a beeline for an open doorway, where a small room housed a coffee station. An extremely handsome young man stood inside, his back to them as he rummaged through a box of donuts, the fresh pot of coffee steaming on the counter beside him.

Pixie skidded to a halt in the doorway, her little body trembling with excitement. Then, without warning, she erupted into a frenzy of barking. It wasn't her usual dignified woof, but a full-on cacophony of yaps, growls, and howls.

The man spun around, startled, a half-eaten donut in his hand. Powdered sugar dusted his neatly pressed shirt.

Sarah tugged on the leash, mortified.

"Pixie, stop! I'm so sorry, sir, she's not usually like this."

But Pixie was inconsolable. She continued her tirade, her eyes fixed on the bewildered man, her tail no longer wagging regally but whipping back and forth with an urgency Sarah had never seen before.

Lily caught up, out of breath. "What in the world...?"

Sarah struggled to control the usually well-behaved Pixie without causing more of a disturbance than they already had. Doors opened, and people peeked out into the hallway.

"What is going on with you?" she snapped, yanking on the little pink leash.

The man before them was a bit younger than Sarah, perhaps in his mid-thirties. His blonde hair was styled in that carefully tousled way that suggested both a laid-back attitude and a hefty investment in hair products. It framed a face that might have been at home on a California beach, all sun-kissed skin and easy charm. One of their models, perhaps? He wore close-fitting designer jeans, paired with a crisp white button-down shirt now speckled with powdered sugar.

When he turned, a lanyard hanging from his neck identified him as a Creative Charities employee, though Sarah couldn't make out the name from where she stood.

As Pixie continued her frenzied barking, the man took another step back, nearly bumping into the coffee machine behind him. His easy-going surfer demeanor vanished, replaced by a look of sheer alarm. He held his hands out in front of him, palms facing outward, as if to ward off the small but vocal dog.

"Whoa!" he exclaimed, his voice a mix of surprise and irritation. "Can you please control... that?" He gestured towards Pixie with his half-eaten donut, sending a small shower of powdered sugar to the floor.

His eyes darted between Sarah and Lily, clearly expecting one of them to put an end to the commotion. "Seriously, what's wrong with your dog? Why is it in public?" he asked, a panicked edge creeping into his voice.

Sarah tugged on Pixie's leash, trying to pull her back. "I'm so sorry," she said again, her cheeks flushing with embarrassment. "She's never done this before."

"Get it together, Pixie."

Pixie finally sat, glaring daggers at the man with the donut, just before she started barking again. What was it about this man that had set her off, even though he carried a sweet treat?

Vanessa's heels clacked rapidly against the floor as she hurried towards the commotion, a stack of glossy brochures clutched to her chest. Her professional demeanor was slightly ruffled as she took in the scene before her.

"What on earth is going on here?" she exclaimed, her eyes widening at the sight of Pixie's continued barking frenzy. "I can hear you all the way down in the copy room."

Sarah tugged harder on Pixie's leash, her face flushed with embarrassment now. "I'm so sorry, Vanessa. I don't know what's gotten into her. This never... It just doesn't..."

Vanessa's lips pressed into a thin line as she turned to the man.

"Noah, I apologize for this disturbance." She then looked back at Sarah and Lily, her voice taking on a clipped tone. "This is Noah Delmore, our web designer and contractor. He's been instrumental in our online presence. He worked on the Christmas in July event, as a matter of fact."

Noah nodded tersely, still keeping his distance from Pixie.

"Yeah, hi," he muttered, brushing powdered sugar from his shirt.

"I'm terribly sorry about this, Noah," Vanessa said, her voice strained. "Let's meet in my office in five. I have a few ideas for our event page. I want to hear your input."

She then turned to Sarah and Lily, her professional smile barely masking her annoyance. "Ladies, I think it's best if we wrap up our visit now. Let me show you out."

She began ushering them away from the coffee station, her hand gently but firmly guiding them back down the hallway. Pixie continued to strain against her leash, trying to look back at Noah even as Sarah pulled her along.

"Once again, we appreciate your interest in our work," Vanessa said as they walked, her tone making it clear that their welcome had worn out. "These brochures should provide you with all the information you need for your... project."

As they made their way through the reception area, the atmosphere had noticeably cooled. The same employees who had fawned over Pixie earlier now cast wary glances their way, their smiles strained and professional.

The receptionist, who had been so charmed by Pixie at their arrival, now kept her eyes firmly fixed on her computer screen, only offering a curt nod as they passed.

Vanessa opened the glass doors for them, her careful, professional smile firmly in place.

"Thank you for your visit. Good luck with your project." Her tone made it clear that she hoped their paths wouldn't cross again anytime soon.

As they stepped out into the afternoon sun, Sarah felt a wave of relief mixed with lingering embarrassment. She looked down at Pixie, who had finally calmed down but still seemed on edge, her ears twitching nervously, making the long ear fringe dance this way and that.

"Well, girl," Sarah muttered under her breath, just loud enough for Pixie and Lily to hear, "I guess you've blown your chance at being an advertising model. So much for your dreams of stardom."

Pixie looked up at Sarah, her expression a mix of indignation and determination. She cast a glance back at the huge glass door of the building, where Vanessa was just disappearing, and lowered her head.

Trust me, this was important.

Lily leaned in close as they walked away from the building. "Okay, what in the world was that all about? I've never seen Pixie act like that before."

Sarah shook her head, her mind racing. "I have no idea, but I'm sure it wasn't for nothing. We need to figure out what set her off."

Sarah stopped and looked back over her shoulder at Creative Charities once or twice. Despite the disastrous end to their visit, she had the feeling they had stumbled onto something significant. The question was, what had Pixie sensed about Noah Delmore that had caused such an extreme reaction? And how did it tie into their investigation?

Chapter Eighteen

As soon as the doors of the old orange bug slammed shut, Pixie's thoughts erupted into Sarah's mind, tumbling out in an excited rush."

Sarah! That man—Noah—he's the one! He wore the Santa hat I found in the alley!

Sarah turned in her seat to face Pixie, her eyes wide. "Are you sure?"

Pixie shook vigorously, her ears flying.

Positive! That scent was all over him. It's the same one I picked up from the hat in the alley. No doubt about it!

Sarah's mind raced with this new information.

That's a pretty serious accusation. We can't just—

I know what I smelled, Pixie interrupted, her tone uncharacteristically serious. *Trust me on this, Sarah. That man and the hat are connected.*

Lily, who had been watching this exchange with growing confusion, finally spoke up.

"Uh, Sarah? Want to fill me in on what's going on? Sure about what exactly?"

Sarah took a deep breath, then turned to her friend.

Sarah quickly recounted Pixie's revelation, explaining the Santa hat they'd found in the alley and Pixie's conviction about who had worn it.

Lily's eyes grew wider with each word.

"So, you're saying that this Noah guy... he might be involved in Tyler's death?"

"He might. But there's no proof yet," Sarah cautioned, even as her heart raced with the possibility. "As of right now, he's a random web designer we met at Creative. But it's a lead we need to follow up on."

You better believe we do, she heard from Pixie, and caressed the little dog's head.

"Good luck with that one," Lily said, her hands gripping the steering wheel tightly. "After Pixie's performance in there, it's not like we can just waltz back in and ask, Hey, did you rob a bank by any chance? '"

Sarah closed her eyes for a moment, feeling Vanessa's icy, cool smile on her again.

"Right. We need to find out more about this Noah Delmore character."

Her voice drifted off, and the three of them fell into a thoughtful silence. They had come to Creative Charities hoping for answers, and while they'd left with more questions than they'd arrived with, they also had a solid lead.

Sarah glanced back at Pixie, who sat alert and proud in the back seat.

"Good job, girl," she said softly. "Looks like your nose just blew this case wide open."

Pixie's tail wagged, and she winked.

At least this time, you didn't say I wish I had your nose, Sarah heard, and imagined Pixie was chuckling.

As Lily navigated the car out of the parking lot, Pixie suddenly perked up, her nose pressed against the window.

Right over there, there's his car! she exclaimed, her fluffy tail wagging with excitement.

Sarah and Lily both turned to look where Pixie was indicating. Parked near the entrance was an old Ford, its blue paint faded and chipped in places.

"That old thing is Noah Delmore's car, Pixie?" Sarah asked, squinting to get a better look, trying to match the old beater to the image of the stylish, well-dressed Noah.

Pixie pawed the back window, leaning in close.

Absolutely. His scent is all over it. Not exactly what you'd expect for a fancy web designer, huh?

Lily slowed the car down slightly, allowing them a longer look. "It does seem a bit... underwhelming for someone working at a place like this," she mused.

Sarah studied the vehicle, hoping to spot something distinctive or out of place, but it was just an ordinary, somewhat beat-up old car—a dime a dozen. She sighed and folded her arms in front of her.

"It is something, I suppose," she said, trying to sound optimistic. "But I'm not sure looking at an old Ford helps us connect Noah to Tyler's death or the robbery."

Pixie shook and sat straight, with a regal, haughty look on her face.

Maybe somebody could check if it was parked... oh, by the bank the day of the event, or something?

Lily accelerated again, leaving the Creative Charities building and Noah's car behind.

"What's our next move, then?" she asked, glancing at Sarah.

Sarah squinted with half-closed eyes, only barely registering the landscape as they drove.

"We need to find out more about Noah Delmore. His connection to Creative Charities, his background, anything that might give us a clue about his involvement. If any."

"Uh-huh," Lily set a turn signal. "And?"

"And maybe ask Cory to do a bit of research. He's going to love it. Something about this old beater of a car..."

∞

Sarah, Lily, and Pixie arrived back at Thompson Hall, their minds still buzzing with the day's events. Matthew appeared to be at the museum for the day. Emma had left a note; she wanted to check out a support group Penny Harding had mentioned. But as they walked into the den, they found Cory sprawled on the living room couch, his laptop balanced precariously on his knees.

"Hey, research ace," Sarah called out, an idea forming. "Think you could help us with something?"

Cory's eyes lit up, and he sat up straighter and brushed chip crumbs off his shirt. "Any time. What do you need?"

Sarah glanced at Lily and Pixie before turning back to her son. "We're trying to find out more about a guy named Noah Delmore. I believe he does web design work. Think you could dig up anything?"

"Noah Delmore, web designer. Got it," Cory said, his fingers already flying across the keyboard. "Piece of cake. Any particular angle you're looking for?"

"Anything you can find, really," Sarah replied, trying to keep her tone casual. "His work history, clients, that sort of thing. He works for Creative Charities."

Cory stopped momentarily, his face illuminated by the screen's glow, then he nodded. "You got it. This will only take a minute."

As they waited, Lily and Sarah withdrew into the kitchen. Pixie hopped out through the doggie door to deal with some red squirrels who had become entirely too comfortable in the gardens around the house.

After what seemed like an eternity but was probably only about ten minutes, Cory looked up from his laptop with a triumphant grin.

"Okay, I think I might have something interesting."

Sarah abandoned the coffee maker she'd been filling and spread her hands. "What did you find?"

"For starters, this Noah Delmore guy? He's not actually employed by Creative Charities full-time. He's an independent contractor," Cory explained, his eyes scanning the screen. "Looks like he works out of his house, not their office."

Sarah's eyebrows shot up. "Really? That's... unexpected."

Cory nodded. "Yeah, he's got his own business. 'Delmore Digital Designs'. Pretty small-time operation from what I can tell. Creative Charities is probably his biggest client."

"Nice work, Cory!" Lily exclaimed, impressed by the teen's research skills.

"Plain old online search," Cory pulled up one shoulder. "Still..."

Sarah's mind was racing. "Anything else?" she prodded gently.

Cory shrugged. "Not much. His website is pretty basic, lame actually. I could do better. No social media presence to speak of. It's like the guy barely exists online, which is definitely weird for a web designer."

Pixie, who had come back in when she sensed Cory going into the kitchen, sat in front of Sarah and gave her a long look.

A web designer who's practically invisible on the web? I'd call that a little suspicious.

Sarah nodded absently, forgetting for a moment that Cory couldn't hear Pixie's comments.

"You're right, it is a bit odd," she murmured.

"What's odd?" Cory asked, looking confused.

"Oh, just... the fact that a web designer doesn't have much of an online presence," Sarah covered quickly. "Wouldn't that be where all of his clients are? Good catch on that."

"Not really trying if you ask me. The dude could be just lazy. He did the web presence for the Christmas in July event, though."

There it was, that tiny little red thread that connected all of these events. Christmas in July, the bank robbery, and Tyler's murder.

"You can't see webcams on that thing, can you?" she asked, nodding at Cory's tablet.

"Only if they're publicly streamed," Cory said slowly, cocking his head. "Everything else would be... You know, the opposite of legal. What exactly is it you're looking for?"

"Nothing, forget I asked," Sarah said quickly, forcing a smile. "Forget I said anything."

"Sure?"

"Sure."

Cory shook his head and wandered back into the den and games room, while Sarah covered her face with her hands.

"Jesus, I almost asked my kid to hack into traffic cams to check for Noah's car."

"Not that I hadn't thought of it," Lily said, continuing where Sarah had left off with the coffee maker.

"I'm the parent. I'm supposed to make good decisions around here." Sarah jumped to her feet, paced her kitchen, and kneaded her hands. "Maybe this whole looking into this murder and bank robbery is one size too large for us. Maybe I should just..."

"Look, look..." Lily grabbed her hands to still the incessant motion and led Sarah back to a chair. "When I was accused, you moved heaven and earth to help me, even went all the way to see Carlisle at his restaurant."

"I remember," she closed her eyes and shuddered, recalling the man with the steely glint in his eyes and the array of sharp knives behind him.

"But his mind basically told me he was guilty. This Delmore guy? Nothing."

"He triggered something in Pixie."

Sarah reached down, and Pixie came close, leaning into the caress.

I don't like him, but something is up with that man, Sarah heard. *He was basically terrified when I started barking.*

Afraid of dogs? Maybe you are just scary?

Tell me, what do most people do when they see me?

I don't know... speak in a cute baby language, try to pet you?

There.

Pixie shook and walked away.

"Hey," Lily said slowly, putting a finger to her lip. "You think Emma would mind if I borrowed her bike?"

"Her bike? Probably not..." Sarah looked up from where she'd been staring aimlessly into the yard. "Why do you ask?"

"I thought some exercise would do us good, ride around for a little through Rosewood."

Sarah's eyes lit up at Lily's suggestion, quickly catching onto her friend's subtle hint.

"You know what? That sounds like a great idea. I could use some fresh air and exercise."

"Hey Cory," she called into the games room. "Lily and I are going out for a bit."

Cory only waved with the remote control, already engrossed in something else. Sarah moved quickly, grabbing her helmet, the notes Cory had given her, and Pixie's special bike carrier. The little dog, sensing adventure, was already wagging her tail furiously.

"Come on, girl," Sarah said, scooping Pixie up and securing her in the carrier. "Time for a little reconnaissance mission."

Pixie's eyes sparkled with mischief.

You're planning to drive through Delmore's neighborhood, aren't you? Maybe.

Within minutes, Sarah and Lily were pedaling down the street, with Pixie securely nestled in her carrier attached to Sarah's bike. The late afternoon sun cast long shadows as they rode, the air still warm but with a hint of evening coolness creeping in.

"So," Lily said as they turned onto a quieter street, "do you know where Noah's house is?"

Sarah nodded, slightly out of breath from the uphill climb. "Cory found the address when he was doing his research. It's over in the Oakwood neighborhood, not too far from here."

They pedaled in companionable silence for a while, both lost in thought. Pixie's ears flapped in the breeze, her nose working overtime as she took in all the scents rushing past.

As they approached the Oakwood neighborhood, with its neat rows of modest homes and well-manicured lawns, Sarah felt a mix of excitement and apprehension. What would they find?

"There it is," Sarah said quietly as they slowed their pace, nodding towards a small blue house with white trim. A faded Ford—the same one they'd seen at Creative Charities—sat in the driveway.

Lily whistled low. "Not exactly living large for a hotshot web designer, is he?"

Sarah shook her head, scanning the property. "No, he's not. Which makes me wonder... how much money is in all of his contract work?"

As they slowly pedaled past Noah's house, trying to look as casual as possible, Pixie suddenly stiffened in her carrier, her nose twitching furiously.

Sarah, she whispered urgently, *I smell something. Something... familiar.*

They slowly cycled past Noah's house for a second time, and Pixie's nose was working overtime. Her little body was tense with concentration, her ears perked forward.

Suddenly, her eyes widened with realization.

I think I've got it figured out, although it's weird! Sarah heard and slowed her bike, pretending to adjust her helmet as she leaned closer to Pixie's carrier.

"What is it, girl?" she whispered.

Pixie craned her neck toward the house, sniffing the air thoroughly.

Noah doesn't actually live in the house. His scent is coming from the garage!

Sarah brushed the hair out of her face, readjusting her bike helmet. She casually glanced at the property again, noting the small, detached garage attached to the side of the house. It was a simple structure, featuring a single window and what appeared to be a side door, in addition to the main garage door.

"Are you sure?" Sarah murmured, trying to keep her voice down.

Pixie gave her that stern, haughty look she did so well. *Positive. His scent is all over that garage, but it's barely present in the main house. Maybe he's renting it from the owners.*

Sarah signaled to Lily, and they both slowed to a stop a few houses down, pretending to take a water break.

"What's going on?" Lily asked, spreading her hands.

Sarah quickly relayed Pixie's discovery. Lily's eyes widened as she processed the information.

"But why would he be living in a converted garage?" Lily wondered aloud.

Sarah shook her head, her mind racing with possibilities. "I don't know, but it's a little suspicious. A web designer working out of a converted garage, driving an old beater... something doesn't add up."

As they pedaled away from Noah's house, Sarah's mind was whirling with questions. Web design work usually paid well. Why then was Noah living a life more suited to a student that a successful professional? And how did all of this connect to the robbery and Tyler's death? This just added another layer of intrigue to the already complex situation.

Chapter Nineteen

Pixie settled back into her carrier to let the wind caress her little face.

Either he's hiding something, or he's just really bad at his job and at getting clients.

"Could be, but we're only guessing," Sarah cautioned, though she couldn't help but wonder about the possibilities herself.

∞

Once back home, they stored their bikes in the garage. Sarah unclipped Pixie from her carrier, the little dog shaking herself and stretching her legs one at a time.

Inside, they found Cory still engrossed in his laptop. He looked up as they entered, a questioning look on his face.

"Have a nice ride?" he asked, trying far too hard to sound disinterested. He knew they'd been up to something.

"Great," Sarah said, then paused, an idea forming. "Cory, I have another question for you, if you don't mind."

"Of course, you do. What's up?"

Sarah gnawed at her lower lip, choosing her words carefully.

"I was wondering... Do you think Tyler might have known Noah Delmore? Did he ever mention anything?"

Cory frowned, deep in thought. "Noah Delmore... The web designer guy you asked me about?" He thought for a moment. "I don't remember hearing anything specific. Any particular reason you want to know?"

"He's just... odd," Sarah said, trying to keep her tone casual. "I can't put my finger on it."

Cory nodded, already turning back to his laptop. "When you say odd, you mean highly sus. I'll let you know if I find anything."

As Cory began his search, Sarah, Lily, and Pixie retreated to the kitchen for some privacy.

"What are you thinking?" Lily whispered.

Sarah leaned against the counter; her voice low. "I'm not sure yet. But I want to know if there's any connection between Tyler and Noah, it could be the key."

"Because Noah works at Creative, and he reacted to Pixie," Lily asked, pouring herself a glass of water. "I don't know about that."

"That's why I want to know if he and Tyler were friends," Sarah opened her fridge and stared into it, trying to plan dinner in one corner of her mind while sorting through the events of the day in another. "Both the murder and the bank robbery went down at an event connected to Creative Charities. Noah works there and is acting quite 'sus' as my son would call it."

"And Deanna Barnes," Lily asked, the frown on her face deepening ever more. "Where does she fit into all of this, then?"

"Darned if I know." Sarah let the fridge door fall shut again. "I can't make any sense of this. If it weren't for my kids asking me to look into it... I'd probably just walk away."

Lily rose half out of her chair to peek down the hall and into the games room where Cory sat.

"And you are not, you know, sensing anything? Anything at all?"

"You're acting as if I had a radio station in my head I could tune into these things," Sarah complained. "I don't. Half the time I don't know what abilities I have and why. Right now... nothing. And I couldn't tell you if that's good or bad."

Sarah opened her pantry this time and scooped out a glass container of pasta. The ability to sense and know things, to generate power with nothing but the focus of her mind came and went in the strangest situations, quite often without her consciously realizing it, or calling on those powers. It was a massive source of frustration to her. But when she needed it, it had always come through.

Pixie hopped in through the little doggie door and sat pointedly in front of her food dish.

I know who you could ask.

Ask about what?

About this Delmore character. Two... well, beings who can go any-where, see everything without ever having to worry if it's legal or not.

"Amelia and Simon," Sarah sighed, and Lily's head snapped up.

"I thought you'd never ask, Sarah. I'm sure they can get us a ton of intel on how Delmore is connected to Tyler or to Deanna in any way. Great thought."

"Yes, but—"

"I think you should ask them. Right now."

Lily spread her hands with the kind of expectant look on her face, as if she thought Sarah could just pick up the phone and dial. Matter of fact. that was one of Sarah's favorite lines: these two are not dial-a-ghost, and that's not how they work. They decide when, how, and what to do whenever they feel like it.

And besides... Pixie put her paws into the stainless-steel food bowl and began pretend digging. *Dinner?*

∞

Sarah and Matthew sat on the porch swing, gently rocking back and forth as they gazed out at the lush summer garden. The air was thick with the scent of blooming flowers and the gentle hum of cicadas. Despite the peaceful evening, Sarah's mind ran in tight little circles, round and round.

"I can't shake this feeling about Noah Delmore," Sarah said, her brow furrowed. "If he's involved, what's his connection to Tyler? And where does Deanna fit into all of this? Ugh..." she voiced her frustration and gave the swing a little push.

Matthew placed a comforting hand on her knee. "Take it down a notch. This is probably why detectives spend years at police training school and learning the ropes."

Sarah sighed, running a hand through her hair. "I know, I know. Not like I haven't told myself the same thing. But this is upsetting Cory and Emma, and sitting idle doesn't... sit well with me."

"You and sitting idle," Matthew chuckled softly. "That would be a new one. Just take it down a notch. The world does not depend on you figuring this out..."

"No. Just Cory and Emma." Sarah leaned her head on Matthew's shoulder. "Why would Noah be living in a garage unless he's not doing well? And that Santa hat Pixie found, why did he toss it? In an alley? There are too many questions left unanswered."

As if on cue, Pixie trotted out onto the porch, her ears perked up. She sat straight in front of Sarah and draped her fluffy tail around her hind paws. The tip of her tail had the slightest golden gleam, which always meant she was working on something.

"What is it, girl?" Sarah asked, leaning forward.

I think you should come inside.

It's beautiful out here.

Matthew, totally misunderstanding the cue, picked up a little red ball that had been discarded on the porch and bounced it a few times.

"You want to play?"

Pixie didn't move, but she kept her eyes on Sarah.

"She wants me to go inside," Sarah said with a shrug and stopped the motion of the porch swing. "I swear to you if this is a trick to get a cookie..."

Sarah stood up, and held out a hand to Matthew. Pixie spun in a few tight circles in front of them and raced ahead, jumping through the doggie door into the kitchen.

Quite suddenly, she came darting back out and let out a series of sharp, excited barks. Her tail wagged furiously as she dashed back in through the doggie door. This time, Sarah noticed, the golden glimmer on the tip of her tail was quite pronounced.

"What's gotten into her?" Matthew complained and gathered their remaining things. "I was enjoying it out here."

Sarah shrugged, but as they stepped into the den and games room, she froze. There, hovering near the fireplace, their all-time favorite spot, were the translucent forms of Amelia and Simon.

Pixie sat before them, looking rather pleased with herself.

"Well, well," Amelia said, her voice echoing slightly. "It seems your furry little friend has learned a new trick. Summoning the dead? How quaint."

Simon, ever curious, floated down to eye level with Sarah and Matthew.

"I must say, this is quite exciting. We don't often get called upon in this way. What's the occasion?"

Sarah, recovering from her initial shock, glanced down at Pixie, who spun in a joyous circle once again. "Did you... Did you actually summon them?"

Pixie gave a proud little yip and wagged her tail.

Somebody had to do it. You're all standing around wondering how to ask them. So... here they are.

Amelia drifted gracefully to perch on the back of an armchair, her ghostly form barely disturbing the fabric.

"Yes, your droll little animal has apparently expanded her repertoire. Now, darling, what is it you want? We were in the middle of a rather engaging game of spectral chess."

Simon nodded eagerly.

"Indeed! But we're always happy to assist. I have not been in this house for a while, is there a fresh mystery to solve?"

Matthew, still somewhat uncomfortable with the supernatural elements of Sarah's life, cleared his throat.

"Um, yes. We're trying to solve a murder and a bank robbery. They might be connected."

"Delightfully sordid!" Amelia exclaimed, a mischievous glint in her ethereal eyes. "There is a bank teller who is decidedly not acting like one in her position should, and rumors of an illicit affair. Sarah, I might have forgiven you for chastising me over checking on her bank balance. It's quite healthy, you know."

"I well remember, Amelia." Sarah took a step toward the ghost on her chintz armchair. "I - we could use your help. There's a man named Noah Delmore who might be involved. He's acting quite squirrely."

"Squirrely?" Amelia's ghostly form shimmered and sparkled just a bit, which just might pass for her ghostly version of a laugh, even though she kept her face stern and unconcerned. "Is that so?"

"I think he... might be involved. Maybe he has a connection to Deanna..."

Amelia made a disgusted noise.

"Is there any way you could... I don't know, haunt him a little? Maybe find out what he knows?"

Simon clapped his translucent hands together. "A haunting! Oh, how wonderful. It's been ages since we've had a good haunting, hasn't it, Amelia?"

Amelia sighed dramatically. "I suppose we could lend a spectral hand. But do remember, darling, we're not your personal ghost detectives."

Sarah nodded gratefully. "Of course not. But any information you could gather would be incredibly helpful."

As the ghosts began to fade, preparing for their mission, Amelia's voice lingered in the air. "We'll see what we can do. But next time, do try to summon us at a more reasonable hour. The dead need their beauty rest, too, you know."

With that, Amelia and Simon vanished, leaving Sarah, Matthew, and Pixie alone in the suddenly quiet living room.

Matthew turned to Sarah, a mix of amazement and resignation on his face. "That's one way to gather intelligence. What do we do now?"

Sarah smiled, a new determination in her eyes. "Now, we wait. And hope our ghostly friends can uncover something we can't."

Chapter Twenty

For the next two days, Sarah found herself in a state of anxious anticipation. The house had never been cleaner, as she channeled her nervous energy into tidying every nook and cranny. Between dusting sessions and reorganizing drawers, her mind raced with theories about Noah Delmore and the events surrounding Tyler's death.

Was he connected or not? Did he know Deanna Barnes? Was Noah Delmore actually involved? Did he just dislike dogs and dispose of his hats in odd locations? It was enough to boggle the mind.

On the morning of the second day, as Sarah sat at the kitchen table nursing her third cup of coffee, Cory burst in, waving his tablet with the latest edition of the local news on it.

"Mom, you need to see this, right now," he said, his voice allowing no argument and no delay as he held out the tablet to her. Sarah read the bold, screaming headlines, and her eyes widened.

"Local Man Mastermind Behind Daring Bank Heist."

The article went on to detail how police had uncovered evidence suggesting that Tyler Robinson, the victim found dead during the Christmas in July event, had been the brains behind the bank robbery.

"This can't be right," Sarah muttered, skimming through the article. "Tyler? A criminal mastermind? How'd they get to that conclusion?"

Emma, who had wandered in to see what the commotion was about, leaned over Sarah's shoulder. "Most of it is wrong. If Tyler was behind the robbery, why was he killed? And what about the guy who didn't like Pixie, Noah Delmore?"

Sarah looked up, scratching the back of her neck.

"I don't know, honey. This just raises more questions than it answers."

"It's wrong," Cory snapped, taking his tablet back with an angry swipe. "You can't let them print stuff like that. They make him sound like a criminal, just because he was young and he had a few problems."

"I agree with you, there's just nothing I can do about it."

Just then, Pixie, who had been dozing contentedly in her little pink dog bed, suddenly perked up. Her ears twitched, and she let out a series of excited yips.

They're back.

Before Sarah could ask who was back, the temperature in the room dropped noticeably. A familiar, slightly haughty voice filled the air.

"Well, my dears, I hope you appreciate the lengths we've gone to for you," Amelia said as she and Simon materialized in the kitchen.

Simon looked rather pleased with himself and spun in a complete circle.

"Oh yes, I have to get used to visiting on this plane again, but haunting in the digital age is truly a fun little affair. My dear Amelia has taught me a lot about these things you call electronics..."

Amelia's spectral form darkened a bit at that, and Simon wavered.

"Anyway, we've uncovered some rather interesting information about your Mr. Delmore."

Sarah put down her mug and leaned forward. "So, let me have it. What did you find out?"

Amelia smirked, her translucent form shimmering slightly in delightful shades of gold and yellow.

"Oh, it's quite the tale. Your Noah Delmore isn't the brilliant web designer he would want you to think. He could be, mind you, but my father would have called him a sluggard and a loafer."

"A what?" Cory asked, making Amelia's form sparkle again.

"Guy who is lazy and doesn't want to do any work," Sarah supplied. "I think you would call him..."

"Total waste of space," Cory deadpanned.

Simon nodded enthusiastically.

"Indeed! I believe the young fellow has aspirations of being an actor. If he would focus and apply himself, that is. Although females do appear to find him... exceptionally handsome. Even Amelia."

Amelia hissed something incomprehensible, and Sarah covered a chuckle. She didn't even want to guess how Simon had come upon that little fact.

As they listened, Amelia and Simon drifted closer together, and apart again.

"Young Mr. Delmore," Amelia said much like a teacher would have, her ethereal form drifting lazily around the little group in the kitchen, "has been in quite a state these past two days."

Simon nodded enthusiastically, spraying a small shower of sparks. "Oh yes, quite agitated, I would say. We observed him in his office—that wretched garage of his."

"I wouldn't call that dreary hovel a proper office. He is not one for tidiness. Anyway, he's been pacing about like a caged animal, muttering to himself."

"But the most curious thing," Simon chimed in, leaning in with a little smile on his face, "is his behavior with his phone."

"His phone?" Sarah took a step closer to Simon, and Amelia shimmered again.

"Yes, darling. He keeps picking it up, staring at it as if it might bite him, then putting it back down again. It appears he desperately wants to call someone but can't bring himself to do it."

"Or perhaps he's afraid to do so," Simon added thoughtfully.

Sarah's mind raced with possibilities. "Did you happen to see any names or numbers on the phone screen?"

The ghosts exchanged a look. "We tried to peek," Simon admitted, "but every time we got close, he'd snatch the phone away and shove it into his trousers. Terribly rude, if you ask me."

"But I am sure that is not all you found out, is it?" Emma asked, cocking her head. Next to Sarah, she had the closest connection to Amelia and adored the ghost. Amelia's form shimmered with what might have been amusement.

"Oh no, dear child. That's just the beginning. There is so much more..."

"Well then, go on," Sarah urged, her coffee long forgotten. "Don't keep us in suspense."

So far, none of this could be called a breakthrough. Yes, Noah's behavior with the phone could be called curious—and that was it. And it didn't connect to Tyler's death or the bank robbery. For all they knew, it was a dentist's appointment he was putting off.

Pixie sat alert and attentive, her dark, intelligent eyes fixed on the ghosts, the tiniest bit of gold shimmering on the tip of her tail.

"Did Noah catch a glimpse of you by any chance?"

Amelia puffed up with ghostly pride. "Who do you take us for?" she asked, emitting a shower of sparks. "If you must know, we haunted that dreary garage-turned-office of his day and night—quite unseen."

Simon nodded enthusiastically and spun around in a circle again. "Oh yes! We'd drift through the walls, unseen and unheard. Sometimes we'd hover in the corners, other times we'd float right through his computer! You should have seen Amelia. She can..."

"No need to go on at length," Amelia interrupted him. "The man had no idea. He'd shiver now and then, probably thinking it was just a draft. Little did he know he had two of Rosewood's finest ghosts keeping an eye on him."

"We even followed him on his infrequent trips outside," Simon chimed in. "Haunted his car, so to speak. Though I must say, automotive haunting isn't nearly as glamorous as it sounds."

Emma giggled, and even Sarah couldn't help but smile at their enthusiasm.

"Impressive. And a bit unsettling," she admitted. "Please stay out of my car. But I'm grateful for your dedication. Now, what else did all of this haunting uncover?"

Amelia and Simon exchanged a knowing look before continuing.

"Indeed," Amelia began, her ghostly form shimmering with excitement. "We've uncovered something quite intriguing about the connection between Noah Delmore and the deceased Tyler Robinson."

"A connection," Sarah's head snapped up quite suddenly. "What kind of a connection, like they knew one another?"

Simon nodded eagerly. "Oh yes, it's quite the genealogical puzzle!"

Sarah leaned forward, clenched, and then unclenched her hands. "Simon, Amelia, I wish..." She pressed her lips together again. Rushing these two wouldn't get her anywhere.

Amelia cleared her ethereal throat. "One evening, when he had left that little computer open. You know the kind, like the one Cory carries about, and I noticed a message about family trees and distant relations. Naturally, I became quite curious about it."

"So, we did a bit of spectral snooping," Simon added. "It turns out, Noah and Tyler are very distant cousins. We're talking about a connection that goes back several generations."

Sarah's eyes widened. "How distant exactly?"

Amelia waved a translucent hand. "Quite removed, if you must know. Their common ancestor lived in the late 1800s. A great-great-great-grandfather, if I'm not mistaken."

"Five greats to be precise," Simon corrected. "They're fifth cousins once removed."

Sarah furrowed her brow. "That's a massively distant relation. Why would Noah be so interested in this connection?"

"That's the million-dollar question, isn't it?" Amelia said with a smirk. "He seemed quite agitated about this discovery. Kept muttering about family obligations and inherited burdens."

Simon nodded solemnly. "We tried to get a better look at this message, but he was rather protective of that... tablet you call it? He nearly walked right through me at one point!"

Sarah sat back, her mind racing.

"I didn't expect this. A distant family connection between Noah and Tyler... but why is that important to Noah? And how does this relate to Tyler's death and the bank robbery?"

Sarah pulled the hair back from her head and stared unseeing out in the yard. None of this was giving her the answers she sought. On the contrary, the mystery was becoming more complex by the minute.

She sat back in her chair, feeling as if she held a puzzle piece from a completely different game. Something that didn't fit anywhere in this particular mystery.

"This changes the picture," Sarah murmured, more to herself than anyone else. She looked up at her spectral informants. "Thank you, both of you."

"Oh, it was rather enjoyable, Sarah, and with my dear Amelia as a guide, I must say I enjoyed myself."

Amelia preened a bit. "Always happy to assist in a good mystery. Eternity can be so boring."

"But we still don't know what it all means, do we?" Emma asked, her young face scrunched in concentration.

Sarah ran a hand through her hair and idly braided a few strands.

"Afraid not," she said, releasing the strands again. "All of a sudden, everything is on the table again."

"Like what?" Cory asked, pulling his own tablet closer with a finger and inspecting it as if he worried that the ghosts would affect it.

Sarah began ticking off points on her fingers. "Well, first, we need to reassess Tyler's role in all this. The newspaper article painted him as the mastermind behind the bank heist, something we don't believe for a minute. But with this new information..."

"I really liked him, but what if Tyler is guilty after all?" Emma asked, her voice small and uncertain, her face drawn all of a sudden. "What if he and Noah Delmore worked this bank robbery together?"

Sarah reached out to squeeze her daughter's hand.

"I'm sorry, but it's possible. Don't take that newspaper article at face value, though."

"Clickbait," Cory scoffed. "If anything, what if Noah talked him into it? Like you owe me, are we a family kind of deal? Still, he went along."

Simon's ghostly form bobbed in agreement.

"Family connections, even distant ones, can be powerful motivators."

Sarah nodded slowly.

"Could be. And perhaps that is why Noah seems so agitated now. If they were in it together..."

"But then why would he shoot his cousin, even a fifth cousin, and what about Deanna Barnes?" Emma asked, her brow furrowed.

The heavy silence settled onto the little group around the table. Finally, Sarah drummed her fingers on the table and voiced what they were all thinking.

Chapter Twenty-One

"Noah might have killed Tyler," Sarah said quietly. "Maybe there was a disagreement, or Noah wanted to keep all the money for himself."

Amelia's form shimmered darkly with what might have been concern.

But it is still guesswork right now, Pixie said quietly and scrambled up into Emma's lap, cuddling close to the little girl.

"I don't want to believe that," Cory said sadly. "Isn't there anything we can do?"

Sarah straightened up and put a hand on his shoulder.

"Of course there is. We find out what's behind it. We figure out what's up with this family connection between Noah and Tyler and keep a close eye on Noah's movements."

She turned to the ghosts. "Amelia, Simon, if you enjoyed haunting Noah Delmore... would you... Perhaps continue a bit? Any additional information could be crucial."

The spectral pair exchanged a look before Amelia answered. "Well, I suppose we could manage a bit more haunting. It has been rather exciting, hasn't it?"

Simon nodded enthusiastically. "Oh yes, quite thrilling to haunt with you, my dear, indeed!"

As the ghosts faded away to resume their spectral spying, Sarah turned to her children and Pixie.

"There is so much to unpack with those two, I don't even know where to start. Are you okay, Emma?"

She touched her young daughter's arm, and Emma managed a one-shoulder shrug.

"I don't know, Mom. Tyler ended up dead. Thinking that he might have... been involved, brought it on himself. That's tough."

"You said Noah works for Creative Charities," Cory asked, turning on his tablet.

"He created the Christmas in July event website, yes, though he's only a contractor. Why do you ask?"

"I have an idea."

Cory waved her over as he navigated to the event page on the Creative Charities website, and Sarah frowned, torn between his enthusiasm and Emma's sadness.

"Look... live event videos. I knew they'd have them."

They huddled around the laptop as Cory clicked on the list of promotional videos from the Christmas in July event.

"People who donated money want to see themselves on the internet. And if Noah were part of the event team, I'd expect he would be front and center."

They watched the little screen as cheerful holiday music played over footage of the event setup, volunteers in Santa hats, and interviews with organizers. The videos went on and on, the same images and motifs returning, and Sarah quietly took Emma's hand, watching her guarded face. The excitement of Cory's idea began to wane quickly.

"I don't see Noah or Tyler anywhere," Emma finally said, sinking down in her chair a little further.

Sarah wiped gritty eyes. "You're right. For someone who was so involved, he's surprisingly absent from their promotional material."

As they continued watching, Sarah's mind drifted back to the day of the event. She closed her eyes, trying to recall the details of what she'd seen just before Tyler's body was discovered.

"Wait a minute," she said suddenly, her eyes snapping open. "I remember something about two Santas I saw walking away. Matthew and I joked that maybe they wanted to take a leak around the corner." Her face scrunched up in distaste. "Their costumes were identical. Not just similar, but exactly the same, down to the slightest detail."

Cory paused the video. "Identical costumes? That's a little weird, isn't it? Why go through the effort of getting identical costumes?"

Sarah nodded, her mind racing. "Exactly. And now that I think about it, they were both the same height and build, too. It was almost like seeing double."

Emma's eyes widened. "Could it have been the same person? Maybe caught on camera twice?"

"Or it just looked that way from a distance," Cory suggested.

Sarah shook her head slowly. "I don't think so. They were walking away together, side by side. Weird. Could it be someone wanted to make sure you could mistake one for the other?"

She turned back to the laptop. "Cory, can you check if there are any other videos or photos from the event? Social Media? Maybe we can spot these two identical Santas."

"Probably. YouTube, TikTok – somebody was stabbed there. People are going to want to brag that they were there."

Cory began searching for more videos and images, his face glued to the screen with intensity. That detail about the identical Santas was significant, Sarah thought. The absence of Noah in the promotional material was equally puzzling. Could it be he wanted it that way?

"You know," Sarah mused, almost to herself, "for someone who is running his own business, he sure is not using this event to advertise himself."

Pixie, who had been quietly observing, let out a soft whine that Sarah interpreted as agreement. She reached down to scratch behind the dog's ears, drawing comfort from her loyal companion.

"Keep looking, Cory," she encouraged. "If we can find those Santas in any of the footage, perhaps we can spot a face. Anything that might give us a clearer picture of what happened that day."

Digging out her old sketchbook and pencils, Sarah drew a quick sketch of what she remembered of the two Santas and put it in front of Cory. Their costumes were certainly unremarkable—nothing special.

Emma fetched a glass of water and peeked over her mother's shoulder.

"Every online party store has that exact model," she said with a sigh. "That's not a needle in a haystack, that's darn near impossible."

Not for us.

The thought quite suddenly stood between them, and Sarah reached for Emma's hand. As quickly as it had come, the moment was gone.

Emma and Cory continued to scroll through more online videos and pictures, softly chattering with one another, while her mind sifted through all of the possibilities. All of the pieces to this mystery felt unconnected and important in their own way, and still, she hadn't found the red line that connected them all. Other than the one none of them wanted to believe: Tyler Robinson.

❧

Not an hour later, the doorbell chimed softly, breaking the afternoon quiet. Sarah opened the door to find Officer Harding standing on the porch, dressed in casual clothes but still clutching her trademark yellow legal pad.

"Hi, Sarah," she greeted with a warm smile. "Is this a good time? I was hoping to chat with Cory if he's around." She gestured to her jeans and sneakers. "Thought it might help to leave the uniform at home."

Sarah hesitated, but Cory appeared from the den, his expression dark and closed up.

"It's okay, Mom. I'll talk to her."

Officer Harding offered a hand to Cory; her tone gentle.

"I just have a few questions, if that's all right, then I'll be out of your hair. I want to get a handle on Tyler's friends and close... buddies. Did he ever mention hanging out with anyone... unusual? Or any problems he might have been having?"

Cory's eyes narrowed. "Why? So, you can pin this on him, too?"

"Cory," Sarah cautioned softly, but he pressed on.

"I know you think Tyler was mixed up in that robbery. You're looking for an accomplice and the evidence to support your theory. But Tyler wasn't that kind of person. He didn't deserve what happened to him."

Officer Harding's expression softened. "Of course he didn't. I understand you're upset. Nobody deserves to be murdered. We're just trying to piece this case together. For him and his family, as much as the other people in Rosewood. Any information could help."

Cory crossed his arms, his stance defiant, his arms folded in front of his body. "Tyler was a decent guy. We played hockey together and coached kids. He didn't hang out with anybody – weird, and he wasn't into gangs. That's it."

The officer nodded, seemingly satisfied for the time being. "Thank you. If anything else comes to mind, would you please let me know, or..." Her eyes slid over to Sarah. "Or ask someone to do so?"

Cory only nodded and, without another word, went back into the kitchen, where he stood, brooding. Sarah saw out officer Harding and followed Cory into the kitchen to find him digging through the fridge.

"She's just doing her job, Cory."

"I guess."

"You have to admit..."

"That it looks bad for Tyler? Yeah, I get that." Cory found a bag of cold cuts and began piling them haphazardly onto a slice of bread. "You didn't exactly rush her with the Delmore family connection either."

No, Sarah thought, then I'd have to tell her I've been looking into this.

"And I still have not found Noah on those videos... or Tyler for that matter," Cory continued.

He took a bite out of his sandwich, stared at it as if wondering where it came from, and put it back down.

"It... bothers me," he finished simply.

Sarah wrapped her arms around her son, hugging him tightly. "I know, and I'm proud of you. Deanna Barnes, Noah Delmore, Tyler Robinson... there's a definite connection. We just need to find it."

"I'm going back to the videos. At least one of them has got to be there somewhere."

⌒

Later that evening, Sarah and Matthew sat on the porch swing, watching fireflies dance in the twilight garden.

"I feel guilty seeing how much this is bothering Cory and Emma," Sarah said, "And I am trying, but I can't quite connect the dots."

Matthew squeezed her hand. "You've made incredible progress. Don't be too hard on yourself."

"I know. Still." She set the swing in motion with a gentle push. "I just can't figure out what links Deanna, Noah, and Tyler, besides their odd behavior around the time of the robbery and... Tyler's death."

Matthew nodded thoughtfully.

"Tyler. I keep wondering if he seemed distracted lately, or if I am reading into this."

"Cory said the same thing," Sarah replied. "And I'm afraid that Tyler might have stumbled into something that was one size too large for him. Perhaps even without knowing what was going on."

Pixie trotted onto the porch, settling between them. Sarah absently stroked the dog's fur, grateful for Matthew's and her furry companion's constant support.

Emma had another dream, and Sarah suddenly heard and was on her feet immediately.

She did? I have to check on her....

Relax. I slept beside her, and it is over now.

"Everything okay?" Matthew asked, concern etched on his face.

Sarah settled back onto the swing. "Emma had a nightmare, Pixie says. But it's over." She kneaded her hands anxiously. "Ever since she found Tyler, I can feel Emma's abilities developing. On top of everything else, I'm worried she won't know how to handle them."

Matthew wrapped an arm around her shoulders.

"She will. She has you as a guide. What more could she need?"

Sarah spared another glance into the house, as if she could peer through the walls and into Emma's room, then she sat back on the swing, letting it swing gently. Guilt gnawed at her for not seeing the big picture of this robbery and shooting.

The pieces were there: Deanna at the bank, Noah's suspicious behavior, and Tyler's untimely death. All she needed was a roadmap to make them all fit.

Chapter Twenty-Two

T he next morning, Sarah was drinking a cup of coffee on the front porch with Pixie by her side.

"Summer is still my favorite," Sarah said, watching her garden awake. "Everything is so glorious and beautiful."

Pixie sat contentedly beside her, her head on her paws, all while keeping a close eye on a couple of squirrels chasing each other through a tree.

Sarah worried that Emma would have tossed and turned all night with more nightmares, but she surprised them all, appearing bright and bouncy at breakfast, smiling broadly.

"I think I'm going to check out the local gym today," she said, spreading jam on her toast with uncharacteristic enthusiasm. "Maybe try some yoga or a dance class."

Sarah paused, her coffee mug halfway to her lips.

"The gym? That's... new. Who are you and what have you done with my bookworm Emma?"

Emma shrugged, avoiding eye contact. "I just feel like I need to go there. It's hard to explain."

Sarah exchanged a glance with Cory, who raised an eyebrow and said nothing, dumping milk and way too much sugar on his cereal. Just a little while ago, he'd been intensely jealous of his sister's connection to the ghosts and their mother; now he'd found his own place in the world.

"That sounds great, Em," Sarah said carefully. "How about I come with you? We could make it a mother-daughter thing."

Emma's head snapped up, her eyes wide. "Not really!" she blurted, then quickly composed herself. "I mean, thanks, Mom, but I'd rather go alone. I just... need some space to figure things out."

Sarah hesitated, torn between respecting her daughter's independence and privacy, and her immediate instinct to protect her.

"Are you sure?"

"I'm sure," Emma insisted, a note of finality in her voice.

She finished her breakfast and left the kitchen to get ready, and Pixie trotted over to Sarah, her tail wagging slowly.

Something's up with that gym, Pixie said. *I can feel it. But maybe Emma needs to discover it on her own.*

Sarah nodded, absently scratching Pixie behind the ears. *Maybe. But I don't have to like it. I just hope she'll be careful.*

∞

Emma headed out about an hour later, but Sarah still felt the need to stop her at the door.

"Remember, if anything feels off or you need me, just call. I can be there in minutes."

"I will, Mom." Emma rolled her eyes but smiled. "Don't worry so much."

Sarah stood at the kitchen window watching her daughter mount her bike and drive off down toward the road. Every instinct inside her screamed against doing it, but she reached out with her mind toward Emma.

Was she all right? Was something troubling her? Did this have anything to do with her dreams from the night before?

She'd expected a disjointed, chaotic jumble of teenage thoughts, but to her surprise, she was met with a blank wall of white noise.

Emma shielded her thoughts, she said to Pixie, gripping the windowsill tightly. *She's blocking me out.*

And you are surprised?

Yes, I am... No, I'm angry.

Sarah. The gentle pressure of a delicate paw on her foot was Pixie's way of bringing her back to the here and now when her thoughts were spiraling.

Amelia told me I could shield my thoughts, but I... am finding it hard. Emma seems to have no issues.

Trust her.

"Easy for you to say," she said out loud, and Matthew, who'd been reading emails over his tea, finally looked up.

"Something going on?"

"Emma," Sarah said, clearing the dishes. "I'm worried about this sudden idea that she should visit the gym, and now she won't take me along or open her mind to me."

"Hm." Matthew took off his reading glasses and folded them carefully. "Sort of like you when you got an idea last year, that you absolutely had to visit Vincent Carlisle's restaurant?"

"That was different."

"And you went by yourself, and he ended up coming after you?"

"It was so not the same thing. And still that's exactly my point," Sarah argued. "What if somebody does come after Emma?"

Wouldn't get far, Pixie said, rolling on her back, advertising for a belly rub. *As much protective momma bear energy as you're spitting right now, they'd be toast in a minute.*

"I don't know what Pixie just told you," Matthew said, "but I am sure I agree with her."

Sarah headed out into her sun-dappled yard, the scent of freshly mown grass tickling her nose. She knelt beside a flowerbed, her fingers sinking into the cool, damp earth as she plucked errant weeds. Bees hummed lazily around her, their wings glinting gold in the afternoon light.

As she worked, Sarah's eyes kept drifting to the horizon. Her hands moved mechanically, snipping stems and arranging blooms in her wicker basket, but her mind wandered. She closed her eyes, inhaling deeply, trying to quiet the constant whir of her thoughts. In the stillness, she reached out, searching for that familiar warmth, that spark of connection she'd always shared with Emma.

Nothing.

The silence in her mind echoed, vast and empty. Sarah's shoulders tensed, a chill running down her spine despite the summer heat. She opened her eyes, blinking rapidly against the sudden brightness. The flowers in her basket seemed to mock her with their cheery hues. Despite her chores, the nagging worry persisted.

The sharp rap at the door finally startled her from her reverie in late afternoon.

It was Lily, on her way home from the store, arms laden with a tower of books that threatened to topple at any moment. A large bakery bag topped the whole lot, emitting the most delicious aromas.

"You're going to be the death of my waistline," Sarah quipped, but her attempt at levity fell flat. Her eyes darted once more to the kitchen window, scanning the empty driveway as if willing a bike with a teenager to materialize.

Lily shoved up her sunglasses and set down her literary haul. "Oh, I know that look," she said. "Spill it, Sarah. Right at the moment, you look like... well, like you've seen a ghost."

Sarah's fingers twisted the hem of her sweater. "Penny Harding showed up yesterday, sniffing around about Tyler."

"I take it Cory wasn't thrilled?"

"Understatement of the century," Sarah muttered, her gaze unfocused. "But that's not everything... there's something else."

Lily, now as comfortable in Sarah's kitchen as her own, busied herself with the coffee maker. The familiar gurgle and hiss filled the silence.

Sarah slumped into a kitchen chair, the wood creaking in protest. Her hands splayed across her thighs, fingers trembling ever so slightly.

"Emma," she whispered, "decided to go to the gym today."

The spoon Lily had been holding clattered to the counter. "Emma? Our Emma? The girl who'd rather alphabetize my entire inventory than break a sweat?"

Sarah's eyes met Lily's, a storm of emotions swirling in their depths. "She had an... idea," Sarah breathed, bringing her palms together as if in prayer. She pressed them against her forehead, shoulders hunched as if bearing an invisible weight.

The air in the kitchen seemed to thicken, the shadows in the corners deepening despite the afternoon light. Something unspoken hung between the two women, a shared understanding that ideas, especially in this house, were rarely as simple as they appeared.

The gentle flap of the doggie door punctuated Sarah's words. Pixie pranced in, her feathered ears perked and her plumed tail swishing. The tiny Papillon sat primly before Sarah, dark eyes sparkling.

Calm down, Sarah. Emma's fine, Pixie's thoughts resonated in Sarah's mind. *If anyone should be worried, it's her... about your overprotective streak.*

Sarah opened her mouth to retort, but Pixie continued, tail wagging pointedly. *Besides, Emma's coming up Maple Street on her bike right now. So, if I were you...*

The diminutive dog trotted away, positioning herself strategically near the bakery bag on the counter, nose twitching at the enticing aromas.

Lily quirked an eyebrow. "I take it our canine confidante shares my opinion?"

Sarah's fingers raked through her hair in a futile attempt at composure. She grabbed a discarded magazine, feigning nonchalance as Emma's footsteps approached.

"Oh, hi Emma!" Sarah's voice was a pitch too high. "Back already? Want some coffee and cake? Lily brought... something."

Emma removed her hot pink helmet, her gaze sweeping from Lily to her mother. She bent down to ruffle Pixie's silky ears before fixing Sarah with a knowing look. "Mom... You didn't spend the afternoon fretting and worrying about me, did you?"

"Of course not!" Sarah protested weakly. "I know you're responsible."

Emma's eye roll rivaled Cory's best, and she nodded at her mother. "You're reading Gamer's World, Mom."

Sarah's cheeks flushed as she slammed the magazine shut. "Fine. I was... a bit concerned. When you had this so-called idea. I just wanted to keep you safe."

Emma's hand found Sarah's shoulder; her touch was gentle.

"I am. I know you went through some pretty bad experiences last year."

"Kind of," Sarah admitted. "So you see..."

"Yes, I see," Emma said softly. "We have a gift, and I want to practice that. Trust me. It won't be easy, but it will keep us safe, always."

Sarah's gaze dropped to her lap. "When did you get so wise all of a sudden?" she murmured.

Emma's laugh was soft. "Not wise at all. I need a lot of help, and I'm hoping you won't mind. And that you'll want to hear what I found at the gym."

Chapter Twenty-Three

"Yes, please!" Lily chimed in, setting down coffee and fruit tarts. "Spill... why the gym, and what did you discover?"

The kitchen fell silent, save for the gentle gurgle of the coffee maker. The rich aroma of freshly brewed beans wafted through the air, intertwining with an almost palpable tension that crackled like static electricity. Emma's fingers drummed a nervous rhythm on the worn wooden table as she took a deep breath.

"So, I had this dream last night," she began, her voice barely above a whisper.

Sarah's eyebrows shot up. "A nightmare, Pixie said," she corrected, leaning forward.

Emma's eyes glazed over, lost in the memory. "It was... intense. But I felt Pixie, and I knew I was safe. When I finally woke up from it, I just knew I had to check out that new gym downtown. No reason, no explanation, but this... invisible thread was tugging me there."

Sarah snorted, her mug clinking against her teeth. "Bunch of meatheads there, probably. I hope they didn't hit on you."

She paused, catching Lily's warning glare, and mimed zipping her lips.

Emma's lips quirked into a small smile. "It's not like that. There are two sides to this place – men and women. Anyway, I asked for a tour and to look at some of the amenities, and one of the instructors walked me around."

Sarah nodded grudgingly, stabbing a fork into a glistening fruit tart. "Smart thinking. And? Did you figure out why you needed to go there?"

Emma's shoulders slumped. "Not really. I was getting mad at myself. Women pedaling away on bikes, others shuffling towards the sauna, but not a single familiar face. I thought, Wow, what a bust. I can't even trust my own intuition. So much for that."

Sarah reached across the table, her warm hand enveloping Emma's. "Please don't ever doubt yourself," she said, her voice thick with emotion. "It's going to take time."

"I know." Emma's eyes sparkled with renewed determination. "The tour guide offered me a smoothie, and I figured, why not? While she blended away, I wandered to the lobby windows, and that's when I saw them."

Sarah and Lily leaned in, hanging on every word.

"Two guys in the parking lot, arguing—hard. Looking ready to tear each other apart," Emma continued, her words tumbling out faster now. "One of them caught me looking and shook his fist at me like he wanted to break the glass."

Sarah's fork clattered to the floor, forgotten, and Emma's voice dropped to a whisper. "And the other one, it was Noah Delmore."

"And you waited till now to tell me this? Are you absolutely certain?" Sarah's right hand clenched into a tight, hard fist.

Emma nodded emphatically. "Absolutely. Remember when I helped Cory research his web design firm? I'd recognize that face anywhere."

Sarah pressed her fingertips to her temples, her mind a whirlwind of possibilities. "Noah Delmore," she muttered. "He keeps popping up like a bad penny. Any idea about the other guy?"

Emma shook her head. "Not right then, but... I'm not done." Her eyes glinted with triumph. "When I was leaving, he practically bulldozed past me, shoulder-bumped me on purpose. But he dropped his locker key, and when I bent down to help, he snatched it back like it was made of gold. His face went beet red."

Sarah's arms erupted in goosebumps.

"Oh, Emma," she breathed, hugging herself. "This could have gone south real fast."

"The lobby was packed," Emma reassured her with a wink. "Besides, I caught a glimpse of his locker tag. Clear as day: T. Barnes."

Sarah's eyes widened. "T. Barnes... Tom Barnes... Deanna's husband?" The pieces began to fall into place. "What in the world is he mixed up in?"

Emma shrugged, a mixture of excitement and apprehension playing across her face.

Sarah reached out, squeezing Emma's hand. "Don't you dare get disappointed with your abilities," she said, her voice low and intense. "I think you just blew this case wide open."

A faint, shimmering light seemed to dance at the edges of their vision, as if the very air was charged with the weight of their discovery.

∞

The old house creaked and settled as night fell, casting long shadows across the living room. Sarah perched on the edge of the worn leather sofa, her fingers absently tracing the rim of her wineglass as she filled Matthew in on Emma's discovery. Upstairs, a warm glow spilled from beneath Emma's door, where she'd retreated with Lily's stack of new releases.

Matthew leaned against the mantle; his face drawn.

"So, Emma..." he began, letting the question hang in the air.

Sarah nodded, a mix of pride and apprehension in her eyes. "She's finding her way into her... special abilities," she confirmed softly. She glanced up at Matthew through her lashes, searching his face. "And not in little steps either. Does that worry you?"

Matthew's shoulders rose and fell in a heavy sigh. "Honestly? I don't know." He ran a hand through his hair, his voice a low rumble. "I should probably be terrified, but I've seen you handle situations most men couldn't dream of. If she's anything like you..."

"Thank you," Sarah murmured, warmth blooming in her chest. She leaned forward, her voice dropping conspiratorially. "What do you make of Tom Barnes arguing with Delmore?"

Matthew's lips thinned. "Barnes sounds like a powder keg waiting to explode, based on Emma's description." He narrowed his eyes and stared. "But I still can't fathom why he'd want to harm Tyler, if it was indeed him."

"No real connection there," Sarah confirmed, frustration creeping into her voice. "Cory's already checked. Barnes has no kids or relatives on Tyler's hockey team. I guess maybe Tyler could have made a delivery to their house at some point, but so what?" She trailed off, the pieces refusing to fall into place.

Matthew picked up a pencil and tapped it against his teeth, the soft rhythm matching the ticking of the old grandfather clock in the corner. Finally, he retreated to the kitchen, returning with two glasses of deep red wine. The liquid caught the lamplight, seeming to glow from within.

"And if you're right about Emma's newfound abilities," Matthew continued, handing Sarah a glass, "then what she heard when she found Tyler—it was just supposed to be fun, or..."

"A publicity stunt, I think," Sarah finished, taking a sip of wine.

Matthew's brow furrowed deeper. "Then that was likely Tyler's...?" He looked at Sarah, searching for the right word.

"Spirit," she supplied quietly. "His spirit, his... soul, if you will. His final thoughts."

A shudder ran through Matthew's body, visible even in the dim light. "I don't like the idea," he muttered.

The air in the room seemed to thicken, as if the very mention of spirits had drawn unseen presences closer. A chill breeze whispered through the room, despite the closed windows, causing the flames in the fireplace to dance erratically.

Chapter
Twenty-Four

Just after breakfast, Cory and Matthew set out for the nearby university. Cory was eager to explore the campus and soak in its atmosphere, given his keen interest in pursuing investigative journalism there in the future. Their agenda also included a promising opportunity: one of the professors had an open position for a research assistant—a role perfectly suited to Cory's interests. They planned to work on his application after touring the grounds.

Emma and Sarah stayed behind, the air between them thick with unspoken thoughts. Sarah had planned to work in her garden or perhaps meet Lily for coffee, but something in Emma's eyes made her hang back. Her youngest daughter sat at the breakfast table, eyes unfocused and mind clearly elsewhere.

Sarah tilted the nearly empty orange juice bottle, watching as the last drops trickled into a glass. She held it out to Emma, her voice gentle.

"Want to finish this?"

"Hmm...?" Emma's head snapped up, her eyes wide with the startled look of someone abruptly pulled from deep contemplation. "What? Oh yeah, just leave it here." She accepted the glass mechanically, setting it beside her untouched plate before resuming her thousand-yard stare.

Sarah pulled up a chair, its legs scraping softly against the wooden floors. She placed a comforting hand on Emma's arm, feeling a faint tingle of energy beneath her daughter's skin. "You seem... preoccupied. Something on your mind?"

Emma's gaze met Sarah's, her face an open book of emotions, confusion, wonder, and just a hint of apprehension swirling in her eyes. Sarah resisted the urge to reach out with her mind, respecting the sanctity of her daughter's thoughts.

"Mom..." Emma began, her voice barely above a whisper as she grappled for words.

Sarah said nothing, simply sitting close by, a steady presence as she waited for the questions she knew would come. As if sensing the tension, Pixie emerged from her crumb-hunting expedition beneath the table. With elegant grace, she leapt into Emma's lap, snuggling in close. Emma's long, slender fingers instinctively began to comb through the little papillon's silky fur.

"What was it like for you?" Emma finally managed, her voice low and trembling slightly. "When you found out that you could do things, I mean?"

Sarah leaned back, memories flooding her mind. "It was just after we moved in. You were barely twelve then, not even a teenager. Do you remember when we saw Amelia for the first time?"

Emma nodded softly, a ghost of a smile playing on her lips. "Cory thought she was here to kill us all, I think."

"That would be like Cory," Sarah chuckled, but her eyes grew serious. "I wasn't sure this house was safe for us to live in. And then she attacked Matthew, and you two were frightened out of your minds."

"You did something with your hands," Emma said, her brow furrowing as she struggled to recall, her fingers forming shapes in front of her. "I don't remember exactly..."

Sarah's gaze grew distant, her voice taking on an otherworldly quality. "It was like I turned into somebody else. Back in Baltimore, when I was still married to your dad, I said 'yes' and 'thank you' to everything; it didn't matter. It was just easier. Then we moved here, and suddenly I was the boss and I had to act like it. And here comes this ghost, daring to threaten my kids and a man I was just developing feelings for... I think I lost it a little."

A little? Pixie's voice echoed in Sarah's mind, tinged with amusement. *I'm surprised Amelia didn't turn to stone or a pile of ashes, given the power you unloaded on her.*

"Yes, well..." Sarah shook her head, focusing back on Emma. "I just held out my hands to stop her, and suddenly there was all of this power, all of this energy. I didn't know where it came from or what to do with it. The point is..." She leaned in closer, enveloping Emma in a warm embrace. "Even if I don't know exactly how, it has always been there when I needed it, when we needed protection. Don't be afraid of it. Trust what it's telling you, and there's no harm in saying, 'stop, not that way' if it takes you in a direction you don't want to go."

Emma's fingers continued to trace patterns on the cheerful, white-and-red-checked tablecloth, her voice small but steady. "I think it's getting stronger. Sometimes I just... know something, without knowing why. Just like, well, going to that gym."

"I'm sorry. I should have trusted you," Sarah admitted, a touch of regret in her voice. Emma smiled, the tension in her shoulders easing slightly.

"It's okay. Cory calls it your mama-bear thing. Honestly, I kind of like it, even if it is a little much sometimes. But I know I'm safe. Nobody would dare to mess with you."

"Still..." Sarah managed a little smile, her eyes twinkling. "I don't know how far this thing is going to go, how long it's going to last, or why we even have it. So, thank you for understanding."

For a long moment, mother and daughter sat quietly, each following their own thoughts. The rhythmic ticking of the kitchen clock and the cheerful birdsong drifting in from the garden were the only sounds breaking the comfortable silence. The thump of mail landing in their bright mailbox outside—a garish orange and black creation Cory had built—startled them both.

Finally, Pixie began to squirm in Emma's lap, her mental voice clear in Sarah's mind.

Hey, how about a little snack?

Little Miss Greedy, how about a little exercise instead? Sarah thought back, her mental voice tinged with affection.

Emma's face suddenly lit up, her earlier melancholy forgotten.

"You want to go for a walk?" she asked, a mischievous grin spreading across her face. "I heard that."

Sarah's eyebrows shot up in surprise, a mixture of pride and wonder filling her heart. As mother and daughter shared a knowing look, the kitchen seemed to hum with an unseen energy, full of mystery and possibility.

Chapter Twenty-Five

Emma fitted Pixie with a pretty pink and rhinestone harness, even though the little papillon glared daggers at her. Sarah filled a water bottle, and moments later, they were strolling down the street, Pixie trotting ahead on a slender leash. The morning sun cast long shadows across neatly manicured lawns, and a gentle breeze carried the scent of blooming jasmine.

"I'm glad we're in Rosewood Hollow," Emma said, pointing at a couple of blue jays squabbling over a tasty crumb in a neighbor's yard. "For a while, I was worried Dad wanted us to go back."

"I have a feeling he was seriously thinking about it."

"And then his girlfriend stayed behind," Emma giggled. "You hear anything from Katelyn recently?"

"I think she's still working at the museum, as a guide by now. I have to remember to ask Matthew."

The peaceful scene shattered all at once. A piercing screech of tires tore through the air as a bright yellow sports car careened around the corner, fishtailing wildly before screeching to a halt, mere feet from where they stood. Sarah instinctively pulled Emma close, her heart pounding. Pixie yapped furiously, straining at her leash, her diminutive frame quivering with indignation.

The acrid smell of burnt rubber assaulted their nostrils, and Sarah's mind raced. The car—bright yellow, sleek, ostentatious, and expensive—looked eerily familiar. The same vehicle had been parked haphazardly in front of Deanna Barnes' house just last week.

The driver's door flew open with a violent thrust, and a man stormed out, his face contorted with rage.

Tom Barnes—a once-handsome man now ravaged by years of hard living.

His salt-and-pepper hair stuck up in angry tufts, and his designer shirt was rumpled and stained. Bloodshot eyes zeroed in on Sarah and Emma, who stood frozen on the sidewalk.

"You!" Tom bellowed, jabbing a finger in Emma's direction. His gait was unsteady as he advanced, reeking of expensive cologne and cheap whiskey. "You think you can just spy on me? Through the window? At my own gym? Who do you think you are?"

Sarah pushed Emma behind her, shielding her daughter from the approaching storm of a man. The idyllic afternoon had vanished. As Tom Barnes closed the distance between them, his eyes wild and fists clenched, Sarah reached for Emma's hand.

Tom Barnes' voice boomed through the quiet street, shattering the last remnants of peace. His words dripped with venom and barely contained violence.

"Stay away from me and my family!" he roared, spittle flying from his lips. "Stop spying on me, or bad things are going to happen!"

Sarah instinctively tightened her grip on Emma, feeling something fluid and powerful building there. Pixie, sensing the energy, had stopped barking and now crowded between Sarah and Emma, touching both with her little body.

Tom took another menacing step forward, his bloodshot eyes fixed on Sarah with burning intensity.

"Don't think I don't know all about your amateur sleuthing or whatever you call it!" His voice dropped to a dangerous growl. "Stay. Away. From. Me. You hear?"

The threat hung in the air, palpable and suffocating. Neighbors' curtains twitched as curious and frightened faces peered out at the unfolding drama.

Sarah's mind raced, torn between confusion at his accusations and fear for her daughter's safety. She opened her mouth to speak, but no words came out. Emma raised her hand in Sarah's just the tiniest bit, and there it was. A stream of energy flowed out from their clasped hands, building between the women and Tom Barnes.

Tom's eyes darted around wildly, as if searching for hidden cameras or lurking spies. His paranoia was out of control now, fueled by whatever demons drove him to this frenzied state. The stench of alcohol on his breath stung Sarah's nostrils, making her recoil.

Tom's face contorted with a final burst of rage. His eyes, bloodshot and wild, narrowed as he spat out a word that was barely disguised as anything but a vicious expletive. The guttural sound hung in the air, crude and jarring against the backdrop of the peaceful neighborhood. For a moment, confusion flickered across his face. He took another step toward them, fully intending to frighten them into submission, but he couldn't advance. As if someone gave him a gentle push, he actually took a step back. He tried again, only to fail in getting closer to them. Furiously, he shook his fists.

"I'm not going to lose everything because of you. Stay away!" he snarled, the barely concealed profanity making Emma flinch and bury her face deeper into her mother's side.

He hauled out with one hand, and it froze in mid-swing. A flicker of confusion flew across his face as he stared at his still hand, half raised. Then, without warning, Tom spun on his heel and stormed back to his car. He yanked the door open with such force that it seemed he might tear it from its hinges. The engine roared to life, a mechanized growl that matched its owner's fury.

Tires squealed against asphalt as Tom slammed the accelerator. The yellow sports car lurched forward, engine snarling, leaving behind the acrid stench of burning rubber. It tore down the street, fishtailing wildly before disappearing around a corner in a blur of violent color.

The sudden stillness in the wake of Tom's departure was almost tangible, settling like a weight. The idyllic peace of their afternoon walk lay shattered around Sarah and Emma like broken glass. Pixie relaxed, exhaling softly, and Sarah just caught the fading golden glow on the tip of her tail.

Sarah stood frozen, her arm protectively wrapped around Emma. The gentle breeze that had carried the scent of jasmine now seemed to whisper ominous warnings.

Sarah's mouth opened and closed, words failing her as she tried to process what had just happened. Emma, her face pale and eyes wide, barely managed to breathe out, "I could feel it... when you took my hand."

Sarah's gaze dropped to their intertwined fingers. A peculiar sensation thrummed between them, like a low-frequency current. She hadn't even realized she'd reached for Emma's hand, the action as natural as breathing. Now, as if burned, she quickly released her grip.

Emma turned her hand over, examining her palm as if expecting to see visible traces of the strange energy. A serene smile slowly spread across her face, chasing away the lingering fear. "That was you, wasn't it? When he tried to get closer, and instead turned back?"

"Well, I'm..." Sarah's words stumbled over each other. She looked away, her eyes darting to the empty road where Tom Barnes' car had vanished. "Actually, I'm not entirely sure," she finished lamely.

Yes, you are, Pixie's voice echoed in Sarah's mind, clear as a bell. *Every time someone threatens those you love.*

"Mama bear mode," Sarah whispered, the realization dawning on her face. Emma playfully elbowed her in the ribs, a hint of color returning to her cheeks.

"I told you, I kind of like it," Emma said, her voice stronger now. "But what on earth was his problem? Just because I saw him arguing with Noah Delmore at the gym yesterday?"

Sarah's gaze remained fixed on the distant horizon, her mind racing. "Emma," she said, her voice barely audible above the rustling leaves. "That was not just me. That was both of us."

"Both...?"

"You and I together," Sarah clarified, turning to face her daughter. "When I took your hand... something was amplified and strengthened. It protected us."

Told you so, Pixie's mental voice chimed in, accompanied by a full-body shake and stretch that rippled through her petite form. *Now, maybe we can head home?*

Sarah reached down, her fingers sinking into Pixie's soft fur. *And you. Don't think I didn't feel you touching both of us, joining in.*

The triangle, Pixie responded cryptically, before sauntering back the way they had come, tail held high.

Emma linked her arm through Sarah's, a chuckle escaping her lips. "She's got the right idea. I think it's best if we head home again. Maybe get some ice cream?"

"Brilliant suggestion," Sarah agreed, relief evident in her voice.

They walked back slowly, their conversation deliberately light and meandering, touching on anything but what they'd just experienced. Sarah found herself reaching out to Emma frequently, a hand on her shoulder or waist, as if needing constant reassurance of her daughter's presence and safety. Pixie's enigmatic 'triangle' comment faded to the back of her mind, overshadowed by the immediate need for comfort and normalcy.

Chapter Twenty-Six

Hours later, they found themselves on the front porch, sharing a dish of tangy lemon gelato. The sun's warm rays and the garden's tranquil beauty worked their magic, gradually easing the tension from their shoulders. Pixie lounged on the porch swing beside them, occasionally receiving a dollop of ice cream on her shiny black nose, which she licked off with exaggerated pleasure.

As the peaceful moment stretched on, Emma finally broached the subject again. "What do you think he wanted?" she asked, her spoon hovering mid-air. "I mean, sure, I saw him arguing in the parking lot at the gym. But that was by accident. It could have been anybody standing by that window, don't you think?"

Sarah savored a spoonful of gelato, buying herself time to finally answer. "Maybe Deanna told him I'd been in the bank with Lily, and then you and I walked in again virtually the next day, looking around?" She paused, her brow furrowing. "I'm not a customer there, so if she is in fact involved, that might have spooked her... and him by extension."

The implications of her words hung in the air, mingling with the sweet scent of nearby flowers and the lingering taste of lemon on their tongues.

Emma's brow furrowed, her spoon tapping against the edge of the bowl slowly.

"But he has no reason," she insisted, her voice rising slightly. "I literally just saw him arguing with somebody. Who's to say I even knew who Noah Delmore was, let alone his involvement in the robbery and the murder, if any? And what's with that cryptic comment, 'I'm not going to lose everything?'"

Sarah paused, her spoon hovering over the gelato. Her eyes narrowed in thought as she carefully chose her next words.

"This," she began, scooping up another spoonful, "is where you discover that the world would be a much better place if people always had good reasons for their actions." She savored the tangy sweetness before continuing, "He panicked. I'd like to know why. There isn't even the slightest hint about an involvement from his side. All he had to do was keep saying, 'I don't know what you're talking about. '"

The quiet contemplation was shattered by the whir of an electric motor. Cory came racing up the road on his brand-new e-bike, his clothes windswept as he hopped off with youthful energy. He leaned the sleek bike against the side of the porch, catching Sarah's pointed look.

With an exaggerated eye roll and a dismissive wave of his hand, Cory unsnapped his helmet. "Yes, Mom, I will put it away in a minute," he said, his tone a mix of exasperation and affection. His eyes lit up at the sight of the ice cream container. "Any more of that left, or did you guys scarf it all down?"

He dropped his backpack onto the porch with a thud, shaking his head. "God, people are such idiots sometimes," he muttered, running a hand through his disheveled hair.

Sarah raised an eyebrow. "No doubt. Where did you leave Matthew? Did he drop in at the historical society?"

Cory shifted his weight, a hint of discomfort in his stance. "He met some people he knew when he was teaching at the university, and wanted to hang out, so I went on ahead. Didn't want it to look like I was sucking up or using Matthew's connections."

"Wouldn't have been any harm in it," Sarah said, holding out the ice cream container to him. Her voice softened as she continued. "And why, pray tell, are people idiots? Or do I not want to know?"

Cory plopped down on a chair, digging into the ice cream with gusto. Between mouthfuls, he explained. "Just a jerk on the road. Guy with this ridiculously expensive sports car had broken down a few blocks east of here. All the lights and the dashboard were flashing like a video game gone insane." He gestured animatedly with his spoon. "Dude looked like he was going to have to walk to the nearest gas station for help, so I wanted to stop, see if I could help."

Sarah leaned forward, her heart suddenly racing. "And?" she prompted, her voice barely hiding her tension.

"And nothing," Cory shrugged, oblivious to his mother's reaction. "He yelled at me from like ten feet away that I shouldn't get too close to his precious yellow baby with my crappy bike, so I flipped him off and kept going." He had the grace to look slightly sheepish. "Sorry. But he deserved it. He was being a jerk."

"Yellow," Sarah echoed, her voice barely above a whisper. Her knuckles whitened as she gripped the arm of her chair. "One of those expensive ground creepers that sound like you've got your head inside the engine?"

Cory's eyebrows shot up in surprise. "The very one. Why, did you see the thing?"

He scraped the last bit of ice cream from the container and held it out to Pixie, who delicately licked the remnants with her little pink tongue.

Sarah and Emma exchanged a knowing look, a slow grin spreading across Emma's face.

"You could say that," Emma said, offering her hand to Sarah for a high five. Her eyes sparkled with mischief. "And I know a couple of... beings, who could take great offense at somebody's rudeness and love nothing more than to mess around with electronics."

Cory blinked in the bright sunshine, confusion etched on his face. Suddenly, realization dawned, and his eyes widened. "Amelia and Simon?"

Emma nodded, her grin now impossibly wide.

Cory leaned in and grinned with glee. "Whatever they did to mess with those two, it's gonna get real expensive with that kind of car. If I don't miss my guess, the techs are gonna take it apart and put it back together without finding anything until those two are done with him." His eyes gleamed with curiosity. "So, what did he do, and does it have something to do with you two?"

"Let me tell you..." Emma began, stopping the porch swing and leaning closer to her brother.

Sarah gathered the empty dishes and spoons, retreating into the house. As Emma's animated retelling faded behind her, Sarah's mind wandered to Tom Barnes. The memory of the sheer hatred in his eyes and the intense wave of anger she had felt rolling off him sent a shiver down her spine. Amelia and Simon's antics might provide a moment of lighthearted revenge, but Sarah couldn't shake the worry that Barnes wasn't done with his campaign against them just yet. The weight of that concern settled in her stomach, a stark contrast to the sweet gelato they had just enjoyed.

Matthew didn't take the news nearly as well when he came back from the visit with his colleagues, just as Sarah was setting the table for dinner. The aroma of roast chicken filled the air, but the tension in Matthew's posture suggested he had no appetite for the meal awaiting him.

"Matthew, there's something we need to tell you," Sarah began, her voice steady but her eyes betraying a hint of apprehension.

As Sarah recounted their encounter with Tom Barnes, Matthew's expression darkened. His jaw clenched, muscles twitching beneath his skin, and his fingers curled into tight fists at his sides. The veins in his neck stood out as he struggled to contain his anger.

"I knew something like this was going to happen," he hissed through gritted teeth, his words sharp enough to cut glass.

"Matthew..." Sarah reached out to touch his arm, but he jerked away.

"Don't 'Matthew' me," he snapped, his voice rising. "That man threatened you and Emma. I don't care that you have some special mojo that prevented anything... physical, from happening—"

The patter of small paws on hardwood interrupted his tirade as Pixie scampered into the room. The little dog's nails clicked against the floor as she approached Matthew, placing her front paws on his shoe and gazing up at him with soulful eyes. Matthew roughly shook her off, his hands clenching tightly suddenly.

"Sarah, what were you thinking?" His voice cracked with emotion.

Footsteps on the stairs announced Emma's arrival, drawn by the commotion. She paused in the doorway, taking in the scene before her. "Matthew, all we did was go for a walk." She moved closer, scooping Pixie into her arms. The papillon nestled against her chest, a warm, comforting presence as Emma stroked her silky fur.

"I saw Barnes yesterday through the window at the gym," Emma continued, her chin lifting defiantly. "If you want to be mad at anyone, be mad at me."

A sound escaped Matthew's throat, part growl, part groan. He yanked at his hair again, his face contorting with frustration and fear.

"The two of you. If something had happened—" he choked out, unable to finish the thought.

"It didn't," Sarah said softly, reaching for him again.

"By the grace of God only," Matthew retorted, his voice thick with emotion. "It's this amateur sleuthing that keeps bringing this kind of danger to our doorstep."

Sarah and Emma exchanged a loaded glance, a silent conversation passing between them. Sarah shook her head almost imperceptibly, deciding now wasn't the time to argue about their abilities.

"Matthew?" Emma's voice was gentle as she placed her hand on his forearm. Her eyes, so like her mother's, held his gaze. "I was the one who heard Tyler when he... passed. And I was the one who insisted he was innocent."

"Emma..." Matthew's anger seemed to deflate. He sagged into a nearby chair, burying his face in his hands. The ticking of the kitchen clock filled the silence for a long moment before he looked up, resignation written across his features. "There's no way I'm going to win against you two, is there?"

"It's not a case of winning," Emma said, her voice soft but firm. "If you want Mom and me to stop looking into this, we will. Promise. But that doesn't change the fact that the police and the media are considering Tyler the main suspect."

"He was involved," Matthew muttered, then threw up his hands in defeat. "Fine then. Fine, I can't stop you. At least allow me to be angry—no, furious—about this Barnes threatening the two of you."

"Always," Sarah murmured. She moved behind him, wrapping her arms around his shoulders and leaning her head against him.

"Thank you."

Matthew leaned into her embrace, some of the tension leaving his body. After a moment, he asked, "What was his deal anyway? Why did he go all gangster against the two of you in broad daylight on a public street? And then Cory, to top it all off, who by his account was only trying to help."

Sarah turned back to the stove, the sizzle of chicken in the pan punctuating her words. "I wish I knew. But he must have some connection to Noah Delmore, or they wouldn't have argued yesterday."

Matthew's brow furrowed, his mind working to connect the dots. "Noah Delmore... vaguely related to Tyler... acting strange around you two at Creative Charities."

"And when Amelia and Simon visited him," Emma chimed in, her voice carrying a hint of excitement at being part of the conversation. Matthew opened his mouth, then closed it again, visibly restraining himself.

"Right," he said, his tone measured. "So, what exactly did he say?"

Sarah's face darkened as she recalled the encounter.

"He said, 'Stay away from my family.'" Sarah shrugged, her spatula scraping against the pan. "He was furious, thought we were spying on him. The point is, what is he doing in this entire story all of a sudden? If Delmore and Tyler planned the robbery together, then how does he fit in?"

Her voice trailed off as a chilling thought struck them all simultaneously. The kitchen fell silent, save for the soft sizzle of cooking food, and Pixie's gentle panting from her spot under the table.

If Noah Delmore had somehow or other engaged Tyler and committed the robbery with him, then either Noah had shot Tyler or... or... Sarah's mouth went dry as she thought of the man who had enough anger to commit this crime.

"What if he," she began and broke off again.

Cory sat back, his eyes fixed on his empty plate. "That's more than a bit of a stretch," he mumbled. "I mean... why?"

"Hatred, jealousy, envy, or revenge," Matthew suddenly recited, his teacher's voice taking over.

"What?" Emma asked.

Matthew leaned back in his chair, putting his hands in his neck. "Apparently, those are the most common motives when people commit murder. I have an assistant who's a real crime junkie. Assuming Barnes didn't hate Tyler, or was envious of his life as a delivery driver and security guard, what does that leave us?"

Cory snorted, a hint of teenage bravado in his voice. "Jealousy? I can't see that. Tyler wouldn't have looked at somebody like Deanna Barnes with a borrowed pair of eyes. She was like—" He caught both his mother's and Matthew's pointed gazes and looked down at his plate again. "Way older than he was," he finished, suddenly very interested in his cutlery.

"Revenge?" Emma suggested, her voice small but curious.

"For what?" Cory asked, throwing up his hands. "Even if he lost money in the same scam Tyler did, that wasn't Ty's doing."

"Okay." Sarah paused, resting her chin on her hand, lost in thought. "Then there's still something we're missing."

They continued to toss theories back and forth throughout dinner, their voices rising and falling as they cleared the table and cleaned the kitchen.

Eventually, Cory wandered outside, the rhythmic thump of his basketball against the driveway filtering through the open windows. Emma disappeared upstairs to her mini library, leaving Sarah and Matthew alone.

Chapter Twenty-Seven

The porch swing creaked gently as Sarah snuggled against Matthew in the cool evening air. For a moment, only the regular slap of Cory's basketball broke the silence.

"Are you still mad at me?" Sarah asked, her voice barely above a whisper.

Matthew sighed, his arm tightening around her. "Of course not," he said finally. "The thought of what might have happened just scared the living daylights out of me."

"I'm sorry."

"No, I think I finally understand. This is something you and Emma share. I know that you can... deal, as Cory would say. Better than anyone else, it seems. I just don't..."

Sarah nestled closer. "I wish it didn't frighten you, though."

Matthew chuckled softly, the sound rumbling in his chest. "I guess that's the life I signed up for, isn't it? Hang on, I'll get us something to drink while you noodle around on your latest mystery."

He stood, stretching, and headed inside. The screen door hadn't fully closed behind him when he suddenly stopped, one foot still on the porch.

"Oh... Sarah?"

Sarah craned her neck, but all she could see was Matthew's leg and foot, frozen in place.

"Something wrong?"

Matthew's voice carried a mix of amusement and resignation. "I think we have guests. That's all I'm going to say."

As if sensing an unseen presence, Pixie's silky ears suddenly stood at attention, her diminutive frame quivering with an electric energy. The papillon's liquid dark eyes locked onto something beyond the porch—a spectral entity that only she, and perhaps Sarah and Emma, could perceive. With a soft yip that hung in the air, Pixie darted between Matthew's legs, her paws barely touching the wooden floorboards as she raced into the kitchen.

Sarah, feeling a familiar tingle at the base of her spine, pushed herself up from the porch swing. The weathered wood creaked beneath her fingers as she stood, her eyes following Matthew's hesitant steps into the house.

The moment they crossed the threshold into the kitchen, the air shimmered and pulsed with an otherworldly luminescence. Amelia and Simon materialized above the kitchen island, their translucent forms casting a soft, pearly glow across the polished countertop. It was as if someone had strung up the world's most elegant fairy lights.

Amelia's ghostly pearls clinked silently around her neck, each bead catching and refracting the light in mesmerizing patterns.

The pair bobbed gently in the air, as comfortable as if they were perched on invisible barstools.

"Amelia, Simon," Sarah said, noting the barely contained excitement in their luminous eyes. "To what do we owe the sudden visit?"

Amelia's voice, tinged with a hint of mischief, floated through the air.

"Well, you did ask us to keep an eye on your friend Noah Delmore. I'm sure you remember."

"Not my friend, I assure you..." Sarah muttered, reaching for a bottle of water. The cool glass felt solid and reassuring in her hand as she poured, a stark contrast to the ethereal visitors floating before her.

She had indeed enlisted the ghostly duo's help in snooping... before Tom Barnes entered the picture and presented them with yet another enigma to unravel. Of course, Amelia and Simon were notorious for their roundabout methods, rarely delivering requested information in a straightforward manner.

Sarah pulled up a chair and settled into it, putting her palms against her chin. "You look like you have news," she prodded, settling into her seat. "I'm ready to hear it."

Matthew stood frozen; his gaze fixed on the ghosts. Despite his frequent assurances of having grown accustomed to the ghostly residents, Sarah could still see the mix of wonder and trepidation in his eyes. His fingers danced a nervous rhythm against his thigh.

Simon's form shimmered with excitement as he spoke. "We finally know who Noah Delmore was so desperately trying to call in the days just after the bank robbery," he announced, punctuating his words with a shower of gold and bluish sparks erupting from his translucent hands. "Do you want to know?"

"Oh, of course she does," Amelia interrupted, her pearls swaying with the force of her words. "It was Deanna Barnes."

"Deanna..." Sarah echoed, her glass hitting the countertop with a sharp clunk. The name seemed to hang in the air as the gears in her mind whirred into motion, piecing together this new information.

Simon adjusted his spectral bowtie, the motion sending ripples through his ethereal form. "I don't countenance that sort of thing, but I believe they might have been carrying on—"

"Get to the point," Amelia cut in, her voice as sharp as cut crystal. "They were having an affair."

Behind Sarah, a choked gasp broke the tension. Matthew finally pulled out a chair and sank into it, his face a mix of shock and disbelief.

"An affair?" he managed, his voice barely above a whisper. "Are you sure?"

Simon's form glittered with golden light once more. "Well, naturally, by the nature of an illicit affair, one is never quite certain of anything-as well, you might or might not know—but in this case—"

"He finally left a message for her," Amelia interrupted, her spectral form pulsing with impatience. Her words seemed to echo in the suddenly still kitchen.

"And he said, 'Deanna, you cannot ignore me forever. We promised each other. That money was meant for our future. Somebody died for it.' Then he hung up."

The revelation hung in the air like a tangible thing, as heavy and oppressive as the summer heat outside. Sarah, Matthew, and the ghostly pair remained frozen in a tableau of shock and revelation, the only movement the gentle bob of Amelia and Simon's wispy forms and the slow, circular wagging of Pixie's tail as she watched with curious canine eyes.

"Noah and Deanna," Sarah mused, her voice barely above a whisper. She brought the tips of her forefingers together, creating a tight steeple.

Her gaze dropped, focusing on her hands as if they held the answers to this perplexing puzzle.

Simon shimmered as he spoke, a hint of mischief dancing in his eyes. "I told you, the females seemed to consider him exceptionally handsome," he offered, his ghostly bow tie bobbing.

No sooner had the words left his translucent lips than Amelia's form crackled with energy. A shower of iridescent sparks erupted from her, accompanied by a hiss that reverberated through the air. The sound was like static electricity mixed with a cat's warning, causing Simon to slide back a few feet, his form rippling like disturbed water.

Sarah's hand shot up, cutting through the argument. Her eyes, sharp and focused, darted between the two specters.

"No need to argue," she said, in the same tone she used with her kids. A wry smile tugged at the corner of her mouth as she continued, "I get it. Some women go for the bad boy type." She turned to Matthew, throwing him a playful wink.

Her expression sobered almost instantly. "Still," she mused, her brow furrowing, "if Noah and Deanna set up this bank robbery, and Tom Barnes got into a fight with him over it, then why shoot Tyler? That makes no sense." The question hung in the air, as tangible as the ghostly pair floating before them.

Amelia and Simon exchanged a look, a silent conversation passing between them in a fraction of a second. It was Simon who finally spoke, his voice carrying an air of finality. "Well, my dear Sarah," he said, adjusting his spectral bow tie, "some things, you will have to figure out on your own. One thing I will tell you, though, on this thing he calls a laptop, he deleted something. An order form for two identical Santa Claus costumes, as far as I could determine."

As he spoke, Amelia drifted behind him, her form seeming to vibrate with barely contained energy.

"You've said quite enough for one evening, Simon."

For a moment, it looked as if she might attempt to push her spectral companion, but instead, she merely hovered, her presence a silent punctuation to Simon's words.

With a final sparkle that lit up the kitchen like a flash of heat lightning, the ghostly pair faded from view. Their departure left behind a lingering chill and the faint scent of ozone.

In the sudden quiet, Matthew's deep exhale echoed off the kitchen walls. His shoulders visibly relaxed as he reached for Sarah's water glass, his fingers leaving faint smudges on the condensation-covered surface.

"I don't think Amelia appreciated the handsome comment," he said, his voice a mix of relief and amusement. He took a long sip of water, his eyes never leaving the spot where the ghostly couple had been, as if half-expecting them to reappear at any moment.

"Noah and Deanna," Sarah muttered.

"Noah and Deanna, what?"

Sarah looked up and found Cory coming in from the front hall.

His eyes darted left and right, and his face fell a little. "I thought I could hear Amelia here..."

"They were both here," Sarah confirmed. "Alas, I think Simon made a bit of a comment she didn't like, and they left again."

"Ghost drama, great." Cory reached for the water bottle and almost put it to his mouth when a sharp look from Sarah made him reach for a glass.

"What was that about, then—Noah and Deanna? You don't mean...?" Cory's voice trailed off, his eyes widening as the implications dawned on him.

Sarah nodded gently, her gaze fixed on the window. The late afternoon light cast long shadows across the yard, painting the scene in muted oranges and purples. Her eyes, unfocused, seemed to be looking beyond the physical landscape, peering into the realm of possibilities.

"That was their theory," she said softly. "And honestly, it makes sense. Deanna Barnes, married to an older man, gets bored... falls for the handsome Noah Delmore." The words hung in the air, heavy with implication.

Cory pulled up a chair, the legs scraping against the kitchen floor. He sat beside his mother, his face tight with concentration. "But why the fake bank robbery? And why Tyler?"

Sarah's fingers drummed a thoughtful rhythm on the table. "I don't know that yet. But, it seems that Noah ordered two Santa Claus costumes. Identical ones, too." She attempted a wry smile, but it didn't quite reach her eyes. Her hand found Cory's shoulder, giving it a gentle squeeze. "Looks like you're right, bud. Tyler had nothing to do with this, other than being pulled into something he definitely couldn't handle."

Matthew leaned forward, his elbows on the table. "Still, I don't get who shot him," he mused. "Deanna?"

A snort of laughter escaped Sarah. "I doubt it. Handling a gun would mess up her entire five-hundred-dollar manicure."

"Noah then?" Matthew persisted. "I can't see that either. He sounds... weak. Besides, Tyler was a cousin, wasn't he?"

"Pretty distant cousin," Sarah corrected, her voice soft.

Matthew picked at a loose thread on his shirt, his fingers working at it absently.

"Even though..." he trailed off, spreading his hands and drumming his fingertips together. "Why would Tom Barnes get all up in arms about it then? And why against you? I'm still..." He shook his head, frustration evident in the set of his shoulders. "No, there's something else. There has to be."

Cory pushed his chair back and got to his feet. "Let me know when you figure it all out," he grumbled. His voice carried a hint of exasperation as he added, "And figure out a way to get all of this information to Detective Harding, so she stops blaming this all on Tyler."

As Cory's footsteps faded up the stairs, Sarah and Matthew remained in the kitchen, enveloped in a thoughtful silence. Outside, the shadows lengthened, stretching across the yard like inky fingers. Still, they sat, minds whirring, unable to piece together the final, elusive threads of the mystery.

Chapter Twenty-Eight

The next morning, golden sunlight spilled through the kitchen windows, announcing a new day. As Sarah set Emma's breakfast before her, her daughter's sharp words shattered the tranquil atmosphere.

"Why didn't you tell me Amelia and Simon were here last night?" Emma's tone was accusatory, her eyes narrowing.

Sarah sighed, gently squeezing Emma's shoulder. "I'm sorry, sweetheart. You were upstairs reading, and they had a... disagreement. They left rather quickly."

As Sarah recounted the ghosts' discoveries, Emma's expression transformed from indignation to fascination. She tilted her head, reminiscent of Pixie when confronted with a particularly perplexing squirrel, hanging on her mother's every word.

"Wait. Deanna and that Delmore guy? Gross," Emma declared, her nose wrinkling in disgust.

Sarah opened her mouth to respond, but Emma plowed on.

"And Delmore brought in Tyler. That tracks. But what is Barnes' problem? His wife had an affair. It happens."

She gave her mother a knowing look, and Sarah managed a tiny smile. Scratch thinking the kids were too young to catch all of it when the same thing had happened to her, she thought.

"That's the million-dollar question," she said softly, her gaze drifting to the yard. Outside, Pixie trotted along her usual route, her tiny form alert as she conducted her customary morning patrol.

"Maybe he just has a temper and had to take it out on someone," Sarah suggested, her voice uncertain.

Emma's eyebrow arched skeptically. "Shouldn't have argued in public then. If I saw them, anybody else could have too. If Penny Harding goes to that gym, she could have. What was it you said? All he had to do was say, 'I don't know what you're talking about?'"

Sarah's shoulders slumped slightly.

"That's the part none of us can figure out," she admitted. "If they wanted quick money, pretending to rob the bank where Deanna works wasn't all that stupid an idea—"

"Mom!" Emma's scandalized tone cut through the air.

Sarah held up her hands in a placating gesture. "I'm not recommending it by any means. But using the Christmas in July event as a cover, figuring that most of the available police forces would be keeping an eye on the event—that's a plan I can understand." Her brow furrowed as she added, "But then what happened?"

Without warning, the tranquil morning air was shattered by a series of shrill, piercing barks. Pixie, her tiny body quivering with excitement, raced along the fence line at the front of the property. Her high-pitched yaps echoed through the yard, a sound only a Papillon could produce with such intensity.

A row of ornamental bushes obscured most of the view of the street and sidewalk, but Pixie halted abruptly, her gaze locked on one particular spot. Her barking continued unabated, each yap more insistent than the last.

"Pixie, for God's sake," Sarah muttered, moving swiftly to the back door. She yanked it open, the cool morning air rushing in. "Stop it!" she called out, her voice sharp with exasperation.

Sarah immediately thought of the young professional couple who had recently moved in next door. While she hoped they were nothing like the Jenkins who had lived there before, she didn't want to start off on the wrong foot with incessant dog barking.

"Pixie..." she tried again, her tone a mixture of pleading and command.

Pixie did not listen. Just then, Sarah caught a glimpse of movement, a shadow darting away. The figure moved low to the ground, just tall enough to be spotted, before disappearing around the corner of the road.

Sarah stood frozen in the doorway, her hand still gripping the handle. A chill crept down her spine, raising goosebumps on her arms despite the warm morning air. Eventually, even Pixie ceased her barking and came racing back, her tiny paws barely touching the ground.

"Pixie?" Sarah asked, her voice barely above a whisper.

The little dog's response came clearly in Sarah's mind: *There is someone there.*

Pixie's tongue lolled out, her chest heaving from her barking marathon.

"Who?" Sarah pressed, her eyes scanning the now-empty street.

I don't know, Pixie replied, a little piqued at being yelled at. *But no normal passer-by would lurk around, watching the house, then scurry away, crouched down.*

"Thank you, Pixie," Sarah murmured, her mind whirring with possibilities.

You're welcome, Pixie responded lightly before disappearing into the yard again, her nose to the ground as she resumed her never-ending hunt for hidden creatures.

Sarah remained in the doorway, one hand still gripping the handle, feeling an odd shiver creep down her back. The peaceful morning had suddenly taken on a sinister edge.

"Mom?" Emma's voice startled Sarah from her reverie. Her daughter had appeared beside her, eyes wide with curiosity.

"What was that all about?" Emma asked, her gaze darting between Sarah and the yard.

"Nothing," Sarah fibbed, placing a reassuring hand on Emma's shoulder. She forced a smile, hoping it looked more convincing than it felt. "Probably just somebody walking by, and Pixie didn't like the looks of them, that's all." Eager to change the subject, she added, "So,... you're going to work with Lily this afternoon?"

Emma's eyes narrowed slightly, and Sarah felt the familiar, gentle pressure of her daughter's mind reaching out. With an effort, she pushed the probing thoughts away. Emma's lips quirked into a small smile, acknowledging the rebuff.

"I think I might," Emma replied, her tone casual. "You?"

Sarah sighed, running a hand through her hair.

"I have to do some shopping, then figure out a way to get all of this information into Penny Harding's hands without mentioning the words 'ghosts' and 'supernatural abilities'."

"Yeah, good luck with that one," Emma said with a broad grin. She turned and headed back into the house, but Sarah couldn't shake the feeling that her daughter wasn't quite satisfied with her answers.

As the door closed behind Emma, Sarah's gaze drifted back to the street. The long shadows across the front yard were highlighted in golden sunlight, but the peaceful scene did little to dispel the unease that had settled in her chest. Someone had been watching them, and Sarah couldn't shake the feeling that this mystery was far from over.

∾

The bell above the door chimed as Sarah stepped into Rosewood Hollow's only grocery store, a blast of cool air washing over her. As her fingers curled around the cart handle, an inexplicable chill slithered down her spine, entirely unrelated to the store's air conditioning. Her eyes darted around, scanning familiar faces, vibrant produce displays, and neatly stacked cans, searching for... something.

Young mothers chatted, clerks restocked shelves, and everyone seemed to belong. Yet an invisible wrongness permeated the air, setting Sarah's nerves on edge.

As she navigated the aisles, selecting items with trembling hands, the hairs on her nape prickled. In the cereal aisle, Sarah paused, feigning interest in a box of bran flakes while her gaze flicked frantically across the reflective surface, seeking an unseen observer. Nothing appeared amiss, but the sensation of invisible eyes boring into her back intensified, her fingers whitening around the cardboard.

At the dairy case, Sarah reached for milk, her distorted reflection wavering in the glass. A flicker of movement caught her eye—a shadowy figure materialized behind her for a heartbeat. She whirled, pulse thundering, only to find Mrs. Henderson contemplating yogurt varieties.

"Everything alright, dear?" the elderly woman asked, concern etching her wrinkled features.

Sarah forced a brittle smile, her voice unnaturally high. "Just fine, Mrs. Henderson. Thought I... forgot something."

As she hurried to check out, Sarah's gaze swept the store obsessively. Nothing appeared out of place, yet the oppressive weight of unseen scrutiny bore down on her. Her shoulders hunched as if to ward off an impending attack, her movements growing frantic as she rushed through payment, desperate to escape.

The ten-minute drive home stretched interminably. Sarah's knuckles bleached on the steering wheel as she compulsively checked the rearview mirror, half-expecting to glimpse a phantom pursuer. The familiar trees lining Rosewood Hollow's streets loomed ominously, their shadows writhing across the road like grasping tendrils.

Sarah's movements were robotic as she put away groceries, her mind racing with nameless fears. Collapsing into the armchair, a forgotten glass of lemonade sweating in her grip, she peeled back the curtain with trembling fingers. Her wide eyes scanned the seemingly peaceful street, searching for any sign of the unseen presence that had stalked her through the store—and perhaps followed her home?

Sarah remained frozen at the window, her eyes scanning the seemingly peaceful street outside. The late afternoon sun cast long, distorted shadows across the pavement, transforming familiar trees into looming sentinels. A gentle breeze rustled the leaves, the innocent sound now sinister to her heightened senses.

What's going on? Something happen at the store? Pixie's voice echoed in her mind.

Sarah's hand instinctively reached down, automatically caressing the velvety softness of Pixie's head.

I don't know, Pixie. Ever since you chased that stranger away this morning, I feel like...

Eyes on you? Pixie finished, her thoughts tinged with concern.

Exactly like that, Sarah whispered, her gaze still fixed on the world outside. *Maybe it's just paranoia.*

Pixie's ears twitched, and her voice took on a serious tone. *I don't think so. Whoever was there was real, staring at the house. And I don't think they came to admire the flowers.*

A shiver ran through Sarah's body. She held out an arm, and Pixie jumped into her lap, a warm, comforting weight against the growing knot of anxiety in her chest.

Everything looked normal—peaceful, even. Occasional cars passed by, neighbors walked their dogs, all oblivious to the tension radiating from Sarah's vigil. Still, she couldn't shake the feeling of unseen eyes boring into her, studying her every move. Her mind raced, desperately trying to connect the disparate threads: the bank robbery, Noah and Deanna's affair, Tyler's involvement, and now this oppressive sense of being watched.

As the shadows lengthened and the sky took on the golden hues of early evening, the sound of the back door opening jolted Sarah from her trance-like state.

"Mom?" Emma's voice called out. "I'm home!"

Sarah blinked, realizing she had been staring out the window for hours. Her joints protested as she stood, calling back, "In the living room, sweetie."

Emma's approaching footsteps seemed to echo in the silence. Sarah cast one last, desperate glance out the window. The street remained as tranquil as ever, but the knot of unease in her stomach tightened, a silent warning of unseen dangers lurking just beyond her perception.

Chapter Twenty-Nine

"Why are you sitting here like this?" Emma's voice softened, filled with sudden understanding. "You look terrified, Mom."

"I'm not really..." Sarah began, but the words felt hollow even as she spoke them.

"Mom?" Emma's laser-blue eyes bore into her, seeing more than just the physical.

Sarah sighed, knowing she couldn't hide much from her daughter, especially as Emma's powers grew.

"Just an unease," she admitted, sinking back into the armchair. "Ever since Barnes came at us and Pixie chased someone away this morning, I've been feeling... eyes on me all day. I know it sounds silly."

"No, it's not," Emma said softly, moving to stand beside her mother. She placed her hand against the curtain, her gaze scanning the street outside. "I felt the same thing. Somebody is watching us."

"Why?" Sarah asked, hating the desperate edge in her voice.

Emma was silent for a moment, her head cocked to one side. Her eyes became unfocused, as if seeing something beyond the physical realm. Then she slowly shook her head, her blonde braid dancing across her back.

"If I had to guess," Emma said, her voice barely above a whisper, "I'd say it's Barnes." Her eyes grew distant, as if peering into an unseen realm. "His words echo in my mind, 'leave my family alone.' But there's more..." She trailed off, her brow furrowing in deep concentration.

Sarah leaned forward, her breath catching. "What is it, honey? What does he think?"

Emma's focus snapped back to the present, her gaze locking onto Sarah's with an intensity that made her mother shiver. "He's convinced we know something—something dangerous. But we don't actually know it. At least, not yet."

A chill ran down Sarah's spine at her daughter's words. Despite the tension, she managed a wry smile, attempting to lighten the mood. "Well, Emma, when you start dating, those poor boys won't have a prayer of keeping secrets from you."

Emma's eyes softened, a small, mischievous smirk playing on her lips. "Nor should they, Mom. Nor should they."

The moment of levity evaporated, leaving Sarah lost in a fog of memories. Emma had been just twelve when her father abandoned them for 'more freedom and better pastures.' In the aftermath, Matthew had entered their lives, a beacon of hope. Now, Emma and Cory were thriving, but Emma... Emma was growing into something beyond ordinary. Her developing powers whispered of formidable potential, their origin a mystery that haunted Sarah's dreams.

A soft, ethereal jingling drew Sarah's attention earthward. Pixie stood between them, her fringed ears quivering like antennae sensing the unseen. As Sarah watched, transfixed, a gossamer golden glow materialized around the tip of Pixie's tail, spreading outward like liquid starlight—the harbinger of Pixie's special brand of magic.

Pixie... Sarah's breath caught, her skin erupting in gooseflesh.

Suddenly, it engulfed her. A cosmic ebb and flow, an arcane current of power surging between Emma, Pixie, and herself. It was as if they stood in a mystical ocean, waves of energy lapping at the shores of their consciousness, threatening to pull them into its depths. Sarah's gaze locked with Emma's wide, awestruck eyes.

"You feel that?" Emma's whisper held equal parts wonder and trepidation, her voice seeming to echo from both the physical realm and somewhere beyond.

Sarah could only nod, the otherworldly sensation rendering her mute.

Pixie? she projected, her thoughts reaching out across the ethereal plane. The bond between them pulsed, stronger and more vivid than ever before.

Pixie's voice resonated within their minds, clear as crystal and potent as thunder: *Nobody in this house will ever have to be afraid.*

A sudden, jarring noise from the front door shattered the mystical moment. As if choreographed by an unseen force, Emma and Sarah pivoted in unison, hands raised defensively, palms angled toward an unseen threat. They stood like sentinels, heads high, eyes narrowed and glowing with an inner light. The golden aura encompassing Pixie's tail flared, casting writhing, otherworldly shadows across the walls.

Matthew's entrance broke the spell. He crossed the threshold, briefcase in hand, only to be confronted by the surreal scene—Sarah and Emma poised for some metaphysical battle, Pixie radiating an impossible light.

His briefcase clattered to the floor as he recoiled, eyes wide with shock.

"Jesus," he breathed, his voice a mixture of awe and alarm. "What in God's name is happening here?"

The mystical energy receded like a tide, leaving Sarah lightheaded. "It's just you," she managed, offering a wan smile as she lowered her arms. Emma mirrored her mother's actions, the unearthly glow in her eyes slowly fading. The power that had flowed between them dissipated with an almost audible snap, leaving behind a residual tingling that danced across Sarah's skin.

"Do I want to know what is actually happening?" Matthew asked, bending to collect his old leather briefcase. "The last time I saw you like this was..." he trailed off, remembering the Jenkins.

"Somebody is watching the house... and us," Emma said in her clear, no-nonsense voice. Sarah took her daughter's hand and squeezed it gently.

"We've both felt it all day," she confirmed, meeting Matthew's concerned gaze. "Pixie spotted a stranger lurking by the gate this morning, and after what Barnes did..."

Matthew's expression hardened. He set down his briefcase once more and crossed the room, enveloping both Sarah and Emma in a tight embrace. "Are you okay?" he asked, his voice muffled against Sarah's hair. He pulled back slightly, looking from one to the other. "You would tell me if anything had happened, wouldn't you? The way you two were standing there..."

Sarah and Emma exchanged a look, a silent communication passing between them. Sarah had only experienced the power flow between Pixie and herself a few times before, never with Emma. This new development was both exciting and terrifying.

"We're okay," Sarah assured him, leaning into his embrace. "Just... on edge. But we'll figure this out together."

As the family stood there, holding onto one another, Pixie wound herself around their legs, her tail still faintly glowing. Whatever challenges lay ahead, Sarah knew they would face them as a unit, a family bound not just by love, but by a magic they were only beginning to understand.

Chapter Thirty

Sarah tossed and turned most of the night, her restless mind amplifying every creak and whisper in the old house. She was sure she heard quiet footsteps crossing the wide entrance hall downstairs. Was there a voice, a whisper? Sarah strained her senses, only to convince herself it was nothing, and force her mind to rest. Each time her eyes fluttered open again, she found Matthew sleeping peacefully beside her, but Pixie's dark, alert gaze never wavered. The tiny Papillon's delicate ears stood at attention, her white and sable fur catching the moonlight filtering through the curtains.

Rest, Sarah, Pixie's voice echoed in her mind. *I'd warn you of any intruder.*

Sarah sighed, burying her face in the pillow. *Thank you, Pixie. I just never felt so vulnerable.*

What about Emma? Sarah wondered.

Pixie's dainty head lifted, her butterfly-like ears casting whimsical shadows on the wall. *Emma is... watchful. Curious. She radiates a sense of invincibility.*

Sarah groaned softly. The innocence of youth, indeed. A sharp crack pierced the night again, and she bolted upright.

Easy, Pixie soothed. *Just the fox in the yard. We have unfinished business, she and I.*

 ∞

As the first tendrils of dawn crept across the sky, Sarah found herself on the front porch, steaming coffee in hand. She watched a russet blur vanish into the misty orchard where it merged with her garden. Despite her unease, she couldn't help feeling her entire body exhale, releasing the tension of the night for just a moment. Rosewood Hollow never failed to present itself as truly magical in the early morning light.

Matthew chose to work from home that day. Sarah could see him peeking through the curtains at the street past their house now and then, and he worked in the kitchen instead of the little room he had turned into an office for himself. Every few minutes, he'd find an excuse to check on her, his worried eyes softening each time he found her safe.

Yet the unsettling sensation of being watched persisted. Whether Sarah was pruning roses or rocking on the porch swing, she felt invisible eyes on her, and fleeting shadowy figures that disappeared around a corner as soon as she had spotted them. Tom Barnes, or just a nosy neighbor? A villain, or a common door-to-door salesperson? Only within the sanctuary of their locked home did the feeling subside.

Emma had vanished hours ago, eager to spend the afternoon at the bookstore with Lily. Cory was out playing ball with friends, leaving Sarah restless and cooped up.

With a decisive thunk, she finally set her mug down on the counter.

"I'm going to lose my mind if I stay inside another minute," she said to Matthew. "Pixie and I are heading out for a walk, maybe into downtown Rosewood."

Matthew glanced at his watch, frowning. "I've got a call in half an hour. If you wait, I can join you."

"No, I don't think so," Sarah replied, a hint of steel in her voice. Frustration bubbled up inside her. Tom Barnes' foolish vendetta wasn't going to keep her prisoner in her own home.

"I'll be fine," she insisted, already fastening a bright pink harness around Pixie's tiny frame. "We're just walking into town, maybe have a coffee and come back."

"Sarah..." Matthew's gaze darted between his laptop and Sarah, clearly torn.

She silenced his protest with a quick peck on the cheek. "I'll be okay, Matthew. You do what you need to do. I've got Pixie, it's busy out there, and if Barnes does show up, you know we can handle it."

"Are you sure this is Tom Barnes, watching the house?"

"He's the only one who has an issue with me, isn't he?"

"Not necessarily," Matthew shook his head. "What if there's someone else, someone who hasn't even shown up on our radar yet?"

"But we would have..."

"Come across him?" Matthew asked. "Maybe. Maybe not. And perhaps that is the very reason he or she is creeping around the house. To prevent that from happening."

Sarah had no answer and pressed her lips into a tight, hard line. As if on cue, Pixie's gentle reminder floated through her mind. Sarah had faced worse before, feeling vulnerable and fragile. Each time, her power had risen to protect her. She might not fully understand or control it, but it was there, a comforting presence just beneath the surface.

"I'll be fine," she declared, her voice laced with resolute determination. Gripping her keys tightly, she stalked toward the door.

As she and Pixie ventured down the walkway onto the sun-dappled street, she could sense Matthew's concerned gaze lingering on her back.

Badass... Pixie's thought carried a hint of Cory's teenage swagger.

Sarah chuckled, bending to scratch behind the papillon's silky ears. *You bet.*

The street ahead stretched quietly under the July sun. Rosewood Hollow was a postcard come to life—flowerbeds bursting with color, window boxes overflowing with blooms. Sarah breathed deeply, savoring the scents of summer.

This walk had been a good idea, she thought. Better than waiting around inside her house for something to come at them. She would drive herself insane if she did that.

Sarah strolled down the lane towards the Rosewood Common, Pixie trotting contentedly beside her. As they rounded a corner, she nearly bumped into Lisa Broadbent, a petite brunette she knew from organizing library events with Emma.

"Hi, Sarah!" Lisa exclaimed, her face brightening. "What a lovely surprise!"

The two fell into step together, chatting about Rosewood and the weather, as well as any topic that steered clear of the bank robbery, the ruined Christmas in July event, and Tyler's death. Their conversation flowed easily as they admired the fountain, once again merrily gurgling in the center of the Common.

"There's a new café that just opened a few weeks ago," Lisa said, pointing at a sign with one hand. "I thought we might—"

She broke off as Pixie suddenly began pulling hard on her leash, straining across the plaza so hard she could barely breathe.

"Pixie," Sarah said with a hint of annoyance. "That's not the way we're going. Come on."

The tiny Papillon leaned into her harness so hard she was almost lying on her side, all five pounds of her blocking their progress. Lisa screwed up her face and chuckled.

"I've heard papillons can be particularly stubborn..."

"Not usually," Sarah replied, tugging a little more insistent on the lead.

What's the matter? she thought.

Pixie's response came with startling urgency. *I'm not sure I can explain it right now, but we need to go this way. We just have to.*

Sarah shaded her eyes, following Pixie's determined pull. Across the road stood the Rosewood Savings and Trust, the very branch where it had all begun. A chill crept down her spine as memories of that fateful day came flooding back.

We have to go there.

"Pixie, no," Sarah warned aloud, gripping the leash even tighter. If she pulled any harder, she would surely lift the little papillon off her feet.

Lisa, oblivious to the silent exchange, rummaged through her purse. "Actually, your pup might be onto something," she said. "I don't think I have enough cash on me. Let me just pop across and use the ATM. Won't be a minute."

"We'll go with you," Sarah offered, her tone deliberately light as she struggled to control Pixie's insistent tugging.

Are you happy now? she thought. *This is why you're dragging me across the road?*

No, it isn't, came the cryptic reply, leaving Sarah to wonder what unseen force was guiding them towards the bank—and what new mystery awaited them there.

Chapter Thirty-One

Lisa had just inserted her bank card into the ATM when a startled cry pierced the air. It wasn't a shriek of terror, but rather pure astonishment that arrested Sarah's casual glance around the plaza.

"It's brimming with cash!" a woman's voice rang out, tinged with disbelief. Lisa and Sarah turned as one to see a middle-aged lady standing by the ornate double doors, clutching a red and white cloth bag emblazoned with the Rosewood Hollow Grocery Store logo. The woman's eyes were wide with bewilderment. "I swear, it was just hanging here. I didn't... I - I don't know what possessed me to peek inside. I just... had to."

A chill of déjà vu washed over Sarah. The scene before her was an eerie mirror image of the incident she'd witnessed mere weeks ago. As if summoned by an unseen force, security guards materialized from within the bank, their faces set with grim determination to prevent any witnesses from slipping away.

Moments later, the wail of a siren cut through the air, and Officer Penny Harding's police cruiser pulled up, its blue and red lights casting an otherworldly glow on the gathered crowd. The woman who'd dis-covered the bag kept repeating her mantra in a trembling voice. "I just found it, I really just found it."

As the familiar drama unfolded, Sarah felt a tingling sensation at the back of her neck. She knew, with a certainty that defied logic, that this was why Pixie had mysteriously urged her to come to the bank today. This very moment in time, and Sarah found herself unwittingly entangled in another puzzle.

Pixie ceased her incessant tugging, fixing Sarah with a wide, canine grin. Her tongue lolled out comically, as if she were privy to some cosmic joke.

Before Sarah could interrogate her about this bizarre turn of events, she found herself face-to-face with the steely-eyed Officer Penny Hard-ing.

"Well, well, Sarah. Fancy meeting you here again," Penny drawled, her gaze boring into Sarah like a laser. "At a bank you don't even use, which was recently robbed. Quite the coincidence, wouldn't you say?"

Sarah shrugged, trying to appear nonchalant. "I was just walking with Lisa Broadbent so she could use the ATM. And from what I gather, this time money hasn't vanished, it's mysteriously appeared. Unless someone accidentally left a bag of cash dangling from the bank doors like a forgotten umbrella."

Pixie's voice echoed in Sarah's mind, causing her to stiffen. *Someone brought it here, or more precisely, brought it back here.*

Sarah gasped involuntarily, hastily disguising it as a cough under Officer Harding's increasingly suspicious scrutiny.

What do you mean, brought it back? Sarah thought frantically, acutely aware of Harding's narrowed eyes still fixed upon her.

"Sorry, went down the wrong pipe," she mumbled, forcing another cough.

"And you're absolutely certain you know nothing about this?" The intensity of the question left no room for ambiguity.

Sarah shook her head, her heart racing.

Lisa Broadbent's voice quavered as she explained, "We only came because I was short on cash. Otherwise, we'd be at that new café..." She trailed off, her gaze darting between Sarah and Penny.

"Surely you don't think... You can't suspect us?"

Penny tucked her notebook away, her eyes scrutinizing both women. Pixie sat serenely beside Sarah, the picture of canine innocence.

"We'll see. I'll need both of you down at the station—"

Before she could finish, the bank's manager, Timo something-or-other, came bursting out, his suit jacket flapping like startled wings. He clutched at Penny's arm, his attempt at whispering more of a stage whisper that Sarah couldn't help but overhear.

"Exactly half of last week's stolen money—the serial numbers match. Precisely half..."

Penny shushed him, her gaze narrowing once more at Sarah. Sarah averted her eyes to look at Pixie.

You knew.

I had my suspicions. I sensed an intent to set something right.

"Please come by the station to give your statements," Penny instructed, already turning towards the bank with the manager. "We'll be in touch."

Lisa's worried chatter faded into background noise as Sarah's mind raced. Someone had returned the money. But why only half?

Why half? she silently asked Pixie, turning when no response came.

Pixie?

Barnes just vanished around the corner, came the delayed reply. *But before you ask, I don't think it was him. His anger is so palpable, I'd have sensed him from a mile away.*

Sarah's eyes instinctively searched for Barnes, but naturally he was long gone.

"Well, there goes our quiet afternoon," she sighed to Lisa. "I might as well stop by the station. I'd rather not have them showing up at my house... again. Neighbors will think we're some kind of criminals." Catching Lisa's sideways glance, she added, "My daughter Emma discovered Tyler Robinson."

The weight of another mystery settled on Sarah's shoulders as she thought about yet another round of questioning, all while pondering the enigma of the returned money.

Chapter Thirty-two

When Sarah finally trudged through her front door hours later than she had expected, the aroma of Matthew's famous lasagna wafted through the air, but even that couldn't lift her spirits. She found him in the kitchen, his back to her as he pulled the steaming dish from the oven.

"You're pretty late," he said, a hint of worry in his voice as he turned to face her. One look at her expression and his brow furrowed. "Oh no. I know that look. What happened?"

Sarah sank into a chair at the kitchen table, Pixie curling up at her feet. "You're not going to believe this," she began, recounting the day's events.

As she spoke, Matthew's face cycled through a range of emotions—concern, disbelief, and finally, exasperation. Finally, he set the lasagna down with a bit more force than necessary.

"Again? Sarah, how do you keep getting mixed up in these things?" He ran a hand through his hair, a gesture she recognized as a sign of his mounting frustration. "And a bank robber returning money? That's... that's just..."

"Bizarre?" Sarah offered, managing a weak smile.

"Unheard of," Matthew finished, shaking his head. "I mean, who does that? Rob a bank and then have a change of heart?"

Sarah glanced down at Pixie, who gazed back with those knowing eyes.

"I don't know," she said aloud. "But as always, Penny Harding thinks I might have some answers."

Matthew sighed deeply, serving up two plates of lasagna.

"You do understand that I worry about you? These mysteries... they're not just exciting little tales. They can be dangerous."

As he set a plate in front of her, Sarah reached out and squeezed his hand.

"I know that. But this time I didn't set out to get involved. I was literally just walking down the street with Lisa. There is something else, though."

Matthew's fork paused halfway to his mouth. "What now?"

"Pixie... she saw Tom Barnes there. He disappeared around the corner just after the money was found."

The clatter of Matthew's fork hitting his plate echoed through the kitchen. "Tom Barnes?" he exclaimed, his voice rising.

Sarah nodded, avoiding his gaze. "The very same."

Matthew pushed his chair back and stood so abruptly it would have toppled, had he not caught it with a quick reach of his hand. He paced the kitchen, running both hands through his hair in agitation.

"I don't think any of us should go anywhere alone anymore. This is getting out of hand."

"Matthew, please—" Sarah began, but he cut her off.

"The kids asked you to help preserve Tyler's memory. Now we've got bank robberies, returned money, and a known troublemaker lurking around us."

Pixie whined softly at Sarah's feet, and she felt a pang of guilt. She knew her involvement in these mysteries worried Matthew, but she couldn't ignore the pull she felt to solve them.

"I understand you're worried," she said softly, "but I can't just ignore what's happening around me. And Pixie—"

"Pixie is a dog," Matthew interrupted, his voice gentler now as he sat back down. "A wonderful, smart dog, but still a dog. She can't protect you from any real danger."

Sarah bit her lip and reached across the table to take Matthew's hand. "I love you for that, but please don't ask me to turn a blind eye to what's going on in our town."

Matthew sighed deeply, squeezing her hand. He thought for a long moment and finally shook his head, spreading his hands in a gesture both helpless and despairing.

"I know I can't stop you entirely," he said.

Sarah nodded, relief washing over her. As she resumed eating her now-cold lasagna, her mind raced with questions. Why was Tom Barnes at the bank? How was he connected to the returned money? Wasn't the gossip in town that he had inherited more money than he could ever think about spending?

∞

Cory and Emma returned just in time for dinner and were just as stunned as Matthew had been when they heard.

"Oh, Mom," Emma chuckled, giving Sarah's hand an affectionate squeeze. "We can't leave you alone for a minute, can we? Pretty soon, Matthew will want to invest in a leash."

Sarah rolled her eyes playfully. "Don't you dare give him any ideas!"

Cory's brow furrowed, his voice low and gravelly. "What a dumbass move," he muttered, shaking his head. "First, you go through all the trouble of pulling off this stupid heist, even shooting Tyler in the process. Then you... what? Have a crisis and return half the loot?"

"Exactly half," Sarah murmured, her gaze distant. The wall seemed to shimmer slightly, as if the very air held secrets.

"Almost like... someone was trying to make amends."

"Fat lot of good that does Tyler now," Cory snapped, his words sharp enough to make Sarah wince.

She shook her head slowly, a glimmer of something—hope, perhaps—in her eyes. "But maybe it does help, in a way. If the person who returned the money feels genuine remorse about what happened to Tyler, then..."

"And who'd feel worse than the guy who dragged him into this mess in the first place?" Cory continued, his voice softening as the pieces started to click into place.

"Yeah... maybe even someone related to you, in some roundabout way."

From the kitchen, the refrigerator door closed with a soft thud. Matthew's voice carried a hint of amusement, despite his stern words.

"I can practically hear the gears turning in that head of yours, Sarah."

Sarah opened her mouth to protest, but a blur of white and sable fur leapt into her lap. Pixie's dark eyes locked onto hers, and a familiar presence brushed against her mind.

He's just scared, her thoughts whispered. *By tomorrow everything will be right as rain again.*

Sarah's fingers sank into Pixie's soft fur. *I hope so, Pixie. I really hope so.*

The clink of glasses on the table drew Sarah's attention as Matthew set down a pitcher of freshly squeezed lemonade. Deep lines of worry still edged his eyes, but a cautious smile already played on his lips.

"So," he drawled, "What else did our esteemed Officer Harding have to say? Other than her barely concealed desire to slap the cuffs on you, of course."

"Well... I..." Sarah groped for words that would sound lighthearted and fun, and not increase Matthew's worry.

"There's an article here on social media", Cory interrupted, staring down at his phone. "If they wanted to keep it under wraps that half the money was returned, they're out of luck. Somebody heard what was going on... and it's blowing up."

"Cory, no phone at the table, remember?" Matthew said, but the admonishment was missing its usual snappiness.

Cory quickly shoved his phone back into his pocket, the faint glow still visible through the fabric of his jeans.

"Sorry," he mumbled, his voice a mix of excitement and unease. "It's just... Mom was there, and this whole thing is totally bizarre and creepy. Why would anyone–"

A bone-chilling breeze swept through the room, cutting Cory off mid-sentence. Sarah's eyes fluttered closed for a moment, a resigned sigh escaping her lips. So much for a quiet family dinner.

"Because they felt guilty, young man," a crisp, aristocratic voice announced.

The gauzy form of Simon materialized in the kitchen doorway, his translucent figure impeccably dressed as always, complete with a jaunty hat and ever-present sketchpad. Matthew's fork clattered against his plate as he set it down with a weary sigh.

"Simon..." he began, a hint of exasperation in his tone. "I'd invite you to join us for dinner, but..."

"Oh, that would be delightful!" Simon exclaimed, entirely missing, or choosing to ignore, the sarcasm. He glided gracefully into the room, hovering above an empty chair.

Emma's eyes darted to the hallway. "Where did you leave Amelia then?" she asked, a note of concern in her voice.

Simon's translucent form seemed to puff up with pride. "Amelia is on a special mission this evening," he announced, his voice dripping with self-satisfaction. "You seem to have given her quite the taste for sleuthing, I must say."

Sarah massaged her temples, feeling the beginnings of a headache. Between the returned loot and a ghost with a penchant for detective work, it was all becoming a bit much.

"So, they felt guilty," she prodded, desperate for any scrap of information. "Do you happen to know who–"

"Of course not," Simon interrupted, his form flickering slightly. "I wasn't there, as you well know. Or perhaps you don't. I suppose I could have been invisible, although you would have noticed the atmospheric changes with which you're now quite familiar..."

"Simon..." Sarah's voice held a warning note.

Cory leaned forward, his eyes bright with curiosity. "Guilty," he mused. "If you don't know who it was, how can you be sure they felt guilty? Some kind of spectral emotional imprint, maybe?"

Simon regarded the boy with a long, piercing stare. His head shook slowly, the motion causing his image to momentarily disintegrate into small wisps before reforming.

"Nothing quite so sophisticated, I'm afraid, young Cory," Simon replied. "In my lifetime, I knew a fair few thieves, but only one who ever returned his ill-gotten gains out of sheer remorse for the pain he'd caused."

A tense silence fell over the room. Pixie sat primly on Sarah's lap, the golden shimmer at the tip of her tail growing more pronounced by the second.

Emma broke the quiet, her voice soft with affection. "So, what exactly is Amelia up to?"

Simon's ghostly chest swelled with pride. "My darling Amelia," he announced, "is at this very moment investigating the mysterious disappearance of Noah Delmore."

Sarah's breath caught in her throat. "Noah has disappeared?" she gasped, her mind already racing. "Why didn't you lead with that? How did you two uncover this? Do you have any idea where he might have gone?"

"One thing at a time," Simon chided gently. He paused dramatically, then erupted into a dazzling shower of gold and silver sparks, his form momentarily lost in the ethereal display.

As the sparks faded, the kitchen was left bathed in an otherworldly glow. The lasagna lay forgotten, cooling on the plates. The kitchen seemed to grow dimmer, as if the very air was absorbing Simon's otherworldly presence.

"Amelia," Simon continued, his voice carrying a hint of pride, "has developed quite the affinity for your electronic contraptions, as you well know." He fixed Cory with a piercing stare, causing the boy to lower his gaze sheepishly.

Simon's brow furrowed, struggling to find the right words. "She was certain she had observed... Ah, how do you call them? Those catalog order sheets somehow displayed on a magical electric screen? Where one uses a peculiar device to select items and fill in details, rather than writing with pen and paper?"

"Online orders?" Cory offered hesitantly.

Simon paused, considering. "Perhaps. In any case, she believed she had glimpsed an order for two identical Santa Claus costumes on Noah Delmore's device, which he subsequently deleted in quite a rush, if you remember. Naturally, she wanted to confirm her suspicions."

Sarah reached for her lemonade, taking a long, fortifying gulp. "Yes, I remember, he deleted those order forms, but that's pretty normal behavior." She paused, brow furrowing. "Besides, I imagine half the town was buying or renting costumes for the Christmas in July event. But go on..."

"Indeed," Simon continued, his form shimmering slightly. "But when she materialized, Noah Delmore was nowhere to be found in that hovel he calls home. And not just him—all of his machines and clothing items had vanished as well. Not a stitch left behind."

Matthew's voice was flat as he offered, "Could have moved."

Simon erupted once more in a dazzling shower of sparks, his exasperation palpable.

"Perhaps, Matthew, perhaps. But would he not have informed his employer of such a relocation?" The ghost's form rippled as he recounted Amelia's findings. "When she appeared at his workplace, the lady who calls herself his... supervisor," he finally settled on the term, "was frantically telephoning, trying to locate young Mr. Delmore. And oh, the foul language she employed! The threats she made should she find him... In my time, a lady would never."

Simon's entire form shuddered, momentarily losing cohesion before solidifying again.

Sarah leaned forward, her eyes sharp. "So, Delmore is missing. Nobody knows where he's gone. But you and Amelia thought, because he's distantly related to Tyler...?"

"He may be the one feeling dreadful remorse," Simon finished softly. "Causing all of his irrational behavior."

With a theatrical flourish, he bowed deeply, his spectral cap remaining perfectly still throughout the motion.

The kitchen fell silent once more, the only sound the soft ticking of the old clock on the wall. The family exchanged meaningful glances, the implications of this new information sinking in.

Pixie's tail twitched, the golden shimmer intensifying. Her dark eyes locked with Sarah's, conveying a silent message that only she could hear. It was clear that this was far from over. The pieces of the puzzle were only just beginning to fall into place, and Sarah knew that she and her unconventional team of sleuths, both living and spectral, were about to be pulled even deeper into the heart of this enigma.

Simon floated around the kitchen for a moment, peering at the set dinner table with curiosity in his eyes.

"Thank you for the invite, kind sir," he said to Matthew. "I would stay, but, alas..."

He giggled, his spectral form wavered, and with a sigh and soft chilly touch, he was gone again. As Simon faded away, the kitchen seemed to exhale, warmth slowly seeping back into the room.

Matthew was the first to break the spell, clearing his throat. "Well, I suppose we should eat before it gets entirely cold," he said, his voice carrying a mix of resignation and amusement.

Sarah nodded absently, her mind still racing with the implications of Noah Delmore's disappearance. Quietly, she stroked Pixie in her lap, the golden shimmer around her tail slowly fading.

Emma reached for her fork, but hesitated. "Mom," she said softly, "what do you think this all means?"

Cory leaned in, his earlier embarrassment forgotten in the face of this new mystery.

"Yeah, do you think Delmore really returned the money? And why would he just vanish like that?"

Sarah took a deep breath, her eyes sweeping over her family. "I'm not entirely sure," she admitted. "Two Santa costumes, half the stolen money returned, and a missing suspect who might be feeling guilty." She paused, a wry smile tugging at her lips. "Just another day in our lovely little town, I suppose."

Matthew raised an eyebrow, fork stabbing at the lasagna on his plate. "Sarah," he said, his tone carrying a note of resignation. "Let's just eat."

She held up her hands in mock surrender. "Of course, dear. That's what I was getting at." But there was a glimmer in her eye that suggested otherwise.

The cozy kitchen was once again filled with the sounds of conversation and laughter, but beneath it all, the undercurrent of mystery and magic remained.

Chapter Thirty-Three

The next day, Sarah felt Matthew's watchful gaze following her every move. He tried to be subtle, but she knew him too well. Once again, he'd set up his laptop in the kitchen, enduring a cacophony of background noises during his phone calls, all for the sake of staying close.

As the morning light filtered through the lace curtains, casting quirky shadows on the floor, Matthew casually inquired about her plans more than once. The old grandfather clock in the hallway hadn't quite struck eleven when Sarah found herself growing weary of his protectiveness.

"Matthew," she asked, mimicking Emma's sweet, innocent tone. "Can I go hang out with Lily?"

He slowly removed his reading glasses, folding them with deliberate care. The lenses caught the light, briefly flashing with a bright gleam.

"Sarah... you know I'm just worried, right?"

Sarah only shrugged, her silence speaking volumes. Actually, she thought, I feel like you're hovering, but she kept her mouth shut, knowing she would only sound silly and petulant.

Finally, Matthew sighed, a sound tinged with both concern and resignation.

"I guess it wouldn't do much good to ask you to stick close until Penny Harding has sorted this all out, and to forget about Deanna and Tom Barnes... and Noah Delmore?"

Sarah twitched a shoulder again, stubbornly opening the fridge and staring into its chilly depths as if it held all of life's answers.

"Not really," she said, without looking at him.

A soft patter of paws announced Pixie's arrival. The little dog placed her front paws on Sarah's knee, gazing up with eyes that seemed to hold ancient wisdom.

You know he means well, right? she heard the little dog say.

Sarah scooped up the tiny canine, giving her a gentle squeeze. *I guess,* she thought.

Give him some credit, Pixie urged, giving her face a quick lick for good measure.

Sarah set her back down and turned to face Matthew. Their eyes met, and for a moment, an unspoken understanding passed between them.

"I know you don't..." They both began simultaneously, then chuckled at the coincidence.

"You first," Sarah offered, a small smile playing on her lips.

Matthew's expression softened.

"I know you don't want me to hover," he said, his voice low and tinged with worry. "And because Emma found Tyler, you feel a responsibility to get to the bottom of this..."

Sarah looked down at her shoes, scuffing the toe against a spot on the floor.

"I know you don't want to fence me in, and you're just worried," she supplied.

"So?" Matthew prompted, his eyebrows raised in question.

Sarah took a deep breath, the scent of Matthew's tea and the flowers outside filling her lungs.

"So, all I'm planning to do is go into town, meet Lily, hang out for a while, and gossip. And yes, we probably will talk about Barnes and Delmore... I couldn't not do that. But unless somebody drops another bag of money or shoots somebody in the middle of Rosewood Common..."

"Heavens beware," Matthew muttered, a wry smile tugging at the corners of his mouth.

"We'll be fine, Matthew, I promise. I'll take Pixie with me, okay?" Sarah reached down to scratch behind the dog's ears. Pixie's tail wagged in agreement, her eyes twinkling with an almost human understanding.

Matthew opened his mouth to say something, then closed it again. He'd long ago given up reminding her and the kids that perhaps Pixie was a bit too small to be everyone's protector. But as he watched the tiny dog's alert stance and the way she seemed to be listening intently to their conversation, he knew she was at least partially right.

∞

"I can't even blame him," Sarah sighed a little while later, her voice barely audible over the gentle splashing of the fountain in Rosewood Common. She and Lily sat on the weathered stone bench, their takeout coffees warming their hands despite the summer heat. A fine mist from the fountain danced in the air, offering a welcome respite from the sweltering day.

"I keep getting into these scrapes," Sarah continued ruefully, her eyes distant, recalling past adventures. "But, to be fair, I never asked to have ghosts in the house, or find an enchanted sapphire, or find myself with powers I don't even understand."

Lily's eyes softened with a mixture of gratitude and lingering sorrow. "Or figure out who killed Luke," she added wistfully. "You only did that for me."

Sarah gave her friend's hand a gentle squeeze, the gesture speaking volumes. For a long moment, the women sat in companionable silence, lost in their own thoughts. Pixie darted about, her tiny paws barely touching the ground as she chased a vibrant yellow butterfly.

Sarah's gaze drifted towards the imposing facade of Rosewood Savings, its windows reflecting the summer sun like watchful eyes. "Noah Delmore is missing," she finally murmured, her voice tinged with curiosity. "Wouldn't that lend credence to the theory that he committed the robbery?"

Lily only shrugged, taking a contemplative sip of her coffee.

"Simon, on the other hand, thought..." Sarah glanced sideways at Lily, searching for any reaction. Her friend's face remained impassive, but there was a flicker of something—understanding, perhaps—in her eyes. "Simon thought Noah felt so guilty about his cousin being shot—"

"Distant cousin," Lily corrected gently.

"Distant cousin," Sarah amended. "That he felt compelled to return half of the stolen money."

"Half," Lily mused, her brow furrowing. "That is so weird. Doesn't it make you wonder who has the other half?"

"We always suspected Deanna of being involved," Sarah supplied, but even as the words left her mouth, doubt crept in.

Lily shook her head, her earrings catching the light and twinkling briefly. "We're still missing something, girlfriend. If this were a Noah and Deanna thing, with Tyler riding shotgun to help, why would they shoot Tyler in the first place, and why is Tom Barnes suddenly all up in your business?"

As if summoned by their conversation, Penny Harding appeared across the Common, walking down the lane with purposeful strides. Her uniform was spotless and crisp, a beacon of authority in the sleepy town. She greeted the shop owners along the way with polite nods, her keen eyes scanning the area. If she noticed Sarah and Lily, she gave no indication, but Sarah couldn't shake the feeling that nothing escaped the officer's notice.

Pixie suddenly abandoned her butterfly chase and trotted back to Sarah, her tiny body tense and taut. The dog's eyes seemed to convey a silent warning. Sarah felt a chill run down her spine despite the summer heat, a familiar sensation that usually preceded something... unusual.

"I hate this," Sarah whispered to Lily, leaning in close. "I keep thinking that I have all the pieces to this darn puzzle, but still, I can't put them in the right order."

Lily nodded slowly, her eyes never leaving Penny's retreating form. "Welcome to Rosewood," she murmured, a hint of irony in her voice. "Where even the simplest mystery has more layers than you can count."

As if in agreement, a sudden breeze rustled through the trees surrounding the Common, carrying with it the faintest whisper of secrets yet to be uncovered.

Chapter Thirty-Four

S arah narrowed her eyes and nudged Lily just the tiniest bit. "Speak of the devil," she said softly and nodded across the plaza. Immediately, Lily's head snapped up, and the hand holding her coffee cup dropped into her lap.

There, beyond the fountain and all the pretty flowers, Tom Barnes had just stepped out of the Rosewood First Savings building, glaring left and right.

"Nice day to do a bit of banking," Lily breathed, sitting up a little straighter. The very air around them seemed to thicken with tension and barely hidden anticipation all at once.

"Could have just dropped in to take his wife for lunch," Sarah whispered, moving a little closer to Lily, but neither of them believed it.

Tom stood on the bank steps for a moment, his stance alert and defiant. His eyes darted around the square, reminiscent of a predator scanning for threats. Penny Harding had vanished around a corner, but Tom's posture screamed challenge, as if daring anyone to take him on... and lose.

"Loaded for bear," Lily confirmed, pulling her feet up on the bench and huddling behind her knees. The fountain's mist seemed to coalesce around them, as if trying to offer concealment.

But it was too late. In his scan of the area, Barnes' gaze locked onto them. His face contorted with recognition and barely contained fury. He bounded across the plaza with aggressive strides, each footfall echoing ominously in the quiet square.

"And here I told Matthew nothing would happen," Sarah whispered, shrinking down a bit herself. The chill running down her spine had nothing to do with the fountain's spray.

In mere seconds, Barnes loomed over them, his shadow falling across their seated forms like a physical weight.

"You," he snapped at Sarah, shaking a fat forefinger in her face. His voice dripped with venom, eyes blazing with an almost unnatural intensity. "Don't you try to hide from me, lady. Since you came into this town, you've brought nothing but unrest and strife. You and that rat of a dog."

His foot lashed out towards Pixie, but the little dog moved with uncanny grace. She evaded him with an almost lazy maneuver, as if he were not even worth her time. For a split second, Sarah could have sworn she saw a flicker of amusement in Pixie's eyes.

The air around them crackled with unseen energy. The fountain's spray caught the sunlight, creating a momentary rainbow that arched protectively over Sarah and Lily. Tom's angry words hung in the air, vibrating with malevolent intent.

Sarah felt a familiar stirring in her chest, the same feeling she'd had when facing down ghosts in her home or Luke's killer. She straightened her spine, meeting Tom's glare with a calm she didn't entirely feel.

"Mr. Barnes," she said, her voice steady despite the pounding of her heart, "I understand you're upset, but I assure you, I have no idea what you're talking about."

Lily shifted beside her, a subtle movement of solidarity. Pixie positioned herself between Sarah and Tom, her tiny form somehow managing to radiate an aura of protective power.

The standoff stretched, the very air holding its breath. In that moment, Sarah knew with certainty that this confrontation was just the beginning.

"Leave me and my family alone!" Barnes bellowed, his finger still jabbing the air in Sarah's direction. His voice echoed across the Common, causing a few nearby pigeons to take startled flight.

Curious onlookers began to gather, their whispers creating a backdrop of hushed speculation. Sarah felt her cheeks burn, wishing she could melt into the weathered stone of the bench. The unwanted attention was likely the only thing preventing Barnes from becoming physical. Still, his rage was palpable, distorting the air around him like a heat haze.

Pixie let out a low, rumbling growl, impossibly deep for her tiny frame. Barnes glowered at the dog, his eyes narrowing to slits.

"Just leave us alone," he screamed, spittle flying from his lips. "Stop checking on Deanna, or driving by our house... or dropping into a bank you don't use. Or I swear to you—"

"Or what?" Lily interjected, rising to her feet with fluid grace. She positioned herself between Barnes and Sarah, her stance protective yet defiant.

Barnes unleashed a torrent of obscenities, each word hanging in the air like a noxious cloud. He kicked viciously at a crumpled paper cup on the ground, clearly imagining it was Pixie. Then, with a final glare that could have curdled milk, he stomped off toward the parking lot where his ostentatious yellow sports car waited, its dented bumper a stark reminder of recent events.

As Barnes retreated, the tension in the air slowly dissipated. The onlookers began to disperse, their excited murmurs fading into the background hum of the town.

"Thanks, Lily," Sarah sighed, her hand trembling slightly as she reached out to Pixie. "Okay, girl?"

Pixie's eyes, wise and alert, locked onto Sarah's. A clear voice, tinged with concern, echoed in Sarah's mind.

Watch out. This is not the end.

Sarah felt goosebumps crawl on her skin again, despite the heat of the day. She glanced at Lily, wondering if her friend sensed the same thing, but Lily's attention was still focused on Barnes' retreating form.

"You know," Lily said softly, settling back onto the bench. "For a man who claims to want to be left alone, he certainly goes out of his way to make a scene. Leave my family alone," she mocked. "What a—" She swallowed the cussword at the end of the sentence and took Sarah's hand.

"Okay?"

Sarah nodded, absently stroking Pixie's fur. The little dog's warmth was comforting, but it couldn't entirely dispel the sense of foreboding that had settled over her.

"I wish I knew what drives him and his tirades," Sarah murmured, her eyes scanning the Common as if searching for hidden clues. "They're always the same—leave us alone, I won't lose everything because of you—like there's something there he thinks I know."

Suddenly, Pixie froze. Her tiny body became a statue, fur bristling, one paw raised in tense anticipation. Her gaze was fixed on the Rosewood First Savings, unwavering and intense. Sarah followed the dog's line of sight, her hand instinctively reaching for Lily's. With a subtle nod, she directed her friend's attention across the street.

The bank's imposing double doors swung open once more, this time revealing Deanna Barnes. She emerged onto the wide stairs, resplendent in a soft, buttery yellow suit that shimmered in the afternoon light. The effect was somewhat marred by the clear distress etched on her face.

"Tom," Deanna called out, her voice laden with frustration and a hint of desperation. "Tom, for crying out loud..."

Her words were drowned out by the sudden roar of an engine and the angry squeal of tires. Tom's yellow sports car peeled out of the parking lot, leaving behind only a cloud of exhaust and the lingering tension of their earlier confrontation.

Deanna stood frozen on the steps, her arms dropping helplessly to her sides. As if they were watching a movie, every passerby suddenly slowed and stared, their casual strolls becoming meandering loops around the Common. The air crackled with electric anticipation, as if the atmosphere itself yearned to be part of the unfolding drama.

For a long moment, Deanna remained motionless, a statue of distress against the backdrop of the austere bank. Then, with a sudden, jerky movement, she clapped a hand over her mouth, the other diving into her pocket to retrieve a tissue.

"Get a load of that," Lily murmured, her voice a mix of fascination and skepticism. "Is she gonna start crying? Won't that ruin her make-up?"

Sarah felt a sudden wave of empathy wash over her, surprising in its intensity. "Take it easy on her," she said softly. "Obviously, something is going on between her and Tom. Why and how that fits into the robbery, who knows? But she seems... at the end."

Distraught, Pixie's voice echoed in Sarah's mind, clear and tinged with concern. The little dog shuffled closer, pressing against Sarah's leg as if offering comfort. *I can smell the desperation and stress all the way across the Common.*

Sarah blinked and glanced down at Pixie, whose eyes seemed to hold an almost human understanding of the unfolding drama.

The fountain's mist caught the sunlight again, creating another sparkling rainbow over the Common. For a fleeting second, Sarah could have sworn she saw shapes in the colorful light, indistinct figures that seemed to be watching the scene with as much interest as the human onlookers.

"Just got fired," a voice murmured from the growing crowd, the words rippling through the onlookers like a stone dropped in still water. "Between the robbery, her bad attitude, and Tom making a fool of himself in there several times, they decided to let her go."

"Serves her right," came a swift, harsh reply and a cackle. "For thinking herself better than the rest of us, just because she married a wealthy guy with family money? Jeez..."

"I hear he thought they should be above all suspicion and exempt from questioning, because of who they are..."

"Yeah," someone chuckled. "My niece works there, says he yelled at the bank manager about sullying the Barnes' family name with suspicions."

"Old man Barnes always went on about a stable home life... wouldn't have liked this one."

"Serves them right."

On and on the gossip went.

Sarah slowly rose to her feet, drawn by an inexplicable force towards the unfolding drama. The sight of Deanna, exposed and vulnerable in the harsh sunlight outside the bank, intensified the surge of empathy coursing through her.

"Sarah, don't," Lily cautioned, reaching for her hand, but it was too late. Sarah was already crossing the Common with determined strides, Pixie trotting faithfully by her side.

"Deanna," Sarah said softly as she approached, extending a hand in a gesture of peace. "Is there anything I can do for you?"

Deanna looked up, her carefully crafted facade crumbling. Her eyes were red and swollen, makeup streaked by tears that continued to spill down her face. Her hand trembled visibly as she regarded Sarah with a mix of disbelief and barely contained fury.

"You, do something for me?" she shrieked, her voice cracking like thin ice. "Well, that would be something new. After you ruined my life with your constant meddling, poking your nose into..."

"Deanna, I assure you I have not done anything of the sort," Sarah protested, her eyes darting around the Common. Penny Harding was long gone, Tom had roared off in a huff, and Lily was across by the fountain, disposing of their empty cups. She felt suddenly, acutely alone.

"Didn't you?" Deanna's voice rose to a screech, and more passersby slowed their walks. "Didn't you come into the bank the very next day after the robbery, checking me out, staring at me? Didn't you come back with your daughter just a day after?"

"But I was just... with Lily," Sarah stammered, feeling the situation spiraling out of control.

"With Lily," Deanna mocked, her words dripping with venom. "Sure. You and your reputation for mysteries in this town; you were just with Lily Morrison. And were you with Lily as well when you drove by my house, asking my neighbor about me, and when you came to Noah Delmore's agency? You do not fool me for a second, Sarah Anderson."

Deanna lunged forward, grabbing Sarah's shoulders and pushing her backwards. Had it not been for her sturdy running shoes, Sarah would have tumbled down the bank's steps.

"I came here to see if I could help," Sarah said, lowering her voice in an attempt to defuse the situation. "But it's clear to me you don't need—"

"Help... isn't that precious?" Deanna screeched, the last vestiges of her socialite mask crumbling away. "You are—"

As Deanna moved to push Sarah again, Pixie sprang into action. The tiny dog placed herself between the two women, letting out a series of warning barks that seemed impossibly loud for her size. For a moment, Sarah could have sworn she saw a shimmer of protective energy surrounding her faithful companion.

Amidst the chaos, Sarah's mind latched onto a crucial detail. *And when you came into Noah Delmore's agency,* she repeated the words in her mind. *How did Deanna know we had been there—had asked around even—unless Noah himself told her?*

The realization hit Sarah like a bolt of lightning, sending her intuition tingling. She felt the pieces of the puzzle shifting, realigning themselves in her mind. The Common fell away, leaving only her, Deanna, and the palpable tension between them.

"Deanna," Sarah said, her voice steady despite the hammering of her heart, "I think we both have some questions that need answering. Why don't we—"

"I don't have any questions, and you don't deserve any answers," Deanna screamed, her voice raw with emotion. She wiped at her face with the heels of her hands, smearing her once-perfect makeup.

"Noah... Noah is still missing. The love of my life, gone because of you."

The words hung in the air, heavy with unintended revelation. Sarah watched as realization dawned on Deanna's face, her eyes widening with the horror of having said too much. She wiped her face again, more forcefully this time, and tried to turn away abruptly.

Sarah, driven by an instinct she couldn't quite name, reached out and placed a gentle hand on Deanna's shoulder. The contact crackled with the unseen energy of secrets longing to be revealed.

"Were you and Noah..." Sarah began, the unfinished question hanging between them. Together, she wanted to say, but the word never left her lips.

In a flash of movement, Deanna's hand connected with Sarah's cheek in a resounding slap. The sound echoed across the Common, causing nearby pedestrians to duck away visibly. Sarah cried out, her hand flying to her stinging cheek as she stumbled back a step.

Pixie, on the other hand, leaped into protective mode. The tiny dog launched herself at Deanna, her bark ferocious and carrying a power far beyond her size. Sarah saw a flicker of otherworldly light in Pixie's eyes, a glimpse of something ancient and fierce.

Deanna tore away, her movements frantic and uncoordinated. But in that brief, charged moment of contact, Sarah felt as if her eyes had been opened.

In that fleeting touch, she saw it all, the deep, aching grief for Noah Delmore, tinged with a bittersweet longing for what could have been. She felt the weight of secrets, the suffocating pressure of lies, and beneath it all, a desperate, clawing fear.

As Deanna stumbled back, her eyes met Sarah's. For a split second, there was a flash of recognition, as if Deanna sensed that Sarah had seen far more than she should have. Then the moment passed, replaced by a mix of terror and defiance.

The deafening roar of an engine shattered the tense quiet of the plaza, much closer than it should have been, given the distance to the road. Sarah's head snapped around, her eyes widening in disbelief at the sight before her. Tom Barnes' canary-yellow Lamborghini, a blur of violent motion, tore straight across the Common, headed straight for them.

Time seemed to slow, each second stretching into an eternity. The car's engine screamed, drowning out the startled cries of onlookers. Sunlight glinted off its polished hood, now aimed like a missile directly at Sarah and Pixie. The acrid smell of burning rubber filled the air as the tires left dark streaks on the pavement.

In that frozen moment, Sarah caught a glimpse of Tom's face through the windshield. His features were contorted with rage, eyes wild with a dangerous mix of fury and desperation. Veins bulged at his temples, and a thin line of spittle trailed from the corner of his mouth. This was no accident; it was an attack.

Sarah's heart pounded in her chest, her breath catching in her throat. Time seemed to stand still as her mind raced through a thousand possibilities, each more terrifying than the last. *This can't be happening,* she thought frantically. *Not here, not now.*

Pixie's warning bark cut through Sarah's shock, the sound unnaturally loud and commanding.

Move! The word exploded in Sarah's mind, jolting her into action.

Just as Sarah reached down to scoop up Pixie, she felt a hard push from behind, propelling her forward with unexpected force. She stumbled, nearly losing her balance as she clutched Pixie to her chest. The yellow sports car roared past, missing them by mere inches. Sarah felt the rush of displaced air, heard the squeal of tires as Tom swerved at the last second.

As she hit the ground, Sarah curled protectively around Pixie, feeling the world spin around her. The scent of burned rubber filled the air, mingling with the acrid smell of fear that seemed to emanate from every pore of her body. Gravel bit into her palms, and she tasted blood where she'd bitten her lip.

Screams and shouts erupted from all directions as the car careened across the plaza, narrowly missing other pedestrians before smashing into the fountain with a sickening crunch of metal and spray of water. The sound of twisting metal and shattering glass echoed across the Common, followed by an eerie silence broken only by the steady hiss of steam rising from the crumpled hood.

Sarah struggled to her feet, her legs shaky, still clutching Pixie tightly to her chest. As she regained her bearings, she heard a familiar voice filled with concern.

"Sarah! Are you all right?"

Amelia called out from a cloud of white and silver, rushing towards her, her wide, worried eyes scanning Sarah wildly.

As the chaos unfolded around her, one thought crystallized in Sarah's mind like a blinding flash: this was no longer just a mystery to be solved. This had become a fight for survival, and the stakes were higher than she could have ever imagined.

Chapter Thirty-Five

"Sarah!" Lily's scream cut through the chaos, echoing across the plaza. Sarah weakly raised an arm to signal she was alright, mostly. In her sudden leap to safety, she'd collided with Deanna, sending the once-elegant woman tumbling into a nearby rosebush.

"Deanna," Sarah called out, her voice hoarse with shock. She reached out her free hand to steady the disheveled woman. "Are you okay?"

Tears streamed unchecked down Deanna Barnes's face, cutting trails through the dirt smudged on her cheeks. Her crisp yellow suit jacket sported an ugly tear, and bits of leaves and twigs nestled in her once-immaculate hair. She allowed Sarah to help her to her feet, then collapsed against her chest, face buried against Pixie, who remained surprisingly calm in Sarah's arms.

"He's just so angry now," Deanna sobbed, her words muffled against Sarah's shoulder. "All of the time, he is just so angry. Claims his family's hundred-year-old reputation is sullied now, for good. That's all he talks about, how we ruined a legend. But we-we never thought he would take it so hard. We thought he'd be okay."

Sarah felt a chill run down her spine, sensing they were on the brink of a major revelation. "We?" she prompted gently, her heart racing with anticipation and fear.

Deanna raised her tear-filled green eyes to meet Sarah's gaze, her expression a mix of guilt, fear, and a strange sort of relief. "Noah and I," she confessed, her voice barely above a whisper. "We only wanted to be together, leave town, and start a new life together. Then Tom found out, completely by chance. His ego wouldn't handle a wife who left him, and bring shame to him and his family. I didn't know... I didn't know his family trust had conditions about a stable home life. He forbade me to leave, and if I did anyway, I would leave with nothing."

The words hung in the air, heavy with implication. Sarah felt as if the ground beneath her feet had suddenly shifted, the pieces of the puzzle rearranging themselves in her mind. Her thoughts raced, connecting dots she hadn't even known existed moments before.

Pixie squirmed in Sarah's arms, her eyes seeming to glow with wisdom and understanding.

There's more, her voice echoed in Sarah's mind. *So much more.*

As if on cue, the fountain behind them sputtered and coughed, water spraying in erratic patterns from where Tom's car had impacted it. The mist caught the sunlight, creating a momentary radiance around Sarah, Deanna, and Pixie. For a fleeting second, Sarah could have sworn she saw shapes in the colorful light again, indistinct figures watching the unfolding drama with keen interest.

In the distance, sirens wailed, growing louder by the second. The peaceful facade of Rosewood had been shattered, revealing a web of secrets, lies, and dangerous passions that Sarah now found herself entangled in.

"And Tyler," Sarah breathed, the name barely a whisper on her lips. She almost didn't dare to ask, but the need for truth drove her forward. "What about Tyler?"

Deanna's sobs intensified, her words tumbling out between gasps. "Tom was going to leave me with nothing, and he had an army of lawyers to make sure that would happen. I was young and foolish, and I signed a prenup. I didn't think." Deanna sobbed again, wiping her sleeve over her eyes. "Noah wanted to be an actor... move to LA, we needed the money. Tyler was only supposed to make the robbery look better," she confessed, tears welling in her bloodshot eyes again.

"It had to be believable. But then... Tom got enraged... and he wanted to shoot Noah, so he'd have me all to himself again."

"All of it was your fault. Because your damned useless, lazy boyfriend bought identical costumes."

The harsh voice froze Sarah in place, her arm still draped protectively over Deanna's trembling shoulders. Time seemed to slow as she turned, her movements feeling as if she were underwater. The air grew thick with tension, making it hard to breathe.

The yellow sports car stood wedged against the fountain's retaining wall, its once-sleek front now a crumpled mess. The windshield was a spiderweb of cracks, glinting ominously in the sunlight. The airbags had deployed, now draping limp across the interior. Somehow, impossibly, the driver had managed to force open the door and extract himself from the wreckage.

Tom Barnes towered over them, a menacing figure materializing from the mayhem he had unleashed. Blood trickled from a deep gash on his forehead, steadily dripping onto his once-pristine white shirt. His suit hung torn and soiled, clinging to his frame in a way that made him look both disheveled and dangerous. But it wasn't the blood that sent a chill down Sarah's spine; it was the gun clutched in his bleeding hand, aimed with steady precision at Sarah and Deanna.

Pixie growled softly in Sarah's arms, the sound vibrating through her chest. The little dog's eyes now glowed bright with fury, her tiny body tense and ready to spring into action.

The plaza around them had fallen eerily silent, as if the whole world was holding its breath. The fountain's spray created a misty halo around Tom's silhouette, lending an almost surreal quality to the scene. Droplets of water clung to his hair and eyelashes, giving him a wild, unhinged appearance.

Sarah felt Deanna's body trembling against her, a faint, terrified plea escaping her lips.

"Oh God, Tom, please, not again..."

Sarah's eyes locked onto the barrel of the gun, her mind racing desperately, searching for a way to defuse the tension of this perilous standoff.

The distant wail of sirens grew louder, but Sarah knew that whatever was going to happen would be over long before help arrived. She took a deep breath, steeling herself for what came next, acutely aware that her next words or actions could mean the difference between life and death.

"I gave you everything," Tom said to Deanna, his voice cracking with emotion. "Everything." His bloodshot eyes took on a wistful glaze, a moment of vulnerability breaking through his rage. "My money, my family's reputation. All I wanted was to stop you from running off with that skinny computer jerk and come back to me. Why couldn't you just have done that?"

Sarah desperately searched for the right words to defuse the situation. She could feel Pixie's rapid heartbeat against her chest, echoing her own frantic pulse. The weight of the moment felt oppressive, each second stretching into an agonizing eternity.

"You shot a kid," Deanna spat, her words laced with venom. Sarah winced at the harshness in her tone, fearing it would only escalate the situation.

"Well, I didn't mean to, now did I?" Tom's voice rose, tinged with desperation. His hand tightened on the gun, causing Sarah to pull Deanna closer instinctively. "But that idiot was too dumb and too lazy, and he got two identical costumes. How was I to know? How was I to—"

"Stop it. Just stop it. Please. There doesn't have to be another tragedy." Sarah adjusted her stance, one arm around Deanna's shoulders while still clutching a squirming Pixie. The little papillon clearly wanted to get on the ground, but Sarah didn't dare let go. She could feel sweat beading on her forehead, her mouth dry with fear.

"Just put the gun down," she pleaded, striving for calm. Her voice sounded strange to her own ears, steadier than she felt. "Before anybody gets hurt. Nothing's happened yet—"

"Nothing's happened... really? Do you have any idea what's at stake here? If she leaves, I lose everything! My inheritance, my status, all of it! The money only comes if I'm in a stable marriage. I can't let that happen!"

Tom let out a mirthless laugh, brandishing the gun wildly. Panic rippled through the crowd as screams pierced the air and people scrambled to back away. It was only then that he turned his head slightly, a flicker of awareness dawning as he realized he had an audience.

Sarah's heart leapt into her throat as the gun's aim wavered. She could almost feel the weight of all those eyes on them, the collective breath of the onlookers held in terrified anticipation. The scene felt eerily familiar to Sarah: the crowds, the excitement, the undercurrent of tension. It was just like that fateful Christmas in July day when everything had changed.

And then, with a jolt of horror, she saw the door to Lily's bookstore open as if in slow motion, and Emma stepped out, walking calmly towards the tense standoff. Sarah's maternal instincts screamed at her to protect her daughter, but she remained frozen in place, afraid any sudden movement might set Tom off.

Chapter Thirty-Six

Tom had seen Sarah glance over to the bookstore and watched Emma coming toward them, his expression hardening with anger.

"What do you want, kid?" he snapped at Emma, his voice sharp with irritation. The gun wavered slightly in his grip, causing Sarah's heart to skip a beat. "Your mother send you to do her spying for her again?"

Sarah's heart raced as she watched Tom's eyes narrowing at Emma, her arms aching from the effort of restraining Pixie. The little dog's body trembled with barely contained energy, mirroring Sarah's own turmoil.

She could feel Pixie's muscles tensing, ready to spring into action at any moment.

Emma, please, Sarah silently pleaded, her eyes darting between her daughter and Tom's wavering gun. Tragedy was only a slip of Tom's finger away. What if Pixie broke free and charged him? The possibilities whirled through her mind, one chasing the next.

She tightened her grip on Pixie, feeling the dog's rapid heartbeat against her chest. The summer heat only intensified, sweat beading on Sarah's forehead as she fought to maintain control, both of Pixie and her own rising panic. She wanted nothing more than to rush to Emma, to shield her daughter from danger, but any sudden movement could spell disaster.

"Nobody sends me, Tom Barnes," Emma replied, her voice clear and steady.

Sarah blinked, hardly recognizing her 16-year-old daughter in this moment of poise. There was a quiet strength in Emma's stance, a certainty that seemed beyond her years.

Emma stood tall, her chin lifted slightly in defiance. The late afternoon sunlight caught in her hair, creating an almost ethereal glow around her silhouette. Sarah watched in awe as her daughter's usual teenage awkwardness melted away, replaced by an air of quiet authority that seemed to radiate from her very being. There was something else, too. Something Sarah couldn't quite put her finger on. The air around Emma shimmered ever so slightly, like heat rising from sun-baked asphalt. It was barely perceptible, a faint distortion that could easily be dismissed as a trick of the light.

"Tyler was a friend, and he didn't deserve to die."

Tom's face contorted, a mix of anger and guilt flashing across his features. "I told you all I didn't mean to—"

"It was still wrong, Mr. Barnes, and you know that." Emma's words cut through the air like a knife, sharp and unyielding.

Tom flinched as if Emma's words had physically struck him. His face contorted, a kaleidoscope of emotions flashing across his features – anger, guilt, fear, and something deeper, more primal. The hand holding the gun trembled more visibly now, his knuckles white against the metal.

For a moment, the facade of the angry, controlling man cracked, revealing the broken soul beneath. His eyes, usually hard and cold, now shimmered with unshed tears. The weight of his actions—the accidental shooting, the cover-up, the spiral of lies and violence—crashed down on him all at once. He opened his mouth as if to speak, but only a choked sound escaped.

"Emma, run!" Sarah screamed, still struggling with Pixie. If she let go now, the dog would run straight at Barnes to attack.

Sarah blinked, momentarily distracted. The hot, muggy summer day and the spray from the fountain painted dozens of rainbows in the air, but just at the edge of her awareness, slightly above and behind Emma, she saw something extraordinary: a misty haze shimmered, gold, silver, and pink, almost disappearing into the fountain's mist. Emma was protected.

Sarah's breath caught in her throat as she blinked rapidly, trying to make sense of what she was seeing. The shimmering haze behind Emma pulsed gently, its colors shifting and swirling in a mesmerizing dance. It was as if a veil had been lifted, allowing Sarah a glimpse into a world that had always existed just beyond her perception.

A tingling sensation spread across her skin, raising goosebumps despite the oppressive heat. The air seemed to thicken, charged with an energy that made the hairs on the back of her neck stand on end.

Let me go, Sarah, Pixie pleaded. *I can stop him. I will.*

He has a gun, Sarah responded, still holding tight. *And neither you nor the ghosts can stop bullets.*

All I want is a chance.

Emma's voice cut through the tension, barely above a whisper. "Just put down the gun, Mr. Barnes."

Her quiet command seemed to hang in the air, cutting through the oppressive silence that had fallen over the scene. The assembled onlookers held their collective breath, frozen in place as if under a spell. A mother pulled her young child closer, shielding his eyes from the unfolding drama. An elderly man gripped his cane tightly, his knuckles white with tension.

In the distance, the faint wail of police sirens pierced the air, growing steadily louder with each passing second. The sound seemed to break the trance that had fallen over the crowd. Hushed whispers rippled through the gathered spectators, a mixture of fear and morbid fascination evident in their wide-eyed stares.

A group of teenagers huddled behind a nearby tree, their phones held aloft as they surreptitiously recorded the standoff. The fountain's steady splash provided an eerily mundane backdrop to the life-and-death drama playing out before it. A flock of pigeons, startled by the approaching sirens, took flight from a nearby rooftop, their wings beating a frantic rhythm against the sky.

Deanna finally tore away from Sarah and Pixie, her ruined suit jacket hanging in tatters as she flicked a hand toward Tom. A feral glint flashed in her eyes, a mix of rage and something primal.

"Hardly," she scoffed, her voice taking on an unearthly timbre. "He's nothing without that gun in his hand. Are you, Tom? It's just like that ridiculous yellow car—all for show, trying to convince the world you're something you're not."

Tom's face contorted into a mask of anguish and rage, his features twisted almost beyond recognition. Sweat beaded on his forehead, trickling down his temples, and mingling with the dried blood from his earlier injury. His eyes, wide and unfocused, darted frantically between Emma, Sarah, and the growing crowd, like those of a cornered animal searching desperately for escape.

His breath came in short, ragged gasps, each inhale a struggle against the crushing weight of his own actions. The vein at his temple throbbed visibly, a physical manifestation of the war raging within him. Tom's hand, still gripping the gun, shook more violently now, causing the weapon to waver dangerously.

A string of incoherent mutters escaped his lips, fragments of thoughts and regrets tumbling out in a barely audible stream. "Didn't mean to... just an accident... can't let them... no way out..." His mumbled words trailed off into a low, keening sound that seemed to come from the very depths of his soul.

The façade of the strong, controlling man had crumbled entirely, revealing the broken, terrified individual beneath. Tom Barnes stood on the precipice of total mental collapse, teetering between surrender and one final, desperate act of violence. The air around him seemed to vibrate with the intensity of his internal struggle, as if the very fabric of reality was being warped by the force of his deteriorating psyche.

Deanna advanced, her movements unnaturally fluid. Sarah wanted to reach out to pull her back, but something held her in place. It was as if she were watching a scene unfold on a movie screen, powerless to intervene.

Sarah watched in horror as something within Tom shattered. The light in his eyes dimmed, replaced by a terrifying emptiness. He raised the pistol, his movements mechanical, and took aim at Deanna and Sarah. Time seemed to slow, each heartbeat thundering in Sarah's ears.

As Tom's vacant eyes locked onto her, Sarah felt the world around her grind to a halt. The thundering of her heart drowned out all other sounds, each beat stretching into an eternity. In those endless seconds, a torrent of thoughts and emotions crashed through her mind.

Images flashed before her eyes in rapid succession: Emma's first steps, Cory's gap-toothed grin, Matthew's warm embrace. The life she had built, the love she had found, all of it teetering on the edge of oblivion. A wave of primal fear washed over her, threatening to paralyze her completely.

Yet beneath the fear, something else stirred, a fierce, protective instinct that burned like fire in her veins. Her arms tightened around Pixie, feeling the dog's rapid heartbeat echoing her own. Sarah's gaze darted to Emma, standing so bravely just feet away. In that moment, Sarah knew with absolute certainty that she would do anything, endure anything, to keep her family safe.

Time stretched like taffy, each millisecond an agonizing eternity as Tom's finger tightened on the trigger. Sarah's mind raced, searching desperately for a solution, a way out, a miracle. The air around her felt thick, charged with an energy she couldn't explain but somehow understood on a visceral level.

In that suspended moment, balanced on the knife-edge between life and death, Sarah felt something shift within her. A connection to something greater, older, and more powerful than herself.

As Tom's empty eyes bored into her, Sarah silently called out to her own power, praying it would be enough to save them all. She raised one hand, feeling the tendrils of power gathering around her. The energy might not stop a bullet, but perhaps it would distort his aim, sending the shots astray.

As if she'd read her mind, Emma sprang into action. She lunged forward, her hands outstretched, pushing Sarah and Deanna with surprising strength. Pixie tumbled from Sarah's arms, miraculously landing on her feet with a grace that seemed almost magically choreographed.

As Emma moved, the air around her seemed to crackle with energy. Her movements were fluid and purposeful, imbued with a strength that belied her slight frame. Time appeared to slow even further, the world narrowing to this singular, critical moment.

The crack of gunfire split the air.

One. Two. Three.

The sound reverberated through Sarah's body, each shot feeling like a physical blow. She instinctively curled into herself, waiting for the searing pain of a bullet. A pain that never came.

Chaos erupted around them. People screamed and scattered, their panicked cries mixing with the approaching wail of police sirens. Some dropped to the ground or sought refuge behind the fountain's monolith. Sarah's heart pounded in her chest as she realized she could no longer sense Emma's presence.

"Emma!" she screamed, struggling to her feet and shoving Deanna aside. Her voice was raw with fear and desperation. "Emma, answer me!"

Pixie's bark pierced through the commotion, long and shrill, almost as if she were calling out to something unseen. Above it all, a voice boomed through a megaphone:

"This is the Rosewood Hollow Police. Put down your weapons and stand with your hands raised."

Sarah scrambled across the pavement, her hands scraping against the rough surface as she searched for Emma. Relief washed over her as she found the girl sitting up, rubbing her elbow with a grimace. The world seemed to come back into focus, sounds rushing back in a cacophony of sirens and shouting.

"What in blazes were you thinking?"

Sarah grabbed Emma's shoulders, checking her for injuries. Her hands trembled as they moved over her daughter's arms and face, her heart still racing from the terror of the moment. To her amazement, aside from a few bruises and a scratch on her elbow, Emma appeared entirely unharmed.

Behind them, Deanna stumbled to her feet, muttering violent curses as she brushed off her ruined suit. Inexplicably, she too was unscathed. "I felt you trying to unbalance him," Emma said, her voice trembling. "He was aiming right at you."

Tom, where was Tom Barnes? Sarah's head snapped around again, searching for the gunman.

"I... I missed?" Tom mumbled, his voice barely above a whisper.

His words trailed off, lost in the chaos erupting around them. Sarah watched as the realization of what he'd almost done—and somehow failed to do—washed over him. The anger engulfed him in a hot, furious moment, and his eyes narrowed at Sarah as his hands tightened on the weapon once more.

Officer Penny Harding's voice crackled over the megaphone, a hint of desperation in her tone now.

"Mr. Barnes, put down the gun and kick it away. Please, let's end this peacefully." The urgency in her voice sent a fresh wave of fear through Sarah. This wasn't over yet, and Tom Barnes was beyond reason.

With practiced precision, he ejected the magazine and reached into his jacket pocket. The metallic click of a fresh clip sliding into place sent a shiver through the gathered crowd. Sarah instinctively pulled Emma closer, her mind racing for a way out of this nightmare. She could feel Amelia and Simon's presence and the ghost's frustration because they couldn't neutralize the gun. Her hands still pulsed with magical energy, but one glance at the bustling common filled her with dread about unleashing something she couldn't control.

"You want to see if you're twice lucky?" Tom snarled at Deanna, his eyes wild with a mixture of rage and something darker. Spittle flew from his lips as he spoke, his entire body trembling with barely contained fury.

"Tyler wasn't, though he took the bullet meant for your wretched lover."

Sarah's breath caught in her throat. The pieces were falling into place, painting a picture more horrifying than she'd imagined. She glanced at Deanna, seeing the guilt and fear etched across the other woman's face.

Behind them, police officers moved with silent efficiency, ushering bystanders away from the Common, getting into position to take out Tom if needed. The air grew thick with tension, as if the very atmosphere sensed the impending danger. Sarah could hear the rustle of leaves from the nearby trees, the sound oddly amplified and comforting in the tense silence.

Emma's small hand found Sarah's, their fingers intertwining. A warm energy spread between them, both comforting and electrifying. Sarah looked down at her daughter, struck by the calm determination in Emma's eyes. There was something there, a knowledge or power that Sarah couldn't quite grasp.

Pixie trotted over, her little paws making no sound on the pavement as she settled between them. Her fur now shimmered brightly with an otherworldly light, barely perceptible but undeniably there. Sarah felt a strange sense of calm wash over her, at odds with the chaos of the situation.

Her gaze met Deanna's, and she saw the moment realization dawned in the other woman's eyes. The gentle, iridescent mist from earlier began to materialize around them, barely visible yet undeniably present. It pulsed with an energy that spoke of ancient protections and unseen guardians.

"Stand behind us," Sarah said softly to Deanna, her voice carrying a quiet authority that surprised even herself. Without hesitation, Deanna stepped back, sheltering herself in the ethereal cocoon.

A piercing scream cut through the air. Matthew's voice, Sarah realized with a pang of guilt. She wanted to call out to him, to reassure him, but she didn't dare take her eyes off Tom Barnes.

In slow motion, she watched as he adjusted his stance and narrowed his eyes as he aimed. Sarah felt the words of an old prayer rushing into her mind, but just as Tom's finger tightened on the trigger, an unexpected and powerful gust of wind suddenly swept through the Common, gathering speed and power as it rolled toward them.

It came out of nowhere, bending the branches of the nearby trees, rustling leaves, and sending litter, sand, and debris swirling through the air. The force of it hit Tom squarely in the chest, blinding him momentarily. The sting of dust in his eyes caught him off guard, making him stumble.

The gun's report echoed across the Common again, followed by gasps and cries of terror. Sarah's heart stopped, waiting for the impact, for the pain. Her hand almost crushed Emma's. But again, no bullet found its mark. Instead, she heard the distinctive thud of bullets embedding themselves in wood.

Sarah's eyes snapped open—she hadn't even realized she'd closed them—to see Tom staring at his gun in disbelief. The mysterious storm gust died down as quickly as it had appeared, leaving an eerie calm in its wake.

"What the...?" Tom muttered. Rage contorted his features as he stared at his weapon and back at the women in disbelief.

"What kind of insanity is this?" he roared. His eyes darted wildly between Sarah, Emma, and Pixie. Fear began to creep into his expression now, replacing the rage.

Not today, Sarah heard in her mind, and felt the energetic imprint on her leg where Pixie touched her.

"It's no trick, Mr. Barnes," Emma said, her young voice ringing out with unexpected clarity. There was a wisdom in her tone that belied her years, a certainty that sent chills down Sarah's spine. "It's Rosewood Hollow. The town protects its own."

As if in response to Emma's words, a gentle breeze stirred the leaves of the ancient oak trees lining the Common. Their branches seemed to sway in an intricate dance, casting dappled shadows that moved in impossible patterns. The fountain behind them surged, the sun glittering in its spray once again.

Tom Barnes' eyes darted wildly, taking in the scene before him. The gun slipped from his trembling fingers, clattering to the ground as the fight drained from his body. He sank to his knees, head bowed in defeat. The sound of the gun hitting the pavement seemed to break the spell that had fallen over the Common.

The police officers swarmed in as one to apprehend Tom Barnes, and Sarah felt the mystical energy around them begin to ebb away like a receding tide. She glanced down at Pixie, who wagged her tail with an air of satisfaction, offering a soft, knowing bark. Her gentle voice, familiar yet ethereal, whispered in Sarah's mind.

We did it. And nobody got hurt.

Sarah's thoughts swirled with a mixture of relief and confusion.

I thought you wanted to hurl yourself at him.

He would have deserved it, came the reply, tinged with a hint of mischief.

Against bullets? But what...?

Sarah's mental question trailed off, overwhelmed by the implications of what had just occurred. Her world had shifted on its axis, revealing depths of mystery and magic she'd never imagined possible in her quiet little town.

Pixie inched closer, her tiny pink tongue darting out to soothe a scrape on Sarah's leg. The touch sent a ripple of warmth through Sarah's body, and with it, more clarity.

Emma, Pixie's voice continued in her mind. *She's coming into her power. Amelia and Simon came to help. They may not be able to manipulate objects, but it seems they engaged nature to do so.*

And you.

Pixie shook hard, releasing the tension in her body, and put her paws against Sarah's knee.

Sarah's eyes widened, her gaze darting to Emma, who stood nearby, looking both exhilarated and exhausted.

You summoned a storm gust? The thought sent a shiver down Sarah's spine, a mixture of awe and fear at the magnitude of what they'd accomplished.

A tinkling sound, like delicate wind chimes in a summer breeze, filled Sarah's mind—Pixie's laughter.

Oh, that's one of the easier ones. It is entertaining, if you don't overdo it.

The casual way Pixie dismissed such an extraordinary feat left Sarah momentarily speechless. She bent down, scooping the little Papillon into her arms. As she straightened, she turned to face the Common once more, seeing it with new eyes.

Emma caught her eye, a knowing smile playing at the corners of her mouth. There was a silent understanding between them, a shared secret that would forever change their relationship.

As curious onlookers began to disperse and the police continued their work, Sarah hugged Pixie closer. She knew that questions would soon come pouring in: from the authorities, from her family, from the town itself. But for now, she allowed herself to bask in the warm glow of their shared secret.

What happens now? she thought, not sure if she was asking Pixie or herself.

Now? Pixie's thoughts were filled with excitement. *Now, the real adventure begins. Explaining all of this to the police.*

Chapter Thirty-Seven

T he cacophony of the aftermath filled the air, sirens wailing, officers barking orders, and the murmur of bewildered onlookers. Above it all, Sarah heard Matthew's frantic cries as he fought his way through the police barrier, desperate to reach them.

Deanna Barnes sagged onto a nearby rock, her carefully cultivated composure gone for good.

"I don't know what you just did," she said, her voice quavering, "but you saved my life." The words hung in the air, heavy with unspoken questions and a hint of awe.

Before Sarah could respond, Officer Penny Harding approached, her face a mask of professional detachment.

"Deanna Barnes, I'm going to have to take you in on suspicion of your involvement in the bank robbery." She placed a firm hand on Deanna's shoulder, then turned to Sarah and Emma with a mixture of exasperation and curiosity. "You two again. Why is it you always turn up when there's trouble in this town?"

The question lingered unanswered as Cory and Matthew finally broke through the crowd, enveloping Emma and Sarah in a bone-crushing hug.

"Mom!" Cory cried out, his voice muffled against Sarah's shoulder. "Are you okay? What happened here? What happened to his gun?"

Sarah met Emma's eyes over the boys' heads, a silent understanding passing between them.

"Amelia, Simon," she murmured softly, hoping to keep the names from Penny Harding's ears. But the officer's head tilted slightly, her sharp gaze flickering with interest.

As if summoned by their names, a cool breeze whispered through the Common, carrying with it the faintest scent of lavender and old books. The ancient oak trees lining the square seemed to lean in closer, their leaves rustling with secrets.

Sarah looked up, her gaze drawn to the tree behind where they had been standing. Three bullet holes marred its trunk, a stark reminder of how close they had come to tragedy.

Penny Harding rolled her shoulders, her face a mask of professional detachment.

"I'm going to need statements from all of you," she said, her eyes narrowing slightly as she took in the scene, Emma, Sarah, and finally Pixie. "And could someone please explain to me how he missed at point-blank range?"

A silent understanding passed between Emma and Sarah. A lucky gust of wind, that was all they could allow themselves to say.

As officers led Deanna away, Sarah hugged Cory and Matthew close, breathing in their familiar scents. Over their shoulders, she watched Emma bend down to scratch Pixie behind the ears, whispering something that made the little dog's tail wag furiously.

The Common was still alive with activity—paramedics tending to shocked bystanders, officers collecting evidence, curious onlookers straining for a glimpse of the action. But beneath it all, Sarah sensed a shift.

Something magical had happened, and for now, she was content to stand in the fading glow of whatever magic had protected them, Pixie a warm presence against her leg. Rosewood Hollow, she now knew, held far more mysteries than she'd ever imagined.

Feeling the crushing exhaustion of the last few hours, she found her legs wobbling and sank onto the nearest concrete bench to sit while a paramedic handed her water and checked the scrapes on her arms and legs. The tension finally drained from her shoulders bit by bit, and a moment later, her eyes locked onto the trunk of the old oak tree again.

To her amazement, the bullet holes seemed to have shrunk, leaving only faint, scar-like marks. Sarah blinked hard, certain her eyes were playing tricks on her. But no, the marks were undeniably smaller than they had been just moments ago.

"Mom?" Emma's voice startled her. "Are you all right?"

Sarah turned to see her daughter approaching, Pixie trotting faithfully at her heels.

"Fine, I just needed to sit for a moment," she replied, her eyes magically drawn back to the tree trunk.

Emma's gaze fell on the fading bullet marks, and a small smile played at the corners of her mouth. "It's like the tree is healing itself," she said softly.

Sarah nodded slowly, a shiver running down her spine despite the warm afternoon. "Emma," she began hesitantly, "that wind today... did you feel anything... unusual?"

Emma didn't speak for a long moment, her eyes fixed on the tree. "I felt... something," she finally admitted. "Like a tingling in my fingertips. And then the wind came."

Sarah pulled her daughter close, breathing in the familiar scent of her hair. "I think," she said softly, "that Rosewood Hollow might have more secrets than we realized."

As if in response, a gentle breeze rustled through the leaves above them. Pixie let out a soft bark, her tail wagging as she looked up at the swaying branches.

Sarah smiled, a mixture of wonder and trepidation filling her heart. She locked hands with Emma and cast one last glance at the old oak tree. A cloud passed over the sun just then, but she could have sworn she saw a faint, silvery glow emanating from the healing bullet marks. But then she blinked, and it was gone, leaving her to wonder if it had been there at all.

Chapter Thirty-Eight

Finally, they were allowed to leave the Common. As the sun began to set, casting long shadows, Sarah couldn't shake the feeling that this was just the beginning of a much larger adventure—one that would unravel the supernatural secrets lurking beneath the quaint facade of their beloved town.

Matthew's eyes searched Sarah's for a long moment, his gaze filled with a mix of wonder and acceptance. Sarah's lips parted, but words failed her, caught in the tangle of emotions and revelations of the day.

"Guess I'm gonna have to get used to these kinds of moments, huh?" Matthew said softly, drawing her closer.

"I... really... I didn't want to..." Sarah stammered, her voice barely above a whisper.

"I know. It just happened."

"Matthew... I tried. I... For you—for us."

"I know," he murmured, his embrace tightening. "Actually, I'm kind of proud..." He glanced around conspiratorially before continuing in a hushed tone. "That was no freak storm gust, was it? That was you making him miss and stirring up the very wind, wasn't it?"

Sarah buried her face against his neck, her words muffled. "Actually, it was all three of us, connecting to nature in a way I've never seen."

Matthew's eyes widened in astonishment.

Cory's voice broke through their intimate moment, still tinged with confusion.

"So, Barnes really did shoot Tyler? But why?"

Sarah pulled back slightly, keeping one arm around Matthew. "He wanted to stop Noah from leaving town with Deanna to avoid embarrassing his family. That would have broken his family trust and cut him off from the family fortune. He would have lost everything. But since Noah had bought identical Santa costumes..."

Cory muttered a curse under his breath as the group began their walk home.

"He just mistook him for Noah? That is... just so not right."

Lily caught up with them, having finally escaped the concerned first responders.

"Sarah, Sarah, Sarah..." was all she managed to come up with, earning a grin from her friend.

"What about the bank robbery?" Cory pressed.

Sarah shrugged. "Deanna was used to the finer things in life. I guess she felt Noah's lifestyle needed improving. He wanted to move to LA to be an actor..." She blew out a hard breath. "I guess that money was supposed to finance it all for them."

"Women," Cory muttered, earning a playful elbow in the ribs from Sarah.

"Where's Noah now?" he asked.

Sarah's expression softened a little. "Don't rightly know. I think when he realized that Tyler died in his place, he kind of lost it, gave back his share of the money, and took off. I assume the guilt was eating him up. Wherever he is—I hope he finds peace. I have a feeling he might turn himself in sooner rather than later."

"If a nationwide manhunt doesn't get him first," Cory said, shaking his head. "Do you have any idea the methods they have nowadays..."

As they reached the house, Sarah sank into the porch swing, the weight of the day settling over her. Matthew disappeared inside to fetch some wine, while Emma quietly took a seat beside Sarah, their hands intertwining. That familiar sense of calm and protection washed over them both.

"Is it always like this?" Emma asked softly. "It just... comes to you?"

Sarah let her head fall back, her gaze drifting over the beauty of her summery yard. The fading sunlight seemed to paint the world in a soft, magical glow. "I wish I could tell you," she replied. "So far, whenever I've needed it, it's just... been there for me, and I knew what to do."

"Is it ever frightening?"

"Not so far." Sarah gave Emma's hand a gentle squeeze. "I guess you and I... somehow we're going to have to figure this out together, won't we?"

Emma's laughter rang out, bright and beautiful, opening Sarah's heart to new possibilities. Matthew and Lily emerged onto the porch, wine glasses in hand. Cory tossed one of his favorite energy drinks up and caught it, just as Pixie hopped through the doggie door to join them. They all turned to admire the breathtaking colors of the setting sun, the sky ablaze with hues of orange, pink, and purple.

As twilight settled over Rosewood Hollow, Sarah felt a sense of peace and anticipation. The day's events had revealed a hidden world of wonder and mystery, one that had always existed just beyond their perception. She knew that challenges lay ahead, questions to be answered, powers to be understood, and secrets to be unraveled.

But in this moment, surrounded by family and friends, with Pixie curled contentedly at her feet and the lingering warmth of magic in the air, Sarah knew they would face whatever came their way together. The ordinary facade of their small town had cracked, revealing the extraordinary beneath, and she couldn't wait to see where this new adventure would lead them.

As the first stars began to twinkle in the deepening twilight, Sarah raised her glass in a silent toast to magic, to mysteries, and to the endless possibilities that awaited them in the enchanted world of Rosewood Hollow.

"Of course we'll figure it out," Emma said so softly that only Sarah could hear. Her voice was filled with quiet confidence. "It's magic."

Coming Soon

Thanks for reading! ***Please leave a review*** for **Christmas in July,** and watch for Pixie's next adventure in ***The Siren's Lament***, the next Magical Papillon Cozy Mystery.

For more fun and updates follow Pixie on TikTok, @papillon_pixie

Want early access to The Siren's Lament? Email me here to get on the list for release updates – **sabine-author@pm.me**. Or use the link below to sign up to get notifications of the release date Pixie's next adventure.

https://docs.google.com/forms/d/e/1FAIpQLSf6wLjWBuZqqJJg uR-_mtBVCHYE1UtbqxHE1uxpKWOPnlY8hA/

Scan to Sign Up

Also by Sabine

Cozy Mysteries: The Magical Papillon Mystery Series
The Mirror and the Matrix
Whispers in the Attic
Sapphires & Secrets
A Pinch of Peril
Christmas in July
The Rosewood Hollow Express: A special Christmas story featuring Pixie and the Andersons. Released in ebook and audible formats in December 2024.

Financial Thrillers:
The Cannabis Preacher Series

1. *Sermon One*

2. *Sermon Two*

3. *Sermon Three*

4. *Sermon Four*

Joyce AI: She knows Everything About You!

∞

Romance Novels (Pen Name, Sabine Keevil):
SoundMaster Romance Series:
Guitars & Cadillacs
Foolish Pride

∞

Coming Soon
The Siren's Lament (A Magical Papillon Cozy Mystery)
The Curator's Inheritance (An Art History/Mystery)
Ghost Mountain Gold (Financial Thrillers)
This Time (SoundMaster Romance)

Reviews for Other Books

Reviews for Other Books by Sabine

Writing as Sabine Frisch:

<u>The Cannabis Preacher Series</u>

GoodReads Review: "The subject matter and title intrigued me having been around some of these sorts of dealings. From the beginning of this book had my attention; I picked it up to "just have a look" and suddenly found myself eight chapters into it. As the main characters were introduced, I started to feel that I had met all of these people before. Read on as Connor, the main protagonist, battles his demons up and down the shady side of Wall Street. There are just so many moving parts for any one control freak to manage. The greatest deal of all time starts to get out of control but every time he seems about to fall, he finds a way to land on his feet. We keep guessing:• Is he our hero or his own worst enemy?• Is this a runaway train or a slow-motion train wreck?• Will he end up in Financial Heaven, Regulatory Hell, or just a Fool's Paradise? Read to the end of this fun little tale and wait for the movie to come out."

Writing as Sabine Keevil

The SoundMaster Romance Series

<u>Guitars & Cadillacs</u> (Semi-finalist in the BookLife Fiction Prize Contest, 2023)

Editorial Reviews:

"Sabine Keevil has constructed the perfect fantasy romance in her novel Guitars & Cadillacs, the latest in the Soundmaster Romance Series... At the same time, she appeals to that part of us that longs to see the behind-the-scenes footage of celebrity lives."-Rachel Jagt, Rambles.net

"Ms. Keevil is a good storyteller, I'll say that right out. She has a good grasp of storyline, she's succinct and to the point, her characters are engaging, and she knows where she's taking them."-Laurie Joulie, Take-countryback.com

"Guitars & Cadillacs is the entertaining story of the fire and fury stirred up by the relationship between Reanne (Parker) and fictional country superstar Colton Wright...Offering surprise twists, intrigue and myst ery...Keep turning the pages to see what happens next in the well-paced plot."- Pat Mandia, Country Weekly, the world's #1 Selling Country Music Magazine

<u>Foolish Pride</u>

Editorial Reviews:

"Keevil spins an engaging romantic tale and does a credible job of taking us backstage into the minds, lives and hearts of her characters." -Pat Mandia, Country Weekly Magazine

"Canadian author Sabine Keevil (Guitars & Cadillacs) has done it again -- she revisits the world of SoundMaster with originality, humour and a large share of romantic spirit.

One of Keevil's strengths as a writer is her ability to create realistic characters, even in the midst of a story about the world of big money show business. She is unpretentious and honest and her characters are likeable from the beginning...Even in two nights, the characters became beloved -- a sure sign of a good story." -Rachel Jagt, Rambles - a cultural arts review magazine

Spotify Playlists

Enjoy the following Spotify playlists with music mentioned or inspired by my novels.

Guitars & Cadillacs:

https://open.spotify.com/playlist/71ymCTx5YJPzro WBg4gWHF?si=fcf531d7a84b46cc

Foolish Pride:

https://open.spotify.com/playlist/1lR5rhB840RyeecFLvb1pG

The Cannabis Preacher:

https://open.spotify.com/playlist/4P90ZeynKOI7gyGUcVF HJE?si=484f28ffa7fb4b2a

Magical Papillon Mysteries

https://open.spotify.com/playlist/46FQGJn3T7qnAnoau63 BxU?si=379b6a6be4874ef3

Free Bonus Book

Thanks for reading! Please leave a review and watch for the next Magical Papillon Mystery novel, featuring Pixie.
You can follow Pixie on TikTok, @papillon-pixie

Want to know how this magical adventure began? Uncover the secrets of the past.

As a special thank you for reading, I'd like to offer a free copy of the prequel to the Magical Papillon Mystery series, **The Mirror & the Matrix.** This short story reveals the heartwarming moments and spooky encounters that led to the enchanting mysteries in the series.

To receive your free Epub copy of **The Mirror & the Matrix,** please follow this link, https://forms.gle/wf6s7GGf8TSbrVv8A or scan the QR code with your phone.

The Mirror & the Matrix